## Praise for *Turtle*

"Mad entirely . . . dialogue to di[e]
if you value your reputation for [s]
could restore your faith in lif[e]
having yourself"

"Irvine Welsh should be taking lessons from Gaye Shortland. You'll laugh, you'll cry, you're unlikely to recommend it to your granny. She's not out spotting trains, she's in the driving seat, effortlessly achieving on every page a cocktail of loud music, rough sex and gritty prose that relegates Welsh and his mob to the anorak class"
*The Examiner*

"One of the funniest books I have read for a long time, funny enough to make me catch my breath and scream aloud with laughter. Not dissimilar to Roddy Doyle, in a style that echoes the manic reality of the characters of Flann O'Brien. But Gaye Shortland is, in my opinion, a superior writer"
*fm*

"An Irish Irvine Welsh with the emphasis on queens rather than junkies. The cast of characters is so strong that each of them could almost warrant a book of their own. Like the Welsh books, once you get the accent in your head, it flows like a gurgling river and will have you laughing out loud"
*QX (London)*

". . . and Shortland's gift for describing the tenderness and physical concentratedness of sex (even when one partner is disembodied), her ability to convey what is decent, even heroic, in her scuzziest characters"
*Gay Community News*

"A startlingly original and wildly humorous jaunt . . . Gaye Shortland is one of Ireland's most talented writers"
Marian Keyes, author of *Watermelon*, *Rachel's Holiday* and *Sushi for Beginners*

"It's doubtful that anyone in Ireland would have the courage to film it: we'll wait for Channel 4 to do it, and then buy it off them"
*The Phoenix*

"Gaye Shortland is a contemporary writer in every sense of the word"
*Hot Press*

"An extraordinary outpouring – the book's energy and anarchy are refreshing, as is its exuberant treatment of gay sex"
*The Irish Times*

"An addictive mix of sexiness and comedy"    *In Dublin*

## Praise for MIND THAT 'TIS MY BROTHER

"The Irish Tourist Board should reprint thousands of copies and use them as promotional material – bugger the Blarney stone."
*Time Out*

"The madness of obsession and the undying lust of the spirit are portrayed in scenes that are bound to offend. I loved it"
*Irish Times*

"A Corkonian Roddy Doyle, with an equally exact ear, but a more subversive sense of humour"    *Cork Examiner*

"Outrageous characterizations abound in this hugely enjoyable first novel . . . a comic masterpiece"    *Gay Community News*

"She writes with the authority of a gay man, which is staggering considering she is a straight woman"    *QX (London)*

"Just one or two lines of Gaye's dialogue justify the price of the book . . . Her books are also very sexy reads"
Michael Carson, author of *Sucking Sherbet Lemons* and *Hubbies*

"If she continues in the same rich vein Shortland could well become to Cork what Maupin is to San Francisco"
*Thud (London)*

"New implausibles are established with increasing frequency in the ferment of Irish culture: here is an Irish stew well seasoned with transvestism and alcoholism, not forgetting descriptions of gay sex that range from the bizarre by way of the hysterical to the transcendent"
*Our Times*

## Praise for POLYGAMY

"Shortland leaves the reader dumbstruck, so striking are her images, so vivid her characters"
*Hot Press*

"Shortland's writing at its most personal, ruthless and rapturous to date; the sense of raw immediacy which leaps out at the reader is shocking . . . as the narrative takes the plunge with a devastating honesty and lyric beauty. It is an engrossing anatomy of a society, a *tour de force* of supple prose and an entrancing cross-cultural love story"
*Munster Literature Centre Magazine*

"The writing is a delight and includes one of the most erotic scenes of love-making I've ever read (and re-read). It takes the reader on an exotic compelling journey"
*Image*

"She comes to the novel with a huge insight into the workings of the sociey and has used it to stupendous effect. The clash of cultures on a sexual plain I have not seen drawn so starkly before. To this reader with a decade of experience of the Islamic world, it rings true blue indigo"
Michael Carson, author of *Sucking Sherbet Lemons* and *Hubbies*

"A love affair that rivals, even surpasses, that of *The English Patient* in its intensity – one woman's breathtaking, gut-wrenching involvement, not with just one man, but with a whole race"
*IT (Irish Tatler)*

"Shortland takes us on an odyssey filled with passion, joy, obsession and – ultimately – pain"
*Evening Herald*

"An affair of stellar lust and deadly attrition . . . the novel is exhilarating and expansive. Shortland has used her intimate knowledge of the Tuareg to paint the necessary recondite and exquisitely detailed background – and for this alone the book should be read"
*RTE Guide*

"A mesmerising, exquisitely written story of love and betrayal, set against the vast and corrupt backdrop of Africa"
Marian Keyes, author of *Watermelon*, *Last Chance Saloon* & *Sushi for Beginners*

"A riveting tale of sexual obsession, based on the author's own experience"
*GNER Magazine*

## Praise for HARMATTAN

"The rhythm of her words conjures up a story that is both magical and convincing"
*Evening Herald*

"She weaves an authentic spellbinding story of a love that must overcome huge differences, in a novel which is different in context and atmosphere from the usual"
*Dublin People/Southside News*

"Develops neatly and to great effect into an engaging drama of cross-cultural love and personal struggle"
*Irish Examiner*

"An utterly convincing portrait of life in the desert. Shortland maps out the difficulties in cross-cultural relationships, whether sexual or merely social with compassion, humour and insight. Ellen's obsession is complex and sometimes dangerous, but it is also utterly persuasive. It is transmitted to the reader with such fervour that it is sorely tempting to get on a plane and see for yourself"
*RTE Guide*

*About the Author*

Born in Cork, Ireland, Gaye Shortland has taught English literature at University College Cork, the University of Leeds, Ahmadu Bello University Nigeria and the Université de Niamey in Niger. She lived for fifteen years in Africa, spending much of that time with the nomadic Tuareg of the Sahara and eventually managing a restaurant for the American Embassy in Niamey. She married a Tuareg and has three children. She began to write in 1994 on her return to Ireland. She is now editor at Poolbeg Press and the author of four critically acclaimed novels. *Mind That 'tis My Brother* and *Turtles All the Way Down* are comedies set in Cork; *Polygamy* and *Harmattan* are set in Africa.

*Also by Gaye Shortland*

Mind That 'tis My Brother
Turtles All the Way Down
Polygamy
Harmattan

# ROUGH RIDES IN DRY PLACES

# ROUGH RIDES IN DRY PLACES

*Gaye Shortland*

POOLBEG

Published 2001
by Poolbeg Press Ltd
123 Baldoyle Industrial Estate
Dublin 13, Ireland
E-mail: poolbeg@poolbeg.com
www.poolbeg.com

© Gaye Shortland 2001

Copyright for typesetting, layout, design © Poolbeg Group Services Ltd.

1 3 5 7 9 10 8 6 4 2

The moral right of the author has been asserted.

A catalogue record for this book is available from the British Library.

ISBN 1 84223 028 X

All rights reserved. No part of this publication may be reproduced or transmitted in any form or by any means, electronic or mechanical, including photography, recording, or any information storage or retrieval system, without permission in writing from the publisher. The book is sold subject to the condition that it shall not, by way of trade or otherwise, be lent, resold or otherwise circulated without the publisher's prior consent in any form of binding or cover other than that in which it is published and without a similar condition, including this condition, being imposed on the subsequent purchaser.

Cover design by Splash
Typeset by Patricia Hope in Goudy 11/14.5
Printed by Cox & Wyman

*Acknowledgements*

Many thanks to my colleagues at Poolbeg, old and new, from below-decks up to the bridge, for their efforts on my behalf.

*To Tony Olden, best of friends,
For his staunch support of my writing
And for keeping Africa alive for me*

## Chapter 1

"*Ah-hah!*" came raucously over the fence. "Slumming again, are we?"

"Oh, God!" muttered Jan Prendergast, twisting around to look over her shoulder.

Ned Bassett was leaning over the corrugated-iron barrier, leering at the little group sitting cross-legged under the makeshift canvas shelter. He had a sheaf of papers in one hand, his pipe in the other, shirtsleeves rolled up his brawny arms to the elbow as usual.

"Greet your friend, Jan!" said Anow in mock reproach, almond eyes glinting with mischief. He waved to Ned and called out in careful English, "Hallo, Ned! How are you?"

Jan pasted a smile on her face. "Hello, Ned!" she called cheerily. "Come to join us?"

"What? Me sit on a dirty mat on a sodding building-site? Not bloody likely!" He grinned, squinting in the sun, baring his unsightly bunch of teeth. Even at twenty feet, Jan could see the sweat glistening on his splotchy skin and darkening his sparse greying hair.

Anow rose to his feet in one graceful movement and strolled languidly, barefoot, towards the fence.

"What an ugly fucking Infidel!" muttered his uncle, Mohamed, in Tamajegh, as he poured a thin golden stream from a small blue enamel teapot into little glasses. Then, aloud, ceremoniously, in Hausa, "*Madame*, call your friend! Let him drink tea!"

Anow was shaking hands with Ned, then inviting him into the site, hand on heart, face alight with smiles.

"Eh? Well, just for a moment then." Ned made his way through a gap in the fence and strode to the shelter. He took up his usual bulldog stance, grinning, fists clutching pipe and papers on his hips, ignoring invitations to sit.

Anow shrugged smilingly and sat down again.

"Who's he then?" asked Ned, nodding at Mohamed, watery light-blue eyes goggling at him through his glasses.

"Anow's uncle," Jan replied.

"Ugly-looking bugger, isn't he? What we can see of him, I mean, which isn't much under that sodding veil! Lords of the Desert, eh? Don't look very lordly at the moment, do they?"

Jan didn't respond; for her that was a painful subject.

"'Ere, Jan – eh, not bloody likely!" The last bit was in response to an offer of tea from Anow.

"It is good, Ned!" Anow insisted. "Sweet!"

"Yes, and how long since you've washed the sodding glass, mate?"

Anow continued to proffer the little glass, smiling encouragement.

"Shouldn't think he has a bloody clue what I'm saying,

eh, Jan? Good-looking though, isn't he? In a nancy-boy kind of way with that head of hair. Not shrivelled up like the old fart." White spittle was gathering at the corners of his parched mouth. "'Ere! What are they guarding anyway? That pile of bricks? Or that clapped-out cement mixer? That's a laugh! Ah-hah-hah-hah! Steal 'em themselves anyway, more like." He waved the sheaf of papers. "'Ere! Jan! Langley handed me this duplicate pair of essays of yours and I've had a look at 'em –" He leant forward from the hips in characteristic fashion, the better to crack his joke. "You didn't think *he* was going to deal with the problem, did you? Not bloody likely, you silly sod! Ah-hah-hah-hah!" The blast of laughter was followed by a little asthmatic wheezing and a few smug pulls at the empty pipe; then he turned abruptly formal. "So if I could have a word with you? Back at the house though, not here in this sodding heat. I mean, I'm sorry to break up your 'tête-à-tête' and all that but – if you wouldn't mind?" Elaborate courtesy.

"Oh . . . OK." Fuck, thought Jan. Still, she might get to hear some usable gossip-fodder – like more on Ned's attempts to bid for that Hausa girl from Samaru. "Work," she said to Mohamed apologetically, with a grimace.

"Necessity," he responded in proper stoic fashion. He hastily thrust the customary third glass of tea – the sweet golden one – into her hand and she drank it down.

"Eh," said Ned. He swivelled on his heel and strode off, hence missing a moment he would have drooled over when Jan, who was experimentally going without underwear that week, almost lost her long cotton wraparound skirt as she clambered laboriously to her feet.

Face flaring red in embarrassment, cursing her own

idiotic notions, Jan twisted the dark-blue and white cloth around her waist again and tucked it in firmly. She felt vulnerable and stupid. Had Mohamed seen? Fuck it. Oh, for the security of a pair of panties . . .

"I'll leave the car here," she muttered to Mohamed, head down, as she shuffled her feet into royal-blue rubber flip-flops. Ned's house was close by.

*"To, Madame!"* he agreed as Jan set off in Ned's wake into the glaring sunshine of Northern Nigeria's hot season, Anow at her shoulder. The sun made the exposed skin on her arms smart immediately, cursed as she was with copper-haired, fair-skinned Irish colouring.

Ned glanced back. "Eh?" He squinted at Anow. "Your toy boy is coming too, is he?"

"He isn't – my 'toy boy'. He's too young."

"I thought that's the way you liked 'em, Prendergast," leered Ned.

Anow was, in fact, the younger brother of her ex-lover Moussa and therefore held something of a position between brother-child-employee-dependant-friend. It was too complicated to explain to Ned in this heat. Besides, she had tried before.

"What is 'toy boy'?" Anow wanted to know.

"Well, tell him, Jan! Tell him! Ah-hah-hah-hah-*hah*!" He strode vigorously ahead, frayed elastic top of his underpants riding as ever on his fleshy hips, between the pea-green shirt and brown trousers.

Behind him, Jan wondered – not for the first time – if it was his mother who had first taught him to tuck his shirt-tail inside his underpants. There was too much pathos in the thought and she shied away from it.

They were now following the shaded, paved walkways that cut through the centre of the campus.

"Cripes! Here comes that daft bugger," said Ned abruptly. "Jasper Carrott to the life and twice as cracked."

Jan raised her head to see Tom Purthill bearing down on them. She held her breath, expecting him to veer away when he saw her, as he always did recently, but he kept on coming. Suddenly, about thirty yards away, he threw his gaunt khaki-clad limbs into a grotesque, high-stepping gait, approaching at full speed like a maddened stork and sweeping past with his knees reaching almost to his chin, long arms flailing wildly.

Two women students had turned and were gaping after him in grinning amazement.

To her horror, Jan realised that she was grinning too.

"God Almighty – a monkey!" said Anow in Tamajegh.

But Ned was rooted to the spot, gazing after Tom open-mouthed and aghast. "Eh, that poor sod has 'ad it, I should think," he mumbled bemusedly at last, thrusting the essays under a sweating armpit. He pulled a small piece of wire out of his pocket and began to dig viciously at the bowl of his pipe with it.

They stood awkwardly, waiting for him.

"But 'ere . . . we'd better get a move on . . ." He stopped his excavations, sucked on the empty pipe and then strode off again. They trailed obediently behind him.

"But, Jan, today I've seen a wonder," said Anow, shaking his head.

She was embarrassed, aware that to Anow all Batures – expatriates – were ungainly, tense and ridiculous and Tom's performance just a cartoon version of the rest.

'Expatriates': an ungainly, tense and ridiculous word – but such a handy neutral label to fall back on to cover the rag-bag conglomeration of foreigners in Nigeria.

She watched Anow as he walked ahead: the long brown limbs, the ease and erect grace, the cloud of blue-black hair. He was beautiful. Grubby and gorgeous. He wore a white traditional robe, open down the sides, over blue jeans. The jeans looked like Levi Strauss had seventeen-year-old Tuaregs in mind when he designed them.

He really was too young.

The bougainvillaea outside the bungalow was a startling mass of pink and purple. Ned fumbled for his keys. "Tell Toy Boy to wait outside. I don't trust these Buzus!" Using the somewhat contemptuous Hausa term for the Tuareg. "Give him a look inside and he'll be back with his mates to rob me!"

Jan flushed. "I can't tell him to wait outside, Ned! Besides, he's been in your house before – several times."

"Well, I don't want 'im!" The lower lip thrust out.

"I can't! Really! He's a friend!" And he's my bodyguard, she thought, and I'm damned if I'm stepping into *your* parlour without him. Especially without my knickers on.

"We *know* that! We *know* he's a *friend*! You are a silly sod!" He wrestled the padlock and chain off the metal frame of the door and unlocked it. "Oh, if you must then! Bring him in!"

They stepped out of the glare into the gloom of his little hallway with its musty, dusty smell. Ned went through the living-room to the kitchen while his guests stood at the entrance of the room, taking in – once more – its salient features.

It was extraordinarily bare – if you didn't take the dust

that clothed everything into account: the usual university-issue wooden furniture regimented against the walls; some papers scattered over the large table at the far end of the room; the tobacco-tin he used as an ash-tray in its perennial position on the coffee table in front of his armchair, burnt matches strewn profusely about it; a couple of side-tables; a few dusty books on the bookshelves opposite; a ceiling-fan, of course. Bare barred windows set high up in the walls. Nothing else whatsoever.

The black tiles of the floor were coated in dust and, through the dust, footprints led along the beaten paths of Ned's existence: bedroom to living-room to kitchen, with a deviation to the armchair, a fainter blurred one to the table and a much fainter one to the bookshelf.

Anow nudged Jan and pointed with the thick leather whip he was carrying. She stared. Something new! Little pawprints in the dust.

"Ned!" she called, intrigued, stepping into the room. "Has there been a cat in here?"

Ned appeared from the kitchen. "Wot? Roger? You don't know about Roger? *Rogeah! Rogeah!* Where are you, you little sod!"

"Don't tell me you got yourself a cat! I thought you hated them?" This was an extraordinary departure from form. It cost *money* to feed a cat.

"So I do but this little beggar was left behind by that French bastard who used to live next door. Starving, he was, when I took pity on him. Sit down, sit down! And get the Sheikh of Araby to sit down over there!" He sat in his armchair – the standard leather and timber version – and began at once to excavate in his pipe.

Jan sat next to him, elbow to elbow, the chairs being ranged side by side flat against the wall. Anow, near the entrance, watched speculatively, playing with his rigid decorated whip which he stroked up and down with slender brown fingers.

Ned was rambling on. "They don't care, do they, those French bastards? Not like us English! 'Ere, some of those old rich farts end up leaving all their money to their cats! Ah-hah-hah-hah-*hah*!" The blast of laughter raised a cloud of dust from the table in front of him and he doubled up in a bout of asthmatic heaving. He recovered eventually, snuffling, face suffused a bright pink. "*Rogeah! Rogeah!*" he yelled suddenly, craning his scraggy neck at the window to the right. "No sign of the little sod. Lucky they gave him a name I can pronounce, not one of those daft French names. 'Ere, maybe you'd know the reason for this – Roger won't eat! Just samples a little and leaves the rest in the dish. *Good* food!" He glared at Jan and sat bolt upright. "Ungrateful little sod! I take him in, feed him and he refuses my food!" Spraying Jan with spittle as he spluttered his indignation.

She tensed. One of his rages was in the offing.

"Ned, about those essays –"

"Hey, wait a minute! I'm talking about *Roger*!"

"Well – OK. Yes. So – what do you feed him on?"

"Pagoda fish, what else? You don't expect me to go and buy him *meat*, do you? Don't be a silly sod!" He waved an arm at her in lordly contempt and, as he spoke, a shadow darkened the window at the end of the room and a decrepit, moth-eaten cat, fur a mixture of black, grey and ginger, stepped cautiously through the security bars and onto the sill.

"Roger!" Ned leapt joyfully to his feet.

The cat tensed.

Ned dived into the kitchen. "Rogeah! Rogeah!" he called gaily. A saucer of tinned fish was pushed with a sweeping-brush along the kitchen floor into Roger's line of vision.

The cat leapt onto the table beneath the window and crouched there tensely.

Ned reappeared in the doorway, a dishcloth in his hand. In dulcet tones he called softly. "Rogeah! Rogeah!"

The cat advanced a step and, after a feint or two, leapt to the ground.

Ned, crouching at cat-level, made a vicious swipe of the dishcloth in his direction. "Ah-hah-hah-hah! You little sod!"

Roger stood his ground. Then he made a short run forward, Ned swiping at him again.

"*Gotcha!* You bastard!"

The cat stood his ground.

Jan watched, grinning and appalled, while Anow kept a faint smile politely pinned to his face for a while but at last burst into incredulous laughter as cat and man continued this manic performance.

Suddenly the dulcet tones sounded again. "Roge-eah! Roge-eah!"

The cat knew his signal and darted forward into the kitchen. He crouched over the saucer and began to devour the food.

In great good humour after this little bout of sadism, Ned began belatedly to play the host. "Would you care for a beer? I put it in the fridge after lunch so it should be cold. Delicious!"

Lukewarm, thought Jan. "Oh, great!"

"I'm not givin' *him* any!" He glared at Anow. "I'm not wasting good money on him!"

"He doesn't drink alcohol. Water for him, please."

"Oh, religious, is he? A far cry from Bogland, isn't it? You know what they say – an Irishman would step over a naked woman to get to the bar!"

"Actually, it's a *row* of naked women – and I guess that's why I'm here, Ned – but at the moment I would leap over a fence of erect penises to get to a drink myself –"

"*Ah-hah-hah-hah-hah!*"

Oh, *Jesus!* thought Jan in consternation. *What made me say that?*

"Oh, you *are* a naughty girl!" He practically rubbed noses with her in his delight.

"The beer?" she said faintly.

"Right!" The glint in his eye boded no good. He went to the kitchen.

She grimaced over at Anow; he grinned back. What was he making of all this? Jesus! What had possessed her to use the word 'penis' in Ned's presence? A *fence* of them! Christ, she must be raving mad!

A big green bottle of Star beer and a bottle of water, with a glass for Anow, were set on the coffe table with a flourish.

"We shall have to share that!" he said, nodding at the Star. "Oh, I suppose you'll need a glass. I was a waiter once, you know . . . but not for long! At London-bloody-Airport . . ." He plunged into the kitchen again. "Delayed a few planes, I assure you! I can tell you some –" He broke off. "'Ere! What did I tell you? Come here! The little sod hardly touched the food!"

But she had seen him devouring it. She put the bottle of water and glass on Anow's side-table and went to the kitchen door. It was true. Roger was gone. The saucer stood there, with just one cavity excavated in its little heap of tinned fish.

"Em, Ned? How long has that fish been in the saucer?"

"Eh, I dunno – a few days I should think!"

"But it's gone off! You'll have to change it –"

"Change it! I bloody well won't! He's the one that let it go bad, ungrateful little bastard! He can jolly well eat it now!"

"Well, then, if he won't eat, give him *milk* –"

"Milk! Milk! You silly sod! How do you expect a cat to sustain himself on milk! You are a silly sod at times!"

"Well, clean the saucer anyway – cats can be quite fastidious –"

*"Fastidious!Him!"* Torn between amusement and outrage. "You *are* daft! Forget about him!" A lordly wave of the hand wafted the existence of Roger away. "Here's your glass. 'Ere! Toy Boy must be saving his water for a desert crossing!"

Anow was eyeing the green slime at the bottom of the water bottle. He hadn't poured any.

Ned settled himself in his armchair and arranged his accessories on the table in front of him: pipe, cleaning-wire, matches, tobacco-tin, ashtray-tin, bottle-opener, crumpled handkerchief. And the essays. A great sigh of satisfaction as he opened the beer with a flourish and poured. He sampled it. "Delicious!" He smacked his lips.

Jan took a gulp. It was warm.

"Now! The essays. Well . . . I didn't bring you here to

talk about the essays. I have a much more delicate topic to discuss."

Jan had that sinking feeling.

"As for the essays – what you do about the essays is this –" He paused, thrust his face to within six inches of hers and snarled, *"Zero!"* – a chop of the hand – *"Zero!"* – another chop. He sat back. "The silly buggers have copied from one another. We don't know which of 'em wrote the original – neither of 'em to judge by the standard of the writing!" He guffawed. "But I'm not about to go through every critical book in the library looking for their source. So: *Zero!Zero!* Fuck 'em! And don't bother Langley any more with silly problems – he don't need 'em! Got enough of his own – the main one being he's a lousy Head of Department! Ah-hah-hah-hah-hah-*hah!*" He lit a match – the fourth one – and let it burn out in his hand as he squinted at Jan. "And you're causing him enough trouble already with this Tom Purthill affair."

"*I* am?" She flushed and her heart began immediately to race in agitation. Anow, always sensitive to her moods, stared at her, instantly alert.

"Now don't you work up your redheaded Irish temper with me! You know he went to the Chaplain and told him you were about to be engaged but you'd thrown him over!"

"I *do* know – trouble is, I *don't* much know Tom Purthill!"

He was now sucking furiously on his pipe. "You saw the – poor bugger – today. End – of the tether!" All in gasps and grunts. "But it's a toss-up – who's nearer breaking-point – him or our revered Head of Department? Ah-hah-hah-hah-*hah!*"

Langley Forrest had taken to locking himself up in his

house for days at a time, leaving his lecture-notes in the library for any students who could be bothered to read them.

"Ned, I can't do anything about Tom. He's suffering from delusions!"

"Appropriate for a teacher of philosophy, wot? Ah-hah-hah-hah!"

"Look, I went twice to his flat for coffee – at midday!"

He sucked in his breath. "Oh, you shouldn't have done that! Not with a queer bugger like that! Mind you, I *like* the bugger – an intelligent fellah and a nice one but a queer sod nonetheless. Lonely people can be dangerous." He leered at Jan. "And you're so attractive."

An image of Tom Purthill's huge erection protruding down the leg of his loose colonial shorts as they drank their coffee flashed on Jan's inward eye. Underwear was a necessity in life and no mistake. She jumped to her feet, remembering to hitch her wrapper round her waist this time. Anow got up at once.

"Look – I'm going now," she said heatedly. "I came to talk about the essays, not Tom. I'm sick of all this gossip about him and me – I'm not responsible for him! He should be sent back to England – he needs psychiatric care!"

"'Ere, don't be like that!" Ned struggled to his feet. "Forget about it! Forget about the silly fart! Fuck 'im! What do I care? I want you for myself anyway."

She bent to pick up her bag.

"'Ere, give's a kiss!"

She straightened up, startled, and his brawny arms closed about her before she could sidestep. Then a wet and nasty kiss landed on her ear as she twisted her head away.

"*Ned!*" came Anow's voice close up.

"Oh, bugger," said Ned ruefully, "I'd forgotten the Sheikh of Araby for a minute!"

Anow stood there, relaxed and smiling, but the leather whip was against Ned's upper arm.

"Cheeky young whippersnapper, isn't he?" said Ned, almost admiringly. He let Jan go.

The whip dropped and Anow stepped back.

"Jealous, of course," said Ned, looking amused. "I reckon he sees me as a threat!" Unconsciously, he thrust his chest out and swaggered a little.

Jan was suddenly very angry. The arrogance of it! The contempt! To believe she was sleeping with Anow and yet to make advances in front of him! She grabbed her shoulder bag and made for the door.

"Jan! Don't take offence!" said Ned, not at all put out. He looked as pleased as Punch, in fact. "You know I think you're attractive! You're so feminine – I can't help myself!"

Jan was at the door. But it was locked, as all Ned's doors always were, inside and out. "Open the door." She shook the door-handle.

"Don't get your knickers in a twist!"

Can't. Not wearing any.

"But I haven't discussed that matter with you! I told you I had something to discuss!" Very aggrieved.

"What matter?" The girl from Samaru? Damn. She hesitated.

"Jan, something is burning!" Anow butted in.

She sniffed.

Ned got the whiff at the same moment. He tore off to the kitchen. "Bugger it! Bugger it!"

Jan stepped back into the room.

"Now look what you've done!" Ned appeared at the

kitchen door, looking like he was going to cry. He was holding a baking-tray, gripping it with a dirty dishcloth. On the tray were two charred lumps. "My onions! My dinner! Ruined! *Ruined!*" He glared at them accusingly, then swivelled and plunged back into the kitchen.

They sat again and waited.

"*Waltzing Matilda, Waltzing Matilda* . . ." Then, very genteel and cheerful, "Be with you in a mo! Just a sec!"

"God Almighty – a madman!" giggled Anow.

Ned emerged, a dinner-plate clutched to his chest. On it: the two burnt onions, two boiled potatoes, a boiled carrot, a small piece of overdone steak and a pile of spaghetti without sauce. "Delicious!" He placed it on the coffee table and settled down to eat.

Anow's dark eyes were wide. In his culture, to sit and eat by oneself was eccentric; but to sit and eat by oneself in company was unthinkable.

Aware of this, Jan was cringing. She spent a lot of her time cringing, actually.

Ned went into lip-smacking action. They both watched as he chawed at his burnt steak and onions. Jan had witnessed it all before on a regular basis. But the spaghetti operation was new to her and mind-blowing to behold, as he repeatedly forked the strands of spaghetti into his mouth, shoved the rest of it in with the flat of his palm and finished the procedure off with a rub to the open mouth with the grubby handkerchief.

Eventually, she managed to overcome her morbid fascination and move on to another subject of morbid fascination. "Em, Ned? What happened about the girl – the fifteen-year-old from Samaru?"

He paused in his tongue-twisting, open-mouthed chewing, then held his hand up like a traffic policeman while he swallowed. "A *whore!*" he said cheerfully. "Oh, Christ, yes!" He leaned towards her conspiratorially, the wooden armrests of the chairs between them blessedly hampering him. "I went to get her in Samaru village. And d'you know what? She had this bloody great bed – with brass knobs on! Ah-hah-hah-hah! 'Ere, but I'm a daft idiot! There I was, driving into the university with this bloody great whore's bed strapped to the roof of my car! *Chir-rist!* Clamped to the roof! A thing that I regard as no more than a piece of bloody junk. Christ, I said, I've invested in a bloody poor asset! Luckily I couldn't get it through the door here – left it in the garage. Anyway, I knew already that I'd been cheated. I paid a small fortune to that bugger who said he was her brother! Told me she was fifteen, then backed down and said she was eighteen, once married and divorced. A clapped-out thirty-five-year-old at the very *least!* With half a dozen kids no doubt, to say nothing of gonorrhoea and worse! And that wasn't all!" He glared ferociously, good humour evaporated. "That night, after we got here, when I'd try to kiss her – she'd turn her head!" Utmost indignation. "She'd turn her head away and make a grimace! As if she was disgusted! With *me!*" He pounded his chest with the heel of his fist. "Well, I wasn't having *that!* In the morning I told her to pack up! Bed and all! Paid her extra! And *do you know what?*"

Jan shook her head, drawing back from the blast. Out of the corner of her eye she could see Anow tensing, over in his armchair.

"*When we arrived in Samaru the cunt refused to get out of*

*the car!* Said it wasn't enough! After I'd already paid that pimp handsomely for procuring her! But I suppose the bastard kept all that for himself – she wouldn't see any! Anyway, I had to drive her around to the Police Station –" he leant forward even more, twisting his torso over the wooden armrests, thrusting his face close to Jan's – "and they took *her side*! Told me I had to pay her *more*!"

"So what did you do?"

"I refused! What else!"

"And?"

He sat back in his chair and suddenly chortled. "Well, I had to pay in the end – to get her out of the sodding car! Ah-hah-hah-hah-*hah*! Well may you laugh! 'Ere, but I do get myself into some rum situations – I *am* a daft bugger at times!" He enjoyed this for a while, crunching on the remnants of his charred onions.

Jan thought this was hysterical. "Later," she said to Anow who was looking over questioningly, "I'll tell you later!"

"No, I'm through with whores. I've decided to get married! A wife! That's what I need! And I'm through with these Hausa and Fulani – lying sods the lot of 'em! This time I'm going for your people."

Jan stopped laughing.

"The Tuareg have no morals and they're all destitute since the droughts drove them down here. Shouldn't be any problem. *Yes!* One of those succulent little darlings! *Ummmuh!*" He bunched his fingers to his lips and threw a kiss to the ceiling. "Imagine having one of those around the house!"

Yes, indeed, thought Jan, and imagine all the lovely lolly

you'd be collecting in British Married Supplementation . . .

"'Ere! What's that you told me before? Force-feed 'em with camel's milk, don't they? Fatten 'em up for the kill, what? Ah-hah-hah-hah-*hah*! Plump, ripe – delicious!"

"Oh, Ned," said Jan feebly, trying to quell her horror, "I don't think you should –"

"Oh, I've made up my mind," he said gruffly and emphatically, "and I expect you to help me." A stern and cautionary look, thick finger raised. "No messing about!"

"Listen, I couldn't take the responsibility –" Jan gabbled, not caring what she said as long as she registered protest before it was too late and she found herself unwillingly in harness. "Honest to God, it would be a disaster. These women are – are *bush* women, Ned. They don't know how to live in a house. Or use a toilet. They never wash!"

"Eh?" He grimaced, raising his nose and upper lip in a way that made him look like a chunky perplexed rabbit.

"They put butter in their hair and rub indigo dye into their skin. They can only cook guinea-corn –"

"I will help you, Ned."

Ned goggled as Jan swung her head around to glare at Anow. "Anow!" she said sharply in Hausa. "Don't get into this! He's full of the love of money – he won't pay a proper bride-price!"

He ignored her. "I can get woman for you, Ned."

"'Ere! He understands! Wot? Wot, mate? You can get me a woman?"

"Yes!"

"For marriage, you understand? With *papers*."

"Yes. *Marriage.*" He pronounced it the French way. "I understand."

"But *young*, mate, a nice *young* girl?"

"Yes, yes, a small girl. A new girl. With *nono* like this . . ." He raised his fists to his chest indicating young high breasts.

Ned practically slavered. *"Chirr-ist!"*

"I will bring her here," said Anow.

*"Chirr-ist!"* said Ned, his eyes popping, all but doubled up in lust and disbelief. *"Jesus!* I think he means *now*!" Face splotchy with excitement he leapt to his feet, wiping his mouth vigorously with the grubby handkerchief.

"Yes. Now. Maybe," said Anow, as if practising grammar.

"Anow! I beg you!" Jan wailed in Hausa. "In the name of God, don't enter this thing!"

"I will bring her here," Anow repeated, making eye contact with Ned, ignoring her.

This was so unusual that she was lost for words. In a flash she realised what had happened. Her unguarded remarks to Ned about 'bush women' and never washing hadn't gone down well.

Anow stood abruptly, slipping the leather loop of the whip over his wrist and slinging his open-sided robe back over his shoulder in a graceful gesture, exposing his golden-brown flank. He slapped the whip against his leg with finality.

"I will bring the girl here – to you," he said to Ned, slender hands emphatically illustrating his words.

Jan was bewildered. Why should he take such offence at what she had said? Not only was it simply a matter of *fact* that the Tuareg were bush people, it was also an everyday joke between them.

"I will go now," said Anow.

Jan got to her feet. Inexplicably, she felt close to tears.

Ned rushed to open the door in a welter of excitement and then Jan was out and away.

She climbed into the Land-Cruiser, which was like an oven pre-heated to cook a Sunday roast, wincing as the hot plastic of the seat scorched through the single thin layer of her cotton wrapper. Yet another reason to wear knickers, a wonderful invention: to prevent one's genitals being fried. To her immense relief, Anow got in – she had been afraid he would stalk off in a huff.

Ned was at the car window, in high glee. "Thank you, Jan! Who would have thought Toy Boy would come up trumps!"

She started up the car. "I'm glad for you, Ned," she muttered to herself.

As they moved down the little drive, Ned's voice sounded in their wake.

"I'll be here, mate! I'll be waiting! And, Jan! Jan! Remember!"

She glanced back as she braked to a halt at the exit.

"The essays: *Zero! Zero!* Finish!" Hands chopping the air. "Fuck 'em! In fact – fuck as many of 'em as you can – that's my policy! Ah-hah-hah-hah-hah-hah!" And he doubled up in laughter at his own wit.

## Chapter 2

Simon Cullen had just given his final lecture of the term to ninety-odd blank-faced, sweating students crammed into a small stifling room, and was heading home in his daffodil-yellow VW beetle. The lecture had been on WH Auden and he was once again ruminating on the folly of forcing such stuff down the reluctant throats of – well, of anyone really, he thought with a grimace – but particularly these mystified Nigerians who didn't even have any cultural clues to help. Like herding a bunch of pre-school kids into an underground cavern, without so much as pencil-torches, and expecting them not only to find their way around but to discourse learnedly on stalactites and stalagmites on their return to the surface. Some of them, heroically, managed to do it despite the odds.

As he approached the roundabout on the edge of the main campus he spotted Jan Prendergast's royal-blue Toyota Land-Cruiser ahead of him. Excellent. He desperately needed someone to talk to and who better than Jan? He accelerated and slid between her and the inner kerb as she took the roundabout. She glanced in his direction, not at all startled by this manouevre. Driving in Zaria was lunatic at the best of times.

They turned off the roundabout and drew up alongside one another, now blocking the road. Simon grinned coyly up at her through his open window, pushing his silky black hair back from his fine-featured face with long brown fingers, eyebrows arched ironically over green eyes. "Darling! I hear you're scandalising the university again! How *do* you do it? God knows I try hard but I just don't have your style! Come and tell me all about it!"

She opened her mouth and, observing the minute hesitation, he knew she was about to say no.

"Iced coffee!" He swiftly flung his parting shot into the tiny pause and sped off along the road to the housing areas, fingers crossed on the wheel. He took the turn to his area and with relief saw that she was following.

It was a profound pleasure as always to step out of the glare of the scorching midday sun and into his shady air-conditioned living-room. He had managed to make the room look light and airy despite the ugly university-issue furniture. The trick was to cover it all up with locally woven off-white blankets in heavy cotton and trailing potted plants. On the walls he had nailed some fine camel blankets, with their characteristic black and rust-red patterns against a creamy background; he was never clear whether these blankets with their rough and scratchy texture were actually *made* of camel hair or were just used as saddle-blankets for camels.

He threw his briefcase on the table and moved into the bedroom area: his room to the left and Kolawole's to the right, bathroom in between. He heard Jan come in the front door.

"Just a tick!" he called. "Must change into something more comfortable!"

He quickly stripped off his embroidered African shirt, figure-hugging cream jeans and skimpy underwear and, turning about, briefly surveyed his smooth lithe tanned body in the full-length mirror. Were those some hairs on his shins? Time for an Immac job again – he sighed and then wondered if there was any left in his precious little store. He put his hand on his cock and squeezed a little, then smirked at the rapid tumescence.

"Oh, dear," he sighed fondly, "whatever will I do with you?" He pushed it back between his legs but it flipped back out and bounced invitingly. "Dear oh dear, *not* very ladylike!" If Jan hadn't been there he would have got out the nude photos Kolawole had allowed him to take and had a leisurely wank.

He stepped into the cold shower and tried not to think of Kola, his live-in Yoruba lover, who was a postgraduate art student.

When he came slinking into the living-room some minutes later, dressed in skimpy white top and his new green, blue and pink woman's cotton wrapper, he found himself playing to an empty house. Jan was asleep in an armchair. He tiptoed up to her.

Her nose was sunburnt, her feet red with dust in their rubber sandals and sweat had left a dusty streak leading down between her breasts. He noticed she was wearing some striking woven Tuareg bracelets in blue and black with touches of red. He must really ask her to get some made for him. Blue, black and white, the Tuareg colours. Lucky for her, with her dark-blue Irish eyes. Her vest-top was dark blue, her wrapper dark blue and white, her sandals blue. He lifted one of her coppery plaits cautiously, testing its thickness with his long fingers and examining the weave. That was another thing – he really must learn to do that four-strand plait – the result was so much thicker.

Poor thing, he thought, as he padded barefoot into the kitchen. Worn out with it all. Screwing the Blue Men of the Desert must be such hard work.

A little while later he nudged her awake, a tall glass of iced coffee in his hand with an iceberg of home-made vanilla ice cream floating on top and a long spoon stuck in it.

"Am I dreaming?" she murmured, looking up at him. "That looks like ice cream."

"Dream come true," he responded archly.

"Where the hell did you get ice cream?"

"I made it, of course."

"You are *so* clever." She sat up and eagerly took the glass from him.

Simon flicked his hair back behind his ears and postured in front of her, hand on hip. "So what do you think of my new wrapper?"

"Brilliant colours!" she said indistinctly, eyes on him but attention obviously on a mouth full of ice cream.

"But wait!" He swivelled round. "*Da-da!* The slogan!" He presented her with his backside. A large round pink circle, the surround decorated with flirtatious almond eyes, sat right on his neat ass. In the centre it read: *Bottom Power*.

Jan exploded in laughter, the coffee sploshing over the top of her glass. "*Aaagh!* I'm losing my precious coffee!" 'Bottom power' was a well-known catch phrase referring to women who used sex to advance themselves in the world.

"Isn't that a scream?" he said. "Found it in Kaduna market and thought 'That's for me!'. Should I wear it to lectures?" With a wiggle, he arranged himself on the leather pouffe in front of her, knees coyly pressed together. "Now tell me all about it!" he breathed in girlish eagerness.

"What? Tom?"

"Yes! It's so thrilling! The man is quite inflamed!"

"Oh, God, Simon," she said with a heartfelt sigh, "when you talk like that it's quite clear you aren't a woman."

"Bitch!" He tossed his head and crossed his knees. "I could teach *you* a thing or two about being a woman!"

"Oh, what do *you* know? You think it's all about wearing a skirt! As if millions of Chinese women don't wear *pants* and still have more woman in their little fingers than you have in – in your *cock!*"

"Darling, that doesn't make any sense –" Oh, dear, that whole Tom Purthill business must have her on edge, he thought charitably. She had flushed and looked quite agitated.

"It's the male ego, I suppose," she rattled on. "Men just can't understand how *repugnant* it is to be pursued by an unwanted male. Actually, *gay* men can't make any sense of the concept 'unwanted male' for starters." She was amused by her last point and looked more cheerful as she started spooning ice cream again.

Simon decided to pout. He pushed his lips out, looked at her askance and held the pose until she looked up.

"Oh, you're sulking!" she said. "Why? Because of what I

said about the Chinese women? Well, I can't take it back. You really have to take your vocation as a female more seriously and get it right."

"But I *am* trying to take it more seriously," he said in the soft namby-pamby tone he used as his female voice. "In fact, I have something important to tell you." He twisted his long outstretched arms around each other, winding his fingers together, and rested them on his crossed knees. With his lanky legs sinuously entwined, he looked like a gangly circus contortionist.

"Yes?" She widened her eyes in encouragement as she spooned more iced coffee in.

He was nervous. He hadn't told anyone else.

'Well . . . I've decided . . . I want to have Kola's baby."

Jan gulped down her ice cream and her eyes widened even more. Froze, in fact, in a startled stare. Then she put her glass down carefully. "What do you mean?" she said cautiously, staring into the coffee, beginning to swirl the last little island of ice cream around with the long spoon.

"I love him – I love him so much it seems that only having a baby can express that love," he said coyly, tightening his contortionist's pose even further. Did that sound glib? Maybe he had over-rehearsed it.

Now she looked him in the eye. "Oh, I understand that!" she said animatedly. "I so much wanted to have Moussa's baby! I was so jealous of every African woman I saw heaving a baby around! Like, it was so simple and matter-of-fact for them but all the forces of society were ranged against me having one!"

Simon well remembered Moussa, the dishy Tuareg man Jan had loved and eventually lost, elder brother of that *sexy* young Anow who hung about with her now. *Very* incestuous. "I *knew* you'd understand!" he said.

"Yes . . . but . . . what do you mean? How can you . . . do that . . . er, exactly?"

"Well, I don't know . . . *exactly* . . . I was hoping you could suggest something."

"Me!" Now she was rattled.

"Well, you know so much about the culture . . ."

"But how can that help? Science hasn't *got* as far as male conception yet, you know! Or have they tried it . . . ? I read something – something about attaching the placenta to the wall of an internal organ like the liver and delivering the baby by caesarian. With the risk of growing breasts." She paused, confused. "Or was that a science fiction story?"

"But I want to be pregnant by him!" he cried, somehow managing to twist his arms together yet another few degrees.

"Eh, yes, but . . . I mean, as you can't . . ." she floundered. "I mean, after all, if you were a woman you could be infertile, too, you know. . ." Her eyes were fixed on him. He could almost hear her brain whirring as she searched for the right thing to say. "So . . . well, what about a surrogate?"

"You mean, hire a woman to have the baby?" He had been waiting for her to suggest that, wanting her to think it was her idea.

"Yes," she said. "But . . ." She now looked like an absorbed researcher flicking through a set of files, checking a multitude of facts. "Very dicey," she said.

He pouted and relaxed his entwined limbs a little. "But *why?*"

"You wouldn't have any legal claim – she could take it away at any time."

"No, she couldn't, Jan! Not if Kola was the father – you know the women have no rights to their children here!"

"True. But – think of this – you'd never get it out of the country – ever. Not even on holiday. If you tried to, *then* she'd have rights – not as a woman but as a Nigerian."

Ah! Here was his cue. "But what if the mother was *not* Nigerian – one of your Tuareg, let's say? Who would ride off into the desert, no complications?"

Jan gave him a funny look that he couldn't interpret – except in so far as it meant 'back off' among other things. Oh, dear, he had been staking everything on that notion.

A slight pause and she continued – without answering his question. "But, in any case, the mother is irrelevant. You know how ferocious Nigerian men are about their paternal rights – he'd whip it away from you if you split up with him, had a row, whatever. And what if you were deported or something?"

Simon untangled himself and began to comb his hair back repeatedly with his fingers in agitation. "But what if I adopted the baby legally? Surely that's possible?"

"I don't know. You could consult a lawyer, I expect. But . . . eh," now she was looking in her coffee-glass again, "what does Kolawole think of the idea anyway?"

"Well, I haven't actually discussed it with him yet," said Simon in a small voice, adopting his naughty-little-girl look, playing with the ends of his hair.

"You'd better do that then, don't you think?" No eye contact.

"I suppose so." He bit into his hair.

Jan drank off the dregs of her coffee and got to her feet. "Got to go. Langley has summoned me to the office at two –

to talk about Tom Purthill, I expect. Can't believe he'll actually be there, of course."

Simon escorted her to the door, reluctant to relinquish his one and only opportunity to talk about his dream. "We must discuss this again. You've given me such hope!"

"Oh, yeah?" she said, apparently mystified.

"Maybe we can have another chat at the picnic tomorrow."

She looked blank.

"Jan! Don't tell me you've forgotten about the picnic?"

"Oh, God, I had. And I wish you hadn't reminded me."

"Oh, don't look so dismayed! It will be *fun*! It's wonderful to get up on that huge inselberg, above all this boringly flat scrub and farmland. Those brawny, macho Peace Corps have absolutely taken it in hand – you've no idea – to the extent of filling up one of those dried-up rock-pools so we can all go skinny-dipping! And there will be camels – well, Land-Rovers too for the fainthearted – to take us to the foot of the inselberg."

"Camels! Where are they getting enough camels? Those mangy things from the market?"

"Hetty Coleman's watchman actually."

"Jesus, I know that guy – a wily old Tuareg who would promise to provide *yaks* if he thought he'd get a 'dash' for trying!"

"Relax, Jan! It's not your problem! You're not involved. Unlike silly me – I volunteered to organise the music – get a sound-system set up to play my soundtrack from *Picnic at Ayers Rock*." He rolled his eyes.

"Oh, excellent – maybe it will serve as a signal to outer space and we'll all be abducted by aliens or whatever happened in the film. God, wouldn't it be marvellous if we could lose some of the party on the rock – like Tom Purthill. Or Langley Forrest, come to think of it."

"Just imagine Langley wandering lost and crazed among the rocks . . . wonderful!" He smiled dreamily over this image for a while.

"We'll all be wandering crazed among the rocks if you ask me," said Jan peevishly as she climbed into her Land-Cruiser. "They could at least have waited for the rainy season."

"But it's an *Easter* celebration! An Easter-egg hunt – with dyed eggs."

Jan stared incredulously. Easter? Easter on Kufena? "The Americans are insane. Just the thought of that bloody sun gruelling down at us, exposed on that merciless inselberg! It's enough to give me sunstroke already!"

"It will be late afternoon! The sun will have mellowed by then!"

"And if we survive to nightfall," Jan continued regardless, "we'll be expected to sit around a campfire and sing Boy Scout songs while swatting mosquitos!"

"Oh, don't be so cynical, Jan! It will be a lark!"

"The trouble with you is, despite the impeccable accent and cultivated pansiness, you are in fact an *Aussi*! And Australians, I believe, hang corks out of their hats and soldier on when normal folk seek shelter under rapidly whirling ceiling-fans."

Simon made a feint at looking camp but then decided to look smug instead. After all, she was complimenting him in a back-handed fashion on all counts.

"G'day, sport! Don't forget to speak to Kolawole!" she called as she swung out the drive.

Oh, dear, yes. Simon waved goodbye and felt far from smug as he re-entered the house.

Jan was pondering on eccentricity as she followed the shaded walkways of the campus. Simon was an absolute nutter, no doubt about it.

God, she wished him luck with Kolawole. She had believed for a long time that Kola was utterly innocent of any sexual interest in Simon – that he was in it for the comfortable rent-free lodgings, fine food, money loans and all the other perks that came with living with a Bature – including future invitations to England, references for jobs and eventual payment of bride-price ('I don't love her, of course, but my family insists . . .'). That may have been true at the start. Now she gathered that, by dint of persistent effort, Simon had managed to lure Kola into some kind of sexual contact.

She remembered a strange conversation she had with Kola one evening when Simon was out. They had ended up drinking most of two bottles of red wine together and . . . well, she couldn't remember, but she must have brought up the subject of Simon's taste for cross-dressing. Worried as always about Simon, she had probably been fishing for indications about Kola's inclinations. At any rate, she remembered him saying that in his culture fucking transvestites was usually perceived to be OK, as it didn't cast doubts on the fucker's masculinity. It was the fuckee who had the problem after all, he said, or words to that effect . . .

That had struck her as the most elegant slice of denial she had ever come across.

God, self-honesty was rare as – chocolate Easter eggs in

Northern Nigeria. Simon wouldn't know it if it jumped up and bit his bum.

Now, Ned Bassett at his best had a raw honesty that was disarming. She grinned. *There* was eccentricity in a full-blown version. You had to give it to him, though – despite his awfulness, he really did have the vital spark. She chuckled aloud, remembering the hideous baiting of Roger. He needed that cat and they were well-matched after all.

She turned into the English Department office and rapped on Langley Forrest's door.

"Enter," came his voice weakly – Nigerian idiom but high-class Bostonian tone.

At least he was there. Surprise, surprise.

He had obviously suffered severely from the shock of coming into the department. His ash-tray was full to capacity already. Somewhere along the line, Langley had decided to save himself from possible cancer by smoking his cigarettes only three-quarter-way down. Their toxicity, he had read somewhere, was reduced significantly by this strategy. The salaries he had been conning out of various overseas departments for a lifetime had made this habit feasible.

He was quite sober, for a wonder.

She sat down across the desk from him. He smiled sweetly at her. She found that ominous.

Jan had a liking for lean men and Langley was undoubtedly lean, so for her he had a sort of residual attractiveness. He was thin and long-boned with a lot of wavy hair which was silver-white and bushy eyebrows under which grey eyes glinted. He wore silver-rimmed spectacles – to set off the hair – a short African shirt in black with silver embroidery, silver-grey corduroy trousers and black leather locally made sandals. Quite an eye for style had Langley. Or perhaps it was his wife Prissie who dressed him.

Jan particularly liked Langley's feet which were lean and brown.

What she did not like was the expression now on his face – one that managed to be petulant and irate at the same time. She also didn't care for the way his hands were trembling, though whether that was from rage or alcohol deprivation she could not yet judge.

"Jan," he said hollowly, making the single word sound like a cry for help and an accusation simultaneously. It was singularly unpleasant hearing her name said like that.

"Um, I need to talk to you –" she began.

"My dear girl," he cut in, in a querulous and nasty tone, "what *are* you playing at?"

"What?" she said, startled at his frontal attack.

"There is no *doubt* but that you've encouraged him –"

"What! Tom Purthill? Encouraged him? But I've explained everything to you! I've told you the man's delusional!"

He looked at her slyly. "So you say. But I saw you myself kissing him goodbye before you went off on that trip at Christmas." He shook another cigarette from the pack with a trembling hand.

Jan gaped as an unwanted memory floated to the surface from wherever she had hidden it. She flushed. "Langley, who told you about that? If you had really been there you wouldn't be describing it like that. I was already turning away and it ended up as a peck on the ear! I didn't even see it coming!"

He glowered at her, lighting up with his silver lighter.

"Langley, I *told* you I had done nothing at all to –"

He cut in. "First, complaints from the Chaplain, next the Vice-Chancellor and now the Immigration Office!"

*Vice-Chancellor! Immigration!* Jan was stunned into silence.

Langley winced, closing his eyes, his lined and fine-boned face looking like that of an irritated saint. Then he opened the eyes again with an obvious effort and with a trembling hand stubbed out his barely smoked cigarette among its fellows. When he spoke he paced out his words as if they hurt him. "They want – to send – Tom home – and deport *you* . . ."

"Deport *me!* *Deport* me! For *what?* Langley, you're not going to let them deport me, surely!" Her heart was thudding in a frightening way.

"I don't know how much I can do . . ."

"You can tell them Purthill's deranged –"

Langley lit up, stubbed the cigarette out immediately and then tried to smoke it nevertheless. "Well, you see . . ." He squirmed and she thought he was embarrassed until she realised he was just stubbing out the already-stubbed cigarette. "It's a political thing. The droughts, you know." He waved the crushed cigarette about vaguely.

"The *droughts? What are you talking about?*" She was all but shrieking, leading to another bout of wincing from Langley.

"Well, you've seen it in the newspapers – the religious leaders are blaming the droughts on the proliferation of prostitutes and persecuting them accordingly . . ."

"And what's that got to do with *me?* Are you saying I'm a *prostitute?*"

"Not at all, but – by extension – single women . . ."

Jan leapt to her feet, outraged. "I'm not staying here to listen to this!"

"Oh, calm down, Jan, calm down! It's a difficult situation – the Vice-Chancellor has to be seen to take some action – the neighbours in the apartments complained, you know."

"Complained about *what?*"

"About the screaming-fits, of course."

*"Screaming-fits?"*

"Didn't you know?"

"No!" She sank back on her chair. "What do you mean – screaming-fits?" Her voice emerged as a near-whisper.

He had lit another cigarette and was now managing to look grave instead of testy. "He has recently taken to locking himself in his apartment and . . . screaming. His neighbours managed to get his door unlocked a few nights ago – the windows are barred, of course – but they couldn't open it because he had piled furniture against it."

"But," Jan whispered, appalled, "doesn't that prove he's sick? That he needs psychiatric help?"

"Well, this is it, you see – the university does want to send him home – but, to the Vice-Chancellor's way of thinking, you aggravated his condition and must be seen to be punished. The femme fatale in *Zorba the Greek* got her throat cut, after all."

Jan's hand shot to her throat. "But – have *you* no say in the matter?"

Langley suddenly began to fumble the cap off a large thermos flask at his elbow. He poured a dark stream of hot coffee into a plastic cup. A pleasant aroma of freshly ground coffee pervaded the office – with a heavy undertone of something else. He gulped at it. "Excuse me. I don't have another cup to offer you some."

Jan murmured pardon.

"Look . . ." He squirmed again. "I'm cursed with my personnel! Christ, I've got Bassett! *You!* That loopy faggot Simon Cullen!" He groaned. "That battle-axe Coleman and her dog! I must be the only Department Head in West Africa to have a German Shepherd on his staff! I can't afford to oppose the Vice-Chancellor – it wouldn't take much for him to see us as a worn-out colonial dinosaur, a rotten mango better plucked off the tree and thrown on the garbage-heap!"

This flight of mixed metaphor had apparently strained him, since he heaved a hollow sigh, grabbed the cup on his desk and drained the coffee in one go. He smacked his lips loudly, filled the cup to the brim again, then paused in the act of raising it shakily to his lips. "But I am prepared to stick my neck out for you."

"You *are?*" Relief flooded through her. He wasn't going to throw her to the wolves after all.

He sipped. "Well, we *are* friends, Jan." He gazed at her. "We are friends, are we not?"

He seemed to expect an answer.

"Um, yes," said Jan.

The plastic cup still teetered crazily because of the tremor in his hands but his eyes were very intent under the bushy eyebrows. "So we are obliged to scratch each other's backs, isn't that so?"

Oh, God, thought Jan, don't make me have to sleep with Langley Forrest!

"Isn't that so?" he insisted.

"Um, yes!" Maybe if I closed my eyes it mightn't be too bad, she thought in desperation.

"So there's a little favour I need to ask you."

"Yes?" she said brightly, quaking.

"I have a very dear friend, a lady . . ."

Oh, thank you, God! A mistress!

"You know her, I'm sure? Marie Ogunbesan?"

"That Frenchwoman married to a Yoruba – she's in the French Department?" Too young for Langley, surely?

"Yes."

"Well, I know her to see." And I've heard all the gossip about her lousy marriage.

Langley nodded and sipped his coffee. A little lip-smacking followed but his grey eyes were still intent. "Well, she needs to travel to Niger – as soon as possible – and you, I know, are driving there within the next few days."

"Yes?"

"Well, I want you to take her with you, Jan. As a special favour to me." He smiled sweetly, inclining his head – and his coffee – to one side.

"Eh, you're spilling your coffee, Langley . . ." She reached out for a toilet-roll which was perched on the extreme edge of his desk and began to mop up the coffee for him. "Em . . . the trouble is . . . I'm committed to taking a Tuareg family with me and I don't know exactly how many – it will be a terrible squash – it always is!"

"No matter! She won't mind at all!"

She lobbed the soaked bog-roll into a metal wastepaper bin whose butt-filled interior looked and smelt like the crater of a long-erupted volcano. "But I'm going straight north past Tahoua and Tchin Tabaraden – I could only take her over the border. And I suppose she's going west to Niamey?"

"No, no. She only needs to get north of the border."

What an odd answer, thought Jan. Then it dawned on

her. Oh my God! That's it! He's planning to elope with her! He's probably going to pick her up on the other side!

"Excellent!" The empty cup wobbled its way downwards until it came to a jittery halt on the desk. "And I will deal with the Vice-Chancellor and Immigration – don't worry a jot about that!"

But he wouldn't be here to deal with it. Oh, God, he was planning to throw her to the wolves after all . . . literally, off the back of his fast-departing sledge. And one of the slavering wolves would be Marie's husband.

He was smiling at her benignly.

She sat there gazing at him.

"Well, off you go then! I will let Marie know."

She got up, scrabbling wildly in her mind for a way out of this situation.

"She'll be at the picnic tomorrow evening," said Langley, "so you'll be able to have a chat with her there." In his enthusiasm he had actually risen to his feet. He rounded the desk now, swaying a little, to show her to the door; but he must have found the motion unpleasant because he changed his mind, went back, clinging to the desk, and collapsed into his chair again.

Then he sat there, smiling his sweetest little-boy smile, the one he must have used on his nanny back in Boston when he had wheedled his way out of her. The sly bastard. "Thank you, Jan. I knew you would want to help. You're a kind person."

The hypocrite.

She was surprised he hadn't told her to have a nice day.

She left him, bent over his desk like a frail and broken reed, smiling his sweet smile.

## Chapter 3

Jan rounded the shoulder of rock and a clatter of long-tailed monkeys scattered shrieking before her. Stone-grey lizards scampered away from her feet.

A small diamond-shaped pool lay in a cleft of rock before her, some eight feet long and four feet across at its widest. A green hose lay coiled like a snake on its edge, betraying the pool's American Peace Corps man-made origins.

But Jan wasn't looking at the hose.

A naked Anow was squatting beside the bare pool, his back to her, head bent, washing his genitals with an intentness that suggested masturbation. He turned his head and flashed a smile at her over his shoulder, then turned again to his task.

She leant against the rock and stared, glad of the large sunglasses that hid her expression. Better again if she had the Tuareg men's veil that hid the mouth. The mouth was more revealing than the eyes, certainly.

He raised his arms and, throwing his head back, twisted

his hair into a knot at the back of his neck, lithe young muscles rippling.

It was such a beautiful pose, she thought, that supple squat that echoed the limber poses of the long-tailed monkeys sitting watching curiously at a safe distance. A posture that accentuated the swell of muscular buttocks. The Tuareg ass was a wonderful thing anyway – she thought of the female version: a jutting, bouncing lure that followed them behind swathed in soft black cotton. A young American had confessed to her over a few beers that he was terrified he might lose control and just pull out his dick in public and stick it into one. Anow's curves would seem almost feminine if they weren't so powerfully muscular.

Made for thrusting.

She let her breath out in a harsh sigh. She hadn't realised she'd been holding it in.

He turned his head again.

"Why don't you enter?" she called in Hausa. Desert habits die hard, she thought. In the desert, she had often seen people washing in this squatting pose with precious water drawn from wells by the sweat of the brow.

"I will enter," he replied.

Then she realised he was soaping himself first to shift the blue indigo dye from his skin. He must have pilfered a bar of soap from the BBQ supplies.

They were alone on the rock as yet. They had arrived early and Anow, as a 'professional' watchman, had been roped into guarding the stuff while a second load of supplies was fetched from neighbouring Wusasa. He and Jan had then clambered around hiding the hardboiled eggs, dyed so painstakingly by the American wives and kids, in any little rock crevice they could find.

Now Anow slid into the water – it came up to his ribcage – and began to rub the soap off. "What about you?" he called.

"No. Bilharzia."

"Fil-what?"

"That worm that lives in ponds and enters your skin."

But the water looked inviting and was fresh, after all.

"Why weren't the monkeys scared of you?" she asked.

"I stayed still and they came close. Look! They are stealing the eggs!"

She looked and sure enough the monkeys were clutching brightly coloured eggs in their fists. There goes the Easter-egg hunt, she thought wryly. They'll have swiped the lot by the time people get up here. Hope everyone's amused . . . she thought wryly of the American wives labouring on the eggs with 'masking-tape' and nylon stockings, vinegar and carrot-tops, cabbage and spinach leaves, onion skins, apple and orange peel and God knows what else, smug in the notion that they were doing the Mayflower or the *Home on the Range* thing or whatever . . . she grimaced. Well, just as long as the creatures didn't start chucking the eggs at people.

Anow freed his blue-black hair from its knot, ducked and drenched it, then pushed it back with supple fingers.

My very own Jungle Book, she thought. Get in the water, Jan – Bali Hai is calling loud and clear.

"Jan! Enter!" His almond eyes were alive with invitation.

Somehow she found herself pulling off her clothes: the

blue scarf around her head, her navy top, her navy bra, her panties – cherry red, if you please – yes, she had reverted to wearing them. She hesitated then, with her dark-blue and white wrapper around her, wanting to step into the water wearing it. Not just modesty – more a residual childhood memory of Bali Hai and 'Happy Talk' where the exotic Chinese-Polynesian beauty had swum underwater, with her lover, in a white sarong which sensuously outlined her body. Jan's cotton wrapper was a 'Java print' and had the dark-blue and white of Dutch Delft ware – a pattern brought back from the Orient in the seventeenth century by the Dutch East India Company. Yes, her Java print merited a tropical douching – but then she would have a soaked wrapper to contend with and darkness soon to fall.

The late-afternoon sun slanted across the rock, reddening it and Anow's brown skin like the critically-derided stage-effect cloud that billowed over the set in *South Pacific*: another happy coincidence that spurred her on.

She slid in modestly, using the wrapper as a shield but leaving it on the rock. She waded a few steps towards Anow and her tropical dream come true.

His gleaming eyes.

His laughing mouth.

His finely muscled arms.

She slid inside their circle.

His long erect penis.

She recoiled.

"What is it?" he asked huskily, encircling her again.

She gazed into the almond eyes that glowed with the red of the sun. She looked down; her breasts were pink ivory against the red-brown of his chest.

His penis was most definitely erect, hard against her belly. Why should that have been a surprise?

What's more, there was a throbbing between her legs.

He dropped his arms to encircle her hips and lifted, breath now rasping, and she wrapped her legs about his narrow hips, her face and lips against his crinkled blue-black hair. Arms about him as they were always meant to be. Her vagina contracted strongly as she felt it come down on the head of his penis. He pushed fiercely and, with the slight squeakiness of water, his hardness slid in, as easy as that. He was in her! Anow! But . . . he shouldn't be . . . she was conscious of the tender slightness of his body compared to that of his brother but the startling largeness of his penis.

She tightened her arms about his neck and pressed her lips against the cool wet skin of his face.

Her vagina closed hungrily about him and, even as she ground her clitoris fiercely against him and gasped aloud, the purity of the moment was lost and her mind was already thinking: *I must stop, I must stop!*

But it was too late. She was already spasming, greedily sucking on his cock. She clung to him as she orgasmed, belly cleft with pleasure like a juicy watermelon torn in two. And in her blind pleasure she felt the throb, throb, throb of his ejecting semen.

His clean brown skin against her mouth. His slender muscled back under her hands.

She pulled herself off him, reluctant to release him. Then she was out of the pool and scrambling into her clothes.

"Jan, what is it?" He was reaching for her from the pool.

She didn't answer, her mind swirling. She tucked the end of her wrapper in.

"What is it?" he repeated, this time in Tamajegh. He reached out and grabbed her ankle in a strong grip.

She squeezed her eyes shut. "Let go!" she muttered through gritted teeth.

"Talk to me!"

"*Let! Me! Go!*" She kicked wildly with each word and on the third kick freed her ankle. Her own violent action fuelled her anger. She turned on him. "So you take me for a whore? Like your brother did?"

"No!"

"Fuck your brother, fuck you?"

"It's not like that, Jan!"

"I thought you were my friend! But you – you were just waiting your turn!" She spun around and left.

What had she done? What had she done? She scrambled up the rock to the picnic area. Christ! Anow! A kid! Moussa's brother!

Her dependant, her responsibility, her child. Her *friend*. She had thrown away that lovely, light, loving relationship for an unthinking *fuck*! What would Moussa think of her protestations of undying love now? *Would he tell him?*

She reached the picnic area and sat on one of the mats laid out there. The trouble was, she thought, as she pressed her face into her raised knees and rocked herself, the trouble was that what she had spoken so wildly down at the rock-pool was in fact the truth. He had broken all the taboos he would have respected if she were Tuareg, if he had really accepted her as a sister, as one of them. He *had* taken her for a whore while she had taken him as blood-brother. It hurt.

"Look at that silly fart Forrest! Ah-hah-hah-hah-*hah*! Now I've seen everything!"

Ned Bassett had been deposited by Land-Rover at the foot of the huge inselberg that crouched like a monstrous smooth-flanked hippopotamus on the scorched plain. He was now smugly watching the arrival of the more adventurous souls who had opted to ride the camels.

"What daft sod put *him* up on a camel?" he scoffed.

"Hush!" said Marie Ogunbesan, a slender brown finger to her lips. "His wife will hear you."

"Excuse me, I'm sure," said Ned and began to chortle into his crumpled handkerchief.

Langley was drunk as a lord to judge from the alarming way he was swaying about on the saddle which, Tuareg-fashion, was tiny and perched precariously towards the front of the hump. He was clinging like a rodeo rider to the three-pronged saddle-horn which he seemed to think functioned like a pilot's joy-stick. Prissie, his wife, her minute but chunky figure attired in a full-length tie-dye violet and white dress, had already dismounted and now, tension in every line of her face under a large Fulani conical straw hat, she was assisting his arrival. This assistance amounted to focusing on her swaying spouse, arms outstretched as if he were attached to her on invisible strings and she was an inept puppeteer making a sad cock-up of a stage performance. On the other side, Hetty Coleman's Tuareg watchman who was leading the camel had the same instinct and held his whip aloft as if to prod Langley into a more stable position. As he gave an order and the camel lunged forward to fall to its knees, as camels do, the guide did actually ram the whip against Langley's chest to prevent him from pitching forward on his face. The camel rocked back to settle on its haunches and Langley executed a full 180-degree circuit in the saddle while Prissie's gestures became exaggerated to the point where she now seemed more like a flamboyant stage magician abracadabra-ing to a climax.

Simon Cullen came up the slope as Ned's chortling changed into asthmatic heaving behind the handkerchief.

"Oh dear, I shan't be the better for that for a long while," said Simon in his campest tones. "Those tiny saddles! It's like riding on a particularly uncomfortable dildo. And I was already a bit raw in that area. My houseboy used a highly corrosive toilet-cleaner this morning which unfortunately splashed up as I was sitting on the loo," – this very coyly and with a slight wiggle –" and hit me in the most delicate part of my anatomy."

Marie Ogunbesan threw him a wide-eyed glance, made an odd fluttering gesture with a hand and went to join a group gathering at the path which led up the inselberg.

Ned gazed after her neat dark-haired figure.

"Well, you certainly frightened her off, mate! Not everyone is into *The Joy of Anal Retention* – or what was that book you had?"

"Ned! Please! *Anal Pleasure Safely*," said Simon with a smirk.

"Yes, indeed – you are rum buggers, you lot! Oh, cripes! Look at that! Ah-hah-hah-hah-hah! The Charge of the Light Brigade, wot?"

A camel came charging across the bush, ridden by a squat, brown-skinned woman with close-cropped greying hair whose conventional cotton dress was blown high around her waist, revealing some sort of old-fashioned beige bloomers. A large German Shepherd was keeping pace with the camel.

"It's our esteemed colleague, Hetty Coleman," said Ned in glee. "My, my, my. They could have done with her at the relief of Mafeking, eh?"

They watched as she swung to the ground and embraced the dog as he put his paws on her shoulders.

"She masturbates that dog, you know," said Simon conversationally.

Ned goggled, jowls shaking. "Eh? Ah, don't be a silly bugger," he said weakly. "There ain't no one would do that."

"Oh, she told me so herself. Does it daily – well, maybe in season, I don't know – do male dogs have a season? To relieve his sexual tension, she says."

"Relieve hers, more like." The 'ah-hah-hah-hah-hah' that followed was half-hearted.

"I daresay. Apparently it's a relatively widespread practice among – ah, ardent dog-owners."

"Not in any circles *I* know of, mate," said Ned.

"Oh, in very respectable circles, I believe. It prevents the dog from trying to rut against the vicar's leg, you know."

"Encourage 'im, I should think."

"Yes. Lucky old vicar."

"Eh? You are a rum lot, you queers!" Ned regarded him wonderingly.

Hetty, Langley and Prissie were now coming up the slope towards them, Hetty supporting Langley by an elbow, all but lifting him off the ground. Prissie was still doing puppet-master as Langley flopped and swayed in Hetty's powerful grip.

"It's scandalous! Scandalous!" Hetty was booming. "How do they propose to guard them? There have been no proper arrangements that I know of – only the odd security guard, a few Tuareg! Priceless works of art guarded by imbeciles!"

Langley dug his heels in and began to fumble in his pocket. A crushed pack had half-emerged when Hetty pulled him onwards with a jerk, leaving Prissie to scramble about in the dry grass picking up a starburst of scattered cigarettes.

"Welcome to the Rock," said Ned in courteous mode, baring his bunch of teeth in a smarmy smile. "No one ever gets off, I believe."

Now, with his Head of Department and ladies present, he would play the gentleman for a while.

"Hello, Prissie," said Simon and kissed her, the big Fulani hat making it an awkward procedure. He didn't kiss Hetty.

Langley stared bemusedly at Ned as if unsure of whether he had ever seen him before. He reached a trembling hand backwards without looking and Prissie thrust the pack of cigarettes into it.

Swaying, he pulled out a lighter and seemed to be attempting to light up the cigarette pack.

"Nice bit of riding there, Langley," said Ned obsequiously but with a faint smirk on his lips.

Prissie came to the rescue and took over the cigarette operation while Langley smiled sillily. He was drunk as a coot.

When at last he was dragging at a cigarette he seemed to muster a degree of sobriety. Squinting through a screen of smoke at Hetty, who was now ignoring them and surveying the scene at large, he said querulously but with amazing clarity and minimal slurring considering his condition, "You can't hold me res-*pon*sible for Boston's stupidity."

Hetty swung back to face him, hands on hips. "You could have told them, Langley."

"I *did* tell them," he said like an indignant child – as if he might follow that with 'I did! I did!'.

"He did," said the half-pint Prissie, nodding the Fulani hat.

"The Nigerian collection –" He dragged on his cigarette. "The Nigerian collection . . ."

They all waited.

"You're talking about the museum pieces sent on loan?" Ned prompted helpfully.

"Boston are imbeciles," said Hetty forcefully. "Call themselves museum curators! I believe they didn't even make investigations as to security and housing – if they had they wouldn't have sent it at all! And as Langley was the one negotiating with them I certainly hold him responsible."

"The Nigerian collection . . ." said Langley.

"Yes?" said Simon.

"The dog," said Langley, gesturing with his cigarette. "What's the name of the dog?"

"Ajax," said Hetty crisply.

"He's sulking in his tent," said Langley. "Or was that Hector?"

Ajax had begun to snuffle beneath his mistress's tent-like navy cotton skirts. Prissie averted her eyes and took advantage of the distraction to shove what seemed like a plastic bottle of water into Langley's hand.

Hetty meanwhile disregarded Ajax's incursions much as a mother would disregard a small child tugging at her skirts for attention – or as an African mother might disregard a child who toddled up and began to tug at a breast.

Langley was taking large swallows from the bottle, smacking his lips.

"You were saying about the Nigerian collection, hon," Prissie said.

Langley, refreshed by the liquid intake, suddenly became articulate. "The Nigerian collection – is a hot potato. Boston are em-*barr*-assed. They shouldn't have it. Belongs here. They have no right to it. They had no choice. They *had* to send it."

All eyes were drawn – darting away in embarrassment, flicking back in fascination – to the spectacle of Ajax under Hetty's cotton dress, now apparently licking her sturdy brown thighs below her beige bloomers. She had put down a fond hand – for all the world as if she were encouraging him.

"They don't care. About se-*curity*," said Langley. "They don't care because they never ex-*pect* to get the coll-*ection* back from the Nigerians. That's the thing. As long as their shot-hot – shot-hot – hot-*shot* lawyers set things up so they *seem* to have satisfied insurance requirements, they don't care. Boston . . . Boston is ready to kiss the collection goodbye. What is that dog up to?"

And with that, all pretence at normality was dropped like so many hot cakes as, to everyone's consternation but Hetty's, Ajax began to rut against her thigh. Indeed, even to a casual observer who hadn't heard the rumours, it was clear she appeared to be lending her squat thigh to the operation.

Now centre stage and apparently appreciating it, Hetty began to wrestle with the dog. "Here, boy, here! Come to Mummy! *Argh! Argh! Argh!*" She wrestled him to the ground.

Silly fixed smiles were married to bulging eyes as a circle of faces hung on the spectacle of Ajax in a headlock, still grinding away enthusiastically, as once again the world was given an unasked-for view of Hetty Coleman's large beige bloomers.

Screaming children at risk of life and limb had pursued monkeys absconding with dyed eggs, parents had pursued said children over the treacherous surfaces sweating and cursing, video-camera-bearing picnickers had scrambled along bringing up the rear, the Peace Corps had skinny-dipped rather coyly in their man-made rock pool (said parents half-heartedly shooing said children away while trying to video the event at the same time), countless photos had been taken, the sun had set, home-made burgers and shoe-leather steaks had been barbecued and devoured. Sloppy Joes had been slopped up. Endless conversations about the dyeing of eggs had taken place.

Now Simon's soundtrack from *Picnic at Ayers Rock* eerily needled itself into the cracks and crevices of Kufena like moon music.

Jan and Marie settled themselves on a rock outcrop and looked out over the dark plain far below with its sparse glimmers and occasional strings of light. Jan was covertly eyeing her companion with envy. Marie had the French trick of looking classically stylish in any setting. How was it done? Flawless olive skin, slim wrists with expensive silver bracelets, a tiny waistline clasped about with the thick leather belt of her cream linen A-line skirt, a neat little black top, dark-brown real-leather sandals, smooth brown legs. How had she scrambled up this rock in flaring heat, eaten Sloppy Joes, chased monkeys and still emerged looking so cool – so *clean*? So *French*? Her black hair swung thick, straight and heavy to shoulder level – a simple cut but with that stamp of expertise. But where in God's name had she got a French haircut in Northern Nigeria? Jesus, what a curse it was to be Irish! Nothing on earth could ever make Jan look like that.

Marie smiled nervously.

"So," said Jan cautiously, with a small sigh, "you want to go to Niger?"

Marie nodded and the expensive haircut bounced. "Yes, I and my two children."

Children? "Children?" *What?*

"Yes, the boy is two years and the girl is four years," Marie informed her chattily.

Damn! Even less room. God knows how many kids the Tuareg family would be hauling. "Eh, Langley didn't mention children . . ." Crafty bastard.

"Yes . . . there are – a few things Langley didn't mention."

You betcha, thought Jan. "Umm?"

Marie fixed earnest dark eyes on Jan. "Please . . . can I trust you?"

"Well, yes." What, what, *what* was going on?

"I can trust you, to confide in you?"

"Yes, you can," Jan nodded. Sure you can – I've been bloody blackmailed and I bet you know it.

"OK."

"OK." Oh God, spare me.

Marie paused and seemed to look at the moon for inspiration. She looked back at Jan. "I am running away from my husband."

Oh, bugger, thought Jan.

"And I must go as soon as possible. He has travelled to the south today and will be gone until next Sunday night. I must go *now*." She looked pleadingly at Jan.

"Oh," said Jan weakly, "I don't know if I –"

"Jan!" A slender brown hand reached out and caught at her wrist while dark eyes pleaded eloquently. "I cannot bear any more what he is doing to me. I met him in France where he was doing a postgraduate degree and he seemed like another man. So free, so different, so full of *joie du vivre*!" Her hands sketched precise expressive gestures. "I lived with him for two years, then came to Nigeria to visit his family and everything seemed wonderful! Then I married him – in France – and came back here to a life like a prisoner."

Jan had heard it all before. So many cases, all exactly the same. And it tore her heart out every time. *But* . . .

"I work but when I come home I cannot even go to the market without his permission. My life is miserable. And . . . he has become quite violent. I tried to complain to his relatives but they see nothing wrong with my situation. I even tried to get my brother in France to speak with him – my husband made many promises but –" she shrugged elaborately, "he did not keep them. Worst of all, he will not allow me to take the children home to France, not even for a short holiday to see my mother. My mother can come here, he says. But he *knows* she cannot – she has the hypertension. I have permission to go to France – but without the children. He knows I will come back for them."

Tears were now glistening in her eyes. She bent her head to wipe them away.

Oh, bugger, thought Jan, how am I going to say no?

Marie raised her head again and tried to speak but her lips trembled and she turned away as her face twisted. Then she threw her head back, brimming eyes closed, tear-stained face to the moon, and bit down on her lip.

Jan's heart quailed at this raw pain. *How was she going to say no!*

In a few moments Marie continued, her voice wobbling. "And now I discover he has another woman and a child in another house down south." She took a deep breath. "I cannot bear it."

This is impossible, thought Jan. For starters, I will have to come back here – and the man will strangle me with his bare hands if he knows I've helped her. That's the worst-case scenario. The best is that I'll be deported anyway for all my pains.

Stealing someone's wife and kids was not going to go down well with the Immigration Officer, a dyed-in-the-wool male chauvinist Muslim.

"Em . . . as we're being frank, can I ask you something?" she said.

Marie nodded.

"Are you – are you running away with Langley Forrest?"

Marie burst into incredulous laughter. "Don't be ridiculous!"

"But why is he so – involved?"

"We are friends."

Jan had to leave it at that.

A thought struck her. "Marie, if your husband's watching you like a hawk and you're fighting about taking the children to France, are you sure he hasn't already alerted the airports and the border crossings?"

"But he has! Because I have tried to escape before." A wry smile twisted Marie's face. "That time I took only the baby – my daughter was with him and I had to leave her."

Jesus! She went without her little girl! God, what kind of desperation did that indicate?

"That is why I must go incognito."

"Incognito? What? With a false passport or something?" Worse and worse.

"No. Langley thought you could disguise me as a Tuareg woman."

"Langley thought *what?*" Jan gasped. The lunatic *nutter*!

"He suggested you could –"

"I heard, I heard! Ah!" She stared bemused at the Frenchwoman.

"I can easily pass," Marie went on eagerly. "I am dark-skinned with brown eyes. My children are half-Nigerian and so their skin-colour looks right. And we speak in French like Nigeriens."

Jan gaped at her. The gall of it. Though what she said was true. In black robes with indigo dye rubbed into her skin and her hair plaited she would look the part. And, in any case, the border-police would probably not even spare a Tuareg woman a glance. "But few bush women would know any French – what if they address you in Tamajegh? What if this is Give-the-Tuareg-a-Fright Week? What if, this week, they step up the policy of harassing illegal migrants?"

Dark eyes widened. "It is my only hope!"

Time for the speech. Jan drew a deep breath and plunged in.

"Marie, don't you see . . . I would love to help you . . . but what you're asking me is terribly dangerous. God knows what could happen. They could decide I was a Libyan spy – they are paranoid about the Tuareg using Nigeria and Chad as a corridor to get to Libya – where, the notion is, they plot the downfall of the government in Niger. And I've promised to take a Tuareg family with me – they could get into serious trouble – imprisonment or worse! I *really* can't do this –"

So what about her agreement with Langley – assuming he wasn't eloping after all? What indeed? But taking her chances in the Tom Purthill affair seemed a cinch compared to these shenanigans.

"I can't," she finished. "No way."

"Then can you find someone," Marie pleaded, "some Tuareg who would be willing to take me across?"

About this Jan had no hesitation. "I couldn't ask any of them to take that risk."

"But what if we avoided the frontier-posts? They do that all the time, do they not? Go through the bush?"

"Yes, but that's worse – you could get shot by the mounted police or, at any rate, hauled in for serious questioning. Better take your chances on the road."

"But could we not bribe the mounted police?"

She had really done her homework. Jan sighed. "You're not getting the point: any of that might work very easily on a lucky day but *it's the risk*. I can't take the risk and I can't ask anyone else to take it."

"But I would pay!"

Jan hesitated. Might there be a fortune in this for one of her destitute friends? "How much?"

"A hundred naira?"

A hundred naira! That did it! Talk about cheap!

"No, I couldn't ask anyone to risk their lives for a hundred naira!"

Did they think the Tuareg were children? A wonder they didn't offer a bottle of Coke in payment like she'd seen some Americans do in reward for a car washed or a yard swept.

She thought of Ned's request for a Tuareg girl and Simon's for a Tuareg surrogate mother who would co-operatively ride off into the desert leaving her child behind. It was obviously open season on the erstwhile Lords of the Desert.

Suddenly she was angry and her anger lent her the strength to be tough. There was only one way out of this situation: walk away before she relented.

She got up. "Sorry," she said, without looking at Marie.

She walked away, uncomfortably aware of Marie's despairing brown eyes fixed on her back.

She stopped at the rim of the rock overlooking the picnic area and stood there, trying to remember the easiest way down.

"Jan! Jan! What are you doing up there, you silly sod? I've been holding this for you for an *hour*!" Ned Bassett's glasses gleamed up at her in the moonlight.

"Oh, hi, Ned!"

"You can get your own food in future!"

There was a small dark square on his palm. An American brownie. He'd been holding it for an hour. And he was peeved and offended.

She almost turned back to discuss illegal border-crossings further with Marie.

She looked up at the fantastic diamond-studded sky embracing the inselberg.

Somebody up there had it in for her.

## Chapter 4

Simon heard the car pull up outside. He peered through the slats of the wicker window-blinds into the glare of the mid-morning sun.

It was Jan. Oh, he thought a little nervously, pulling a face, she'll want to know what Kola had to say about the baby. He hadn't asked him yet.

But Jan didn't look up to much Gestapo stuff as she plodded in.

Dear, dear, he thought, biting his lip – still off form? She was worrying herself to death about Tom Purthill and Immigration. And she'd had a bad fright on Kufena when young Anow did a disappearing act after the picnic. She really had been frantic. With a head full of *Picnic at Ayers Rock* she'd been convinced he had fallen into a crevasse, been abducted by aliens or had thrown himself off the rock in a fit of despair because of some silly quarrel they'd had.

Meanwhile, it seemed, Anow had been safely escorting the camels back to the university.

Poor Jan. She was having a rough ride. "Iced coffee?" he proposed diplomatically.

"Oh, God, yes!" she said fervently. "Can't stay long – I'm leaving for Niger tomorrow morning." She plonked herself down on an armchair. "I'm on my way to Zaria now – have to buy a few more jerrycans."

He shimmied across the room towards the kitchen in his long-time favourite wrapper which was a riot of gaudy cocks of the feathered kind with the slogan *Good Cocks Rise Early* and, as he fluttered his eyelashes over his shoulder, he was rewarded with a wide grin from Jan.

"Life's a stage," he murmured to himself as he took his ice cream from the freezer. "And all the men, women – and especially those in drag – are merely players."

When he emerged she said, "Can you believe it? Just met Ned – I told him I'm travelling tomorrow but he's landed me with getting a cylinder of gas for him in Zaria! And *potatoes*!" She took the iced coffee and gloated over it. "Oh my God, that's beautiful!"

He sat on the pouffe and regarded her. "So why haven't you travelled yet? You usually can't be seen for dust as soon as we get a break."

"Oh . . ."

What was she hiding? It was so unlike her to hedge. "You shouldn't fret so much. I'm sure Langley is blowing all that stuff about Immigration out of proportion – you know how he is."

"People *do* get deported."

They did. "Eat your ice cream – don't let it melt."

She took a spoonful, then gazed at him as if she were about to say more. Her eyes dropped. A further pause. "Anow hasn't turned up."

"You mean – since the picnic?"

She nodded.

"Oh, my God! Was he abducted by aliens after all?" He rolled his eyes.

"No, no, no! He's farting around the university, procuring for bloody Bassett. In fact, he's already done the dirty deed: provided a woman who's squatting outside Ned's door even as we speak while her relatives negotiate marriage . . ."

"Actually outside his door?" He burst out laughing. "Oh, wonderful!"

"Yes. I know it's funny but – oh, stop laughing, Simon – the poor woman! Life with Ned – *sex* with Ned – a fate worse than death!"

"Have you seen her? What's she like?"

"I haven't actually seen her – I've been keeping well away. Luckily, turns out it's a long time since she's seen fifteen but still . . ." She sighed.

"Oh, there you go again! Always fretting about some underdog or other! Cheer up! Think of yourself for a change!"

"Is that your cue for a musical number? 'Happy Talk' would do fine." And, oddly, she winced.

"No, but I'd *love* to do 'I'm in Love with a Wonderful Guy'!"

"Oh, you'd need me for the chorus and I'm really not up to it. All those 'I'm-in-love's' – no way!"

Simon giggled. "But, really, sweetheart, those wily Tuaregs can take care of themselves – as they did for centuries before Jan Prendergast came along!"

"But they weren't destitute and drought-ridden migrant labourers then," she muttered, her head pressed back against the armchair, eyes closed.

Oh, dear, worse and worse. "Oh, *lighten up*, Jan! You know, I keep telling you, a quick fuck from that young pal of yours would straighten you out for the road – what?" As her eyes sprang open and she flushed. "Don't look so shocked – he's *gagging* for it! Oh . . ." He had *definitely* hit a nerve. "Have I said something – close to the bone?"

"Oh . . . he's . . . a bit difficult to handle these days . . ."

"Well, a firm grip does the trick –" He broke off as Jan glowered at him. "Oh, be like that, then!"

He arranged a sultry pout on his face, then bethought himself that there was little hope of discussing his baby-to-be with her in this mood. Noting that there was something juicy to be ferreted out about her young playmate, he quickly replaced the pout with a sunny smile, got up, sashayed over to the bookcase and picked up a newspaper that lay on top. "I've been saving something for you," he said smugly.

She immediately perked up, sitting up in her armchair and gazing at him expectantly, a half-smile on her face.

He struck a graceful pose, one hand on hip, the other holding the folded newspaper like a playscript, and declaimed: *"Did Boa Constrictor Swallow Taxi Driver?"* This was rewarded by an immediate chuckle from Jan. Success already. *"Our report that a taxi-driver was swallowed by a boa constrictor on the Ibadan to Lagos road has been denied. The report said that the driver had lowered his trousers and squatted down to relieve himself at the side of the road, when in full view of his passengers a boa constrictor emerged from the bush and swallowed him. Witnesses said the boa constrictor began to swallow at the buttock."*

"Which one, I wonder?" spluttered Jan.

*"Safe Home Taxi Company said last night that this is a vicious slander spread by their rivals. 'There has never been one of our taxi-drivers swallowed by a boa constrictor on the road in question,' a spokesman said. We apologise to Safe Home Taxi if our facts were not correct.'"*

Chuffed at her guffaws, he was encouraged to greater efforts. "And something else!" He plucked a slim pamphlet-like book from the top row of the bookshelves. "From our favourite writer!"

"Ah-ha! Sunshine Boy's latest!" grinned Jan.

"Indeed. *How to Be Taken Seriously by Women: Sunshine Boy Advises.* No, no! Don't laugh already!"

Jan pressed her fingers against her lips. Her face was glowing red as it always was when she laughed or drank alcohol. Or had sex, Simon supposed. Rudolph the Red-nosed Reindeer in person. Thank God I'm not cursed with Irish skin, he thought with a mental shudder.

"That's better. Right. This is an instruction book on how to write love letters. The heading of this letter is: *Sunshine Boy Proposes.* And it goes like this: *"Dear My Treasure To Be, Love is the porridge of life."* He waited, smirking, finger marking the page, until her laughter subsided. *"Love is the porridge of life and I now write to ask you to be my wife. My head is hanged down in missing you. If you do not answer positively I am feared it will be hanged up. My ears are cocked to hear from you, Oh pack your lips and be ready to hand them over to me when I come.* (She laughs) *I beg to close, Cool kisses – Sunshine Boy."*

"'She laughs' ?"

"Yes – in brackets – like a stage direction. But here comes the reply!"

She waited – grinning, red-faced, chin on hand.

*"Sunshine Boy Receives A Disappointing Reply to the Former Letter.* This is what 'Dear My Treasure To Be' has to say: *Dear Sunshine Boy, I am sorry to disappoint you but my decision is that I cannot marry you because you are not a Minister of Finance."* He had to stop again until Jan calmed down. *"Please take this as not personal as many other men who are not Ministers of Finance have asked for my hand in marriage and I have rejected them all. Keep fit, Patricia Olowu.'"*

"Oh, God! You're killing me!" Jan was swabbing tears from her glowing face.

"Aren't they just unbelievable? I still can't believe Sunshine Boy isn't just taking the piss. Let me see –" He flicked through the booklet. "The endings are best! '*I drop my biro here – Cherryoh! Thanks in full. Signed, Homo Erotico.*' Did you ever! Listen to this –" He broke off, hearing or rather sensing a movement at the door. "Oh, *hello*, Kola!"

Kolawole Aboyade was standing at the door with the air of a man who had been there for some little time. He was wearing slim blue jeans and an African short-sleeved shirt in a dark-green and brown patterned cotton – rainforest colours – with gold embroidery around the neck and sleeves. Against the gold his skin gleamed like dark chocolate in a golden wrapper. He looked slender but stood with a coiled grace that suggested muscle. He was fiddling with a leather bracelet on his left wrist as he fixed a calm speculative gaze on Simon.

Simon quailed a little – he was familiar with that calm

gaze and knew it was hostile – Kola's face had that amorphous grey cloud across it that veiled his features whenever he was pissed off. And to Simon's practised eye, there was tension in the generous lips and slightly bearded chin.

"You're back!" God, that was lame. "We were just –" He bit his lip.

Kola continued to stand there. "Oh, I know what you were 'just'." He smiled politely at Jan, baring an array of perfect teeth in a smile that lacked all warmth.

"Oh, I'll be going now, Kola," said Jan in obvious embarrassment at his peculiar and most un-African attitude.

"No, no," he said courteously. "Sit! Relax!"

Jan got to her feet.

"No, please! Don't let me interrupt you. I want to visit a fellow-student nearby in any case." He gave another smile like a northern winter. "Just enjoy." He went back out.

"Oh, dear, is it something I said?" Jan asked quietly, grimacing.

"No, he was listening at the door," Simon whispered theatrically. "You know how he hates me having a giggle at the newspapers or those pamphlets." He pulled a face. "It has nothing to do with you."

"Oh! Well, I must be off in any case. I'd advise *you* to get in the kitchen and pound some yam for him before he gets back."

"I'll get my little pestle out immediately," he said with a wiggle as he escorted her outside.

"Though I daresay you'd prefer if he did the pounding."

"Beggars can't be choosers," said Simon and then bit his lip. That was giving rather too much away.

At the car she said rather awkwardly, "I thought maybe you had asked him about the baby and he was furious with me for encouraging you."

"No, no – I haven't spoken to him about that yet," he responded shamefacedly.

She climbed in and started up. "Thinking better of the whole idea?"

"No fucking way!" he said fervently. "I'm living for the day!"

"Well, carry on rhyming . . . and, better talk to him . . ."

*I don't much like that doubtful look in her eye,* he thought.

"Oh, I won't see you again until I get back from Niger, I expect."

He stepped back as she got into gear. "Keep fit!" he called.

"Thanks in full!" she responded grinning.

"Cherryoh!"

Simon had been a lot more upset about Kola's stage entrance and exit than he had let on to Jan. His first thought after he went back inside was to hide the newspaper before Kola saw the boa-constrictor report.

He grabbed the newspaper and folded it, and as he did so, his eye fell on a headline: *Two Feet Tall Woman Delivers*.

He couldn't resist. With the hungry glee of an addict he read:

*A two and a half feet tall woman who was delivered of a baby through Caesarian operation is now the focus of attention at Ilorin General Hospital. The woman, Sade Adeleye, was said to have suffered from a disease that affected the cartilage in her joints. She was transferred from her village to the General*

*Hospital when it was clear that she could not deliver her baby in the natural way.*

*It was also said that at first people had mistaken her for a dwarf but later it became clear that she is a human being after she had spoken fluent Yoruba and given her name.*

*Commenting on the mysterious birth Dr EB Ogali, obstetrician, said Sade was a victim of achondroplasia.*

*Sade was unable to tell our reporter who had sexed her.*

"Oh, wonderful!" murmured Simon. It was one for the scrapbook. It and *Safe Home Taxis*, of course. He opened the desk drawer and looked for the scissors but they were nowhere to be seen, Perhaps Kola had them on his desk.

Newspaper in hand, he went to Kola's room. There were the scissors. He bit his lip like a naughty child as he picked them up and began to cut out the two-feet woman report.

He had taken to hiding his precious scrapbook since the day Kola had made a most chauvinistic attack on it.

"You keep it to make a laughing-stick of my people," he had said. Simon's hasty unthinking correction of 'stick' to 'stock' had added fuel to the fire and merited a thunderous scowl.

Kola was right, of course. He kept it for a laugh, yes. And yet . . .

"But what gems, Kola," he had protested. "*Someone* needs to preserve them for posterity! I mean, they are naive art like – like –" he couldn't think what they were like, "like naive art. Like – like Mammy Wagon decorations! People are doing *doctorates* on Mammy Wagon decorations – well, *Americans*, but people nevertheless. And artists like Andy Asshole have even made a fortune *copying* naivety."

"That is different," said Kola. "That is art."

"Yes, but this is the literary equivalent! It's wonderful stuff!"

"You mean it's a perfect opportunity for a giggle at the ignorance of the natives."

It had, of course, blown up into a violent row.

Simon sighed. It was all so difficult. Would they ever be able to rear a child together? Perhaps he was fooling himself.

His eye fell on Kola's wastepaper basket. As usual it was full to overflowing with discarded diagrams and sketches. Lucky for Kola, he was always available to play mother. He straightened the bed, bending to press his face against the pillow and deeply breathe in Kola's aroma.

He was immediately erect. Wanking time, he thought. There might just be time before Kola got back home. He hastily reached for the wastepaper basket and as he lifted it saw the words My Dearest Aminatu in Kola's handwriting. Aminatu? A Hausa name, surely? So, not a relative. Mmm. A little detective work was in order. He picked out the crumpled blue-lined writing paper and smoothed it out. He scanned the couple of lines.

*My Dearest Aminatu,*

*You cannot imagine how stunned I was at your news. But how can I see you when your parents*

Simon stood staring at the scrap of writing for a long time. His heart had started pounding but his mind was blank as a still pond. Then, at last, an intelligible thought fell into it with an almost audible plonk and he scrabbled in the waste basket, searching for the name Aminatu. *My Dearest Aminatu* . . . another.

*My Dearest Aminatu,*

*I was so glad to receive your letter, then stunned with your news. Of course I must see you as soon as possible. We must discuss the problem. But what can I do to get your parents' consent? How can they be so hard? Who can care for you and our child as*

Simon had frozen again. He groped for thought but was only conscious of the fact that his brain felt like a slice of doughy Nigerian bread. When he came to some time later he was trembling uncontrollably. With shaking fingers he began to search the basket again. Then he heard Kolawole arriving back.

## Chapter 5

"Oh, but I am a daft bugger!" said Ned in glee, chortling and rubbing his hands together. He peered once again through the door-pane.

The girl – well, *woman* – was sitting cross-legged on a mat outside. Negotiations had been strenuous since Toy Boy had turned up with her and three men at his door. The men had turned out to be her father, uncle and brother. Or so they claimed, the lying sods!

Ned had been taken aback at the dilapidated cut of the two older men. In their dusty black robes and limp worn turbans, under which they squinted at him from sun-wrinkled faces, they were a far cry from the crisply dressed pimps of Samaru village. The thought had scampered across his mind that these would make rum relatives if he married the girl. Well, if they thought they were going to scrounge any more than the bride-price out of him, they could fuck off! The greedy sods!

He had also been taken aback – well, *gobsmacked* really – at the jib of the girl. She had come in – *waddled* in – and perched herself on the extreme edge of an armchair like a seal Ned had once seen perched, balanced on its belly, on a rock at a zoo. The men had also sat in an uneasy fashion – as if the armchairs were camels likely to rear or bolt at any moment.

The girl, Fatimatu or Fati (Ned had guffawed when Anow told him her name, 'Ah-hah-hah-*hah*! *Fatty*? I *can't* go around calling her that, mate!'), was wearing a white cotton veil instead of the everyday black over her head. It was thrown across her breast and left shoulder and she was holding it across her mouth in bride-like modesty. Above it her eyes were watchful and unreadable. She wore a thick wrapper around her hips in some kind of black satiny material, silver jewellery and blue beads. Her hair was plaited in an intricate way and tiny braids were woven into a sort of blunt horn low over her forehead, looping back from there over her ears which were hung with enormous hooped silver earrings. Her fingernails and toenails were dyed an orangey terracotta shade and her light-brown skin was blue with indigo which was rubbing off onto the white veil.

Ned had vaguely taken all this in. And the fact that her buttocks were gigantic. He had seen how she almost had to throw her feet out as she swung her buttocks along in her wake. He thought seal again, or penguin.

But what had transfixed him and made him quake were her enormous breasts. He had never seen such breasts outside a blue movie or Outsize Boob magazines. Not that he could *see* them, of course, but the outlines were clear where they swayed unfettered under the thin cotton of her clothes. They seemed to be resting on her thighs as she sat there. Seeing is believing, he thought, and he had an unholy urge to pull back the veil, pull up her shirt and actually expose them to the naked eye. He thought of porn-mag pics of DDD-plus-plus-plus ladies making a big deal (and small fortunes presumably) of sucking their own boobs. Chirr-ist! This one could use hers for cushions!

But the *implications* of those boobs! Sixteen years old, my arse! How many suckling kids did it take to produce such bountiful mammary glands? Really, he should be allowed to view the goods! He was buying a pig in a poke! Why should he pay good money for something he hadn't viewed? In fact, he should be allowed – well, a sample. If they wanted to charge him for a sixteen-year-old virgin, the onus was on them to prove she was!

Attempts to suggest this to Anow met at first with blank incomprehension, then with a scandalised stare.

Well, yes, you greedy bugger, thought Ned, of course you would pretend to moral outrage. You bastard! I'm going to watch my step here! Don't you take *me* for a fool! Just because you can wind that silly Irishwoman around your little finger. Or your big prick!

Then he thought, Christ but I really should have asked Jan to be here. At least she can talk to the buggers.

Negotiations had proceeded, the men perching on his chairs, eyes hooded like eagles. The hard-eyed stares that met his bids had made him uncomfortable. Reminded him that these buggers had a reputation for ruthlessness and cruelty. The Blue Men, wot? A picture flashed on his inner eye of himself spreadeagled on the desert sands while the lady in question – Fatty – burned his naked chest with red-hot brands, then began to unzip his trousers. He mentally blacked out at this point.

"Eh? Eh?" He came to himself in his living-room and goggled bemusedly at Anow. His mouth was dry and his tongue felt huge and cumbersome. "What did you say, mate?"

"They say not enough money."

After the first inconclusive session, the girl had settled herself on a mat under a row of trees about twenty yards from his house. Anow explained that, all things going well, she would spend the first night there, the next at his door, the third in his house and the fourth in his bed. Ned had made a mental note to check this out with Jan Prendergast. He had the strongest possible feeling that he was being fed a load of crap.

Negotiations proceeded hammer and tongs. Well, that didn't describe the cool, disapproving stares, the long inscrutable silences, the extended muttered monotoned conversations in Tamajegh. Ned, in despair, had called on Jan for help and enlightenment but she was uncharacteristically adamant: she wouldn't have anything to do with it.

Typical bloody Paddy, Ned thought now, as he peered through the glass door at his bride-to-be. Pliant and fluid as water most of the time and then their anger floated to their rescue like a spar to a drowning man and they grabbed it in their teeth and hung on for dear life. Bogmen. There was only a hair's-breadth between them and the bush people here. Every Irishman or woman on the campus had gone native. Uncivilised cunts. If the English hadn't taught them manners they would still be eating at the trough with the pigs!

Ned savoured that image with satisfaction. Still, he liked the buggers. They were all entertaining sods. And if Jan Prendergast would have him he wouldn't have all these problems in the first place.

His heartbeat quickened. Fatty unguardedly had left her veil down from her face. Beautiful she wasn't – she wasn't even pretty in a culture where looks generally varied from blindingly beautiful to deliciously plump and pretty. No, Fati had a slightly hooked nose and neither the wonderful cheekbones nor the gorgeous sultriness of most Tuareg women. Still, she was handsome as they all were, with fine dark eyes, flashing teeth and a generous mouth.

Jan Prendergast had let him down badly – he *needed* her help! And she didn't care! Prendergast! For Crissake! Some silly French-Norman name! Shouldn't she be called O'Driscoll or McCarthy or something? Mongrel sods, the Irish!

He rapped on the glass pane. Startled, Fati turned her head and pulled her veil over her mouth again. He beckoned to her and was gobsmacked when she rose and languidly waddled to his door.

He opened the door. "Eh? Come in, come in!" Christ, he thought, is she ready?

She made for the armchair she had occupied the first day and sat regarding him.

"No, no, no!" he said, running his tongue around a mouth that was suddenly dry. "Come here, there's a good girl!" He patted the seat next to him.

To his astonishment, she came and sat beside him.

Cripes! Technically, what was the situation now? A price had been sulkily agreed on by both parties. Ned thought it exorbitant – still, he would get it back a hundredfold in Supplementation. He even knew a bugger in Kaduna who would cash British Supplementation air-tickets for him. Catch him taking Fatty back to England! Ah-hah-hah-*hah*! He imagined her waddling across the Arrivals Terminal at Heathrow, a half-caste toddler at each breast! Himself behind, trundling a luggage-trolley! Not bloody likely! You couldn't make a silk purse out of a sow's ear, that's for sure!

"Wait! Let me get you a drink!"

He bustled into the kitchen and brought her a glass and a bottle of water which she surveyed doubtfully. He poured. She lowered the veil and drank, then winced as she felt the unfamiliar coldness of the refrigerated water. She put down the glass and covered her mouth again.

"'Ere, don't do that! I know you lot veil your men and not your women! So what's this false modesty about?" He put out a finger and pulled down the white cotton.

The compulsion to see her breasts came over him again. Now was his chance, with the men out of the way, wherever the silly farts were.

"'Ere, now, give's a look at yer boobs!" He pasted a cheesy smile on his face, running a dry tongue around his mouth, and gently but relentlessly pulled the veil aside.

Then he goggled, face suddenly suffused with mottled red. Two gigantic boobs swung before him. She *had* no shirt. She was naked to the waist under the veil.

His breath began to rasp asthmatically. Topped with great brown nipples, the boobs had prominent tips and hung massively to her knees as she sat. He put a fleshy hand under one and kneaded it. She watched, a faintly puzzled look on her face. Christ! He was beyond coherent thought. What was it he had wanted to do? He foggily remembered something about pigs at troughs or sows' ears – no, no, pigs in pokes.

"Eh, yes," he said. He grabbed the other boob with the other hand.

His mind was seething like a pot on the boil. What rights did he have now? Would they call the deal off if he went too far? Not bloody likely! They wanted their money, the greedy sods!

He shifted both hands to the nearest boob and raised it to his mouth. The thing was the size of two enormous watermelons. The nipple was as big as a saucer. He stuck his tongue out and began to lick the nipple like an ice cream, bottom to top, bottom to top. Cherry on top, he thought, as his tongue ran repeatedly over the the nub which felt as if it were an inch long. Soon he was sucking noisily while she gazed at him inscrutably. He sank his head to her lap and sucked, cursing the wooden armrests that were digging into his ribs, now worrying the breast like a dog with a bone, pushing, kneading, pulling the nipple and tip through his lips again and again. Listening to the clink, clink, clink of her silver and blue-glass bracelets.

Eventually he became aware of another sound. He paused and gazed up at her shortsightedly.

She was laughing at him!

He had let go of the breast. She took the other one in her hands and offered the nipple as she would to a child. A thought struck him and he pushed the breast up to her own mouth. It reached comfortably – Christ, she could have worn it like a muffler – but she shied away, clearly scandalised.

He crammed it into his own mouth and lay there, now conscious of the end of the wooden armrest cruelly digging into his ribs.

It was at this point that another uncomfortable thing occurred. Fatty slipped her supple fingers inside the band of his wristwatch and in a smooth movement pulled it off and onto her own wrist.

He pushed the boob away and struggled upright, his back hurting him cruelly. As he opened his mouth to protest about the watch, he heard a sharp rap at the door.

Jan's nerves were jumping like Mexican beans as she drove into Zaria. Langley hadn't summoned her to the presence yet so she had no idea how he had reacted to her encounter with Marie Ogunbesan on The Rock. She fully expected to come back from her trip to find herself deported. God, if only she could have told Simon the full story about her deal with Langley! But she daren't tell anyone, even him.

And she hadn't told Simon how she'd been frantically scouring the university, pretending casual visits to building-sites and servants' quarters but actually looking for Anow – running the gamut of worry, of not caring, of patience, of anger, of desperation. Knowing she could contact him through Ned but determined not to get involved in the matchmaking shenanigans.

If she got the gas in Zaria for Ned, though, she would have to go by his house. And Anow might well be there. Her heart thudded in anticipation.

Even now, as she drove, she found herself scanning the roadsides, peering into passing taxis and minibuses, in the hope of spotting him.

Her feelings veered from one extreme to another. She was glad he was gone; she was desperate for his return. She was so *so* regretful of her hasty words; she was sorry she hadn't beaten him to death with Easter eggs. She had thrown herself at him; he had taken advantage of her hunger for his brother. She ran through a hundred scenarios and played them out in her head, focusing especially on what she would say when he turned up. In one scenario she embraced him tenderly and dragged him into the bedroom; in another she cuttingly, sneeringly told him to take his worthless bags and baggage and fuck off back to the bush. In yet another she raged at him for his lack of loyalty to his brother, for the insult to her.

What if she were *pregnant*? She had been on one of her periodic rests from the pill since that *bastard – his* brother – had deserted her to marry his young first cousin. And she would blithely cut off *his* paraphernalia, if she got a chance, and fry them for breakfast.

God! She had run smack bang up against that last thought like a speeding car hitting the brick back wall of a cul-de-sac in the dark. Did she actually hate Moussa that much? While she still claimed to love him?

But why didn't Anow *come*? Why didn't he come within range so she could rail at him or embrace him or whatever?

Before he could disappear into the vastness of the Sahara – like his brother – and be beyond the reach of her rage or her tenderness forever.

Ned licked dry lips and smiled his politest cheesiest smile to camouflage his dismay as he gazed at the tiny wizened figure before him.

This was his future mother-in-law and she was standing in his living-room gazing at him in evident horror.

Dressed in dusty worn-out black cotton, naked shrivelled breasts hanging like flaps to her waist, cheeks caved in from yesteryears full of drought and deprivation, she swayed before him.

"Ah!" said Ned heartily, tongue whipping around dry teeth, holding out a hand. "Delighted to meet you, I'm sure."

It was as if she didn't even see the hand stretched out in welcome. Her eyes were riveted on his face with the blind look of one in trance.

Ned lowered his hand, nonplussed. "Eh, what's the matter with her then?" he said to Anow.

"She is afraid," said Anow.

"Wot? Hasn't she seen a European before, then?"

"Yes, she see French people in Niger."

"Well, then . . ."

Anow didn't answer. Instead, he addressed himself to the old woman in wheedling tones, embracing her with an arm and trying to draw her forward. She answered in a guttural stream of complaint that startled Ned by its strength. Its combination of vigour and whine confused him.

Suddenly Fati spoke up from where she sat on the armchair, addressing herself to her mother in a flood of Tamajegh accompanied by vigorous gestures. She beat the back of one hand repeatedly into the palm of the other in a movement that managed to be languorous and violent at the same time. Ned found it frightening. He tried to figure out what was being said. She sounded as if she were berating the old lady for her behaviour but he had the nasty feeling that she might simply be arguing about whose turn it was to cook dinner.

As he stood there unenlightened, there were muttered exchanges behind veils between the men.

Fuck this for a game of soldiers, thought Ned. He stepped forward. The mother recoiled within the circle of Anow's arm.

"Would she like some tea?" he asked Anow. "Tea? A nice cup of tea?" He mimed the drinking of tea for the old woman.

How *could* she be so old? If she was the mother of the girl? But how old *was* she anyway? It was impossible to judge with these people – clapped out at forty all of them.

"Ask her, mate," he said irritably. "Ask her if she wants tea."

Suddenly the old woman let fly with an extraordinary diatribe.

Anow stepped back a little.

Christ, what a language, thought Ned in dismay. He was used to the melodious tonal local Hausa. Christ, this sounded like – what? All guttural, clashing consonants – it sounded like – he didn't know what it sounded like – like something *Martians* might speak.

Abruptly she fell silent to a chorus of murmurs from the men.

Ned saw his opening. Teeth bared in a smile, he leant ingratiatingly closer to his mother-in-law-to-be. She recoiled, like a Hammer Horror heroine confronted by a fanged Dracula.

But her horror could not equal Ned's sense of outrage as she crumpled before him, hitting the floor with an audible thump.

He paled as the men rushed to her. She was out for the count.

A dark-blue glass bracelet on her arm had shattered on the tiled floor.

As Ned stood there, jowls quivering in outrage, Anow produced a little bottle of perfume from his robe and, pulling the cork with his teeth, applied the neck of the bottle to her nostrils. She sighed and stirred and her eyes opened. The men raised her to her feet and assisted her outside, Fati following without a backward glance bearing her succulent mammary glands before her.

Anow halted at the door. "I will come back later," he said reassuringly.

"Eh, mate?" said Ned vaguely, hardly registering what he had said as in utter dismay he watched Fati's retreat – her buttocks bouncing behind her under their soft black wrapper while her breasts swung like Quasimodo's bells from side to side.

Jan swung into Ned's drive, heart in her throat, praying that Anow would be there, busy at his negotiating. But there was neither hair nor hide of a Tuareg around the place. No blushing bride. Not even so much as her mat.

She knocked on Ned's door and peered through the glass panels. Suddenly, and somehow violently, Ned was before her, goggling out.

He unlocked the door and then disappeared. She went inside to find him striding up and down the living-room in violent agitation. Roger the cat was perching tensely on the window-ledge behind him, watching intently.

She pieced the story together as he spluttered his indignation.

"The stupid cunt! Collapsed before me – flat on the floor –" His fleshy hand gestured the flatness. "As if I were effing Frankenstein. What kind of fucking play-acting was that? Oh, all to raise the bride-price, you may be sure! As if she hadn't seen a European before! That boy of yours admitted she *had* seen plenty of those French bastards in Niger! To say nothing of expats around the campus! Silly cunt!"

Jan had a struggle to conceal the glee that possessed her. Serve him bloody well right! She only hoped Fati and family would never darken his door again. Oh, God, the image of Ned confronting his mother-in-law was classic! It deserved to be immortalised on a set of dinnerware.

Ned continued to stride. He was actually slavering at the mouth in rage, white foam caught in the corners of his lips.

"And what's more – *Fatty took my watch*! A *good* one! I bought it in England on my last leave!"

So she had only just missed Anow. "Eh, Ned, was Anow with them?"

"What? Who? Toy Boy?"

"Yes."

"Oh, he was here, the sly cunt!"

The insult hurt her. "Do you expect him back?"

"Eh? What do I know about the greedy cunt? Why are you asking me?"

He paced the length of the room, the dust on his floor still undisturbed as he followed the beaten track from door to the table at the end of the room.

"Um, I got your gas. Can you help me bring it in?"

They hauled the heavy gas-cylinder out of the back of

the car and carried it to the kitchen, to find that Roger had been in like a flash, had scoffed most of a now-clean saucer of fish and was back on the window-ledge licking his chops with gusto.

"'Ere? Hang on! Where are my potatoes?" said Ned belligerently. "You haven't gone and forgotten my potatoes, have you? They were my dinner for the week!"

Jan flushed in annoyance. Rude bastard! "No, I've left them in the car."

"You weren't going to hang onto them, were you? Have I *paid* for them? Where's my change?"

*Hang onto them? Fourteen measly potatoes?* He had counted the number he would need – two a day for the week. She felt that inner quivering that signalled a danger that she might explode in rage. "I forgot – they're on the passenger seat. I'll get them." She went out and came back with the brown-paper bag of potatoes in her arms.

Ned had resumed pacing. He shot her a hostile glance, obviously still suspecting her of trying to steal his fourteen potatoes. And his change. He made no attempt to take the bag from her.

"I'll put them in the kitchen," she said. "I'll have to be off now. As I said, I'm leaving for Niger in the morning –"

"Eh? *What?*" The 'what' was a violent explosion. "You want to bugger off and leave me with this problem!"

"What problem?"

"*What problem! What . . . problem!* Why, you selfish sod! About Fatty, of course! What problem!" He swivelled neatly on his heel to face her in a way that was almost like a dance-step – was almost grace. "*I need your help!* I've decided I definitely want her. And I don't trust Toy Boy any more! I can't be doing with negotiating marriage without understanding a word of their blasted lingo. They've buggered off now because of that silly old bag. But I'm sure it's just a ploy!"

Jan was still angry, in fact furious, that he had called her a selfish sod and Anow a sly cunt and accused her of petty theft. That made it easier for her to say, "Honestly, Ned, I don't want to have any part in it. I don't approve of it –"

"You don't approve of it! Oh, la-de-dah!" Now he was raging again. "But you *approve* of your own shenanigans, do you? Whoring around with all those filthy buggers! Using that little lad as some kind of stopgap until his brother turns up again!"

It was all she needed.

"You insane old *fart!*" she exploded, launching the potatoes, bag and all, at his head. The bag burst and potatoes bounced off him and hopped about the room.

He loomed up close, grimacing, and threatened her with his hammy fists. "Oh, show your Irish temper to me, would you? I can deal with that!"

"You bastard!" she raged. "How *dare* you threaten me with your fists!" She grabbed up two potatoes that had rolled to her feet and belted him with them at close range.

"*Cunt!*" Ned backed off and hammered her with a potato.

"Oh! Fuck you!" *One! Two! Three!* One got him on the shoulder, one on the buttock as he twisted away and the third bang in the chest.

"Take that, you bitch! *And* that!"

"*Ow!*" She got it on the left breast. "*Ow!*" The second

thudded on her right ear. It hurt like hell. There was blood on her hand when she took it from her ear. She grabbed another potato and took aim. *Make it count, Jan!* "Ah-*hah*!" Right in the groin. While he was gasping she grabbed up her shoulder bag and, breath shuddering, rooted out the handful of coins she had put in the side pocket. "And here's your fucking change, you fucking miser!' Kobo coins rained on his head.

Time to retreat. She tore out the door and threw herself into the driving-seat.

The last she saw was Ned shaking his fist at her, yelling "*I shall count my change!*"

An hour later Ned's rage had cooled down. He had picked up the bruised potatoes, picked up his scattered kobos. Picking up the bruised friendship would be more of a problem. He was sorry really, he thought, remembering all the laughs he had had with Jan in the past. Still, she'd get over it.

"Ah-hah-hah-hah!" Crikey, the way those potatoes flew! Oh, she had some temper! Reminded him of Maureen O'Hara in *The Quiet Man*. Now, that was a film – oh, she had stood up to John Wayne like that all right, eyes blazing. He didn't remember Maureen O'Hara's face going puce, mind you, in her altercations with The Big Fellow – but that would have been down to Max Factor. He really must go to Ireland some time – on his next home leave, maybe. Yes.

"Ah-hah-hah-hah!" He delightedly remembered how he had come back at her, gave as good as he got. He swaggered a little. He had always had more than a touch of Wayne in him, particularly in his talent for woman-taming.

His satisfaction waned as he remembered the fix he was now in. Crikey, he'd ruined his chances of getting any help from Jan, that's for sure!

His encounter with Fati's mammary glands had left him in a welter of desire. His initial dream of the pert, plump fifteen-year-old had been well and truly obliterated by now, squashed beneath Fati's ample haunches. All he could think of now was Fati's boobs. They had been within his grasp, all but bought by his hard-earned money to do with as he pleased! His mind boggled at sudden thoughts of what he might do with them as a knock sounded on the glass panels of the door.

They were back!

Christ, maybe it was Jan come to apologise!

It wasn't Fati and it wasn't Jan.

To his great glee, it was the next best thing.

He threw open the door, smiling a huge cheesy welcome. "Cous-Cous! Come in, come in! The very man I wanted to see!"

## Chapter 6

It was after midnight and she had to be up before six. Jan undressed, wound a fresh cotton wrapper around her and went out onto the verandah to have one last long look and listen for Anow. Across the wide stretch of darkened green she saw the lights of a solitary car as it sped up the road to Sokoto. The sight inspired her with loneliness. She went back in despairingly, closed the French door, flicked off the light and lay down on her bed. Above her the university-issue ceiling-fan languidly fought a losing battle against the sweltering air.

But she still fixed her eyes – or ears rather – on the French door hoping to hear his familiar rap on the glass.

Normally the rap would come in the early morning. After his night's guarding – sleeping soundly on his mat wrapped in his blanket, antique sword by his side – he would walk out to her house. She lived in a one-bedroomed bungalow built in the old colonial style, with a deep roof and well established trees about it – not built like a little fortress against thieves like Ned's on campus. Anow would arrive with a brown-paper parcel of hot bean-cakes which they would eat together. He would then spend the day making himself indispensable in every way possible.

Perhaps tomorrow she would wake to the familiar rat-tat on the glass.

Driving home in a fury after the potato fight with Ned, she had suddenly braked, almost causing a taxi behind to ram her. Swinging off the road she had shuddered to a halt and cut out. Then she had turned and driven back to Mohamed's building site: the one place she hadn't looked before because it was too humiliating and obvious to go there. But, after all, she had a cover: she needed Anow's help on the trip – to deal with the jerrycans and emergencies like multiple flat tyres or broken axles.

But Anow wasn't there and his uncle seemed surprised to see her. They had talked at cross-purposes for a while before she realised that he thought Anow was at her house. He was astounded to hear he hadn't shown up.

"But he went!" he said. "Around midday. He made his farewells. I gave him letters to take home and some tea-leaves as a gift for his mother. He went!"

Her heart had lifted in hope and she had come home and waited, amazed at how her other worries had fallen away and her whole body relaxed in gratitude now that he was coming and things would be – well, back to normal again.

But he hadn't come.

But there was still the morning.

Simon knelt at the side of Kolawole's bed, his head resting on the side of it, *"Please!"* he begged.

Not even an answer. Was he actually sleeping? He reached a hand up and touched Kola's mouth. The lips contracted in a faint semblance of a kiss.

"Simon."

"Yes!"

"Please go to bed."

"But I want you."

A sigh and a hand rested briefly on his head. "I am tired. I cannot."

Tears stung Simon's eyes. He pressed his face into the bedsheet, sick with fear and jealousy, refusing to believe he was left with nothing.

Kola had at first refused to talk about the letter from the waste basket. Well, Simon had handled it badly – atrociously, really, in retrospect – immediately plunging in with accusations and distraught reproaches, even throwing the matter of his desire for a baby into the seething mix, using his precious dream as a crude weapon to throw at Kola's head. Unforgivable. No wonder Kola had reacted as if it were an insane notion.

Later, much later, Kola had confessed that yes, the wastebasket scraps were drafts of a letter to a Hausa girl in Tahoua in Niger. Yes, she was pregnant – five months. He had impregnated her when she had visited her aunt in his home town of Ibadan. No, he did not love her, of course not. But somehow he must rescue his child. He was afraid her parents would insist on marriage. He didn't want to marry – and his family would be outraged at the idea of him marrying a Hausa as they had set their minds on a neighbour's daughter. But they would agree that he must claim his child. Ideally, he would like to take the girl down south to his mother to deliver, maybe with an aunt or a sister to accompany her.

Besides, the poor girl was almost suicidal. She was only seventeen, after all, and from a strict Muslim family. Her father might kill her, she had said.

So he needed to move softly, softly, and comfort her heart. But he didn't really love her – of course not. His aim was to rescue his child from Islamic Hausaland and take it to the generous, pulsating South. And then, of course, he would come back to Simon.

"Please," said Simon. *"Please!"* He was desperate for the reassurance of sex.

"I am not able," said Kola from the edge of sleep. "Look –" Kola groped for Simon's hand and placed it on his cock. "I am soft. You know how difficult it is for me. Go to your bed."

Simon lifted his head and took Kola's soft thick penis in his mouth.

There came a sigh from Kola like regret. His hand touched Simon's head as if to dissuade him, then moved away again.

Simon knew it wouldn't take too much time. He'd had plenty of practice after all and knew when to dispense with subtlety. Forceful sucking was in order.

He allowed himself a minute to enjoy the sensation of the flaccid penis filling his mouth. He had recently come to a whole new set of experiences. He sometimes wondered whether he had ever confronted an unwilling and flaccid penis in his life before Kolawole. Eager and rampant was the norm; or languid but sensitive, full of the memories of pleasure after coming.

He had come to enjoy not only the challenge but also

the sensation. When he could get Kola to relax he adored to run through a few tricks from a little repertoire he had developed: rolling the penis on Kola's hard belly with his hand – the springy doughy texture reminded him pleasurably of helping his mother make pastry as a child – or sucking it, pulling the length of it through teeth shielded with his lips – again he was a kid sucking on liquorice strings or pulling on jelly babies until they were elongated and translucent – or cramming his mouth full so it lusciously filled up all the crevices like a huge wad of chewing-gum. Simon had learned to relax into the yumminess of it all – knowing, of course, at the back of his mind that he wouldn't get to sample the whole bill of fare before that glorious moment when it would firm and harden and thrust.

Now he withdrew his mouth, and applying firm pressure with a thumb between penis and anus he subjected the cock to a little merciless handwork. There was a result. He pushed the large erection into his mouth – as always with the thrill at Kola's sheer size and the prayer 'Thank you, God, for an African man' – and for another half minute lapped and swirled but then (he had the timing to a fine art) he headed down the home straight.

His own penis grew ever more rigid as he sucked Kola's to ejaculation. He ground his groin against the side of the bed as he had done on many a night – apart from those special nights when an inebriated or stoned Kola allowed him to linger and caress and even play. And there were those even more special and rare nights when a more sober Kola could be lured into role-play. European dress – make-up, a short skirt, high heels – Simon had learned somewhere along the way that those did the trick very effectively.

Dizzy with desire he brought Kola to orgasm, his own cock ejaculating in twin response.

Moments later he spat Kola's sperm into a little glass jar and took it to bed with him. Was there enough magic in the world to serve his purpose? Exhausted with jealousy and heartache, he barely managed to smear the sperm sleepily and perfunctorily across his belly before he tumbled into exhausted sleep.

Jan was up by six. She had woken with a start and gone straight to the French window, hoping it might have been Anow's rap that had roused her. But there was no one there.

She showered, grabbed breakfast and then did some last-minute frantic packing. Heart pounding, she stood in her bedroom, trying to make decisions like 'Should I bring my travel alarm?' with a mind like a frightened rabbit's. She couldn't think. In the end, she just threw everything in.

By the time she got everything piled up by the door it was eight o'clock and she was late, late, late. With a journey of some eight hundred kilometres ahead of her, she should be long gone. She walked the short distance to her neighbour's house to beg his cook and houseboy to help her get the full jerrycans up on the roof rack. *Where the hell was Anow?*

After she had paid off the lads, she went into the house. A letter had been shoved under the door. Her heart lifted. She snatched it up, hoping to see her name written in Tifenagh, the Tuareg script. But it was addressed in a literate hand, using her full name and correct address. Not Anow then. Her heart tumbled down to the depths and then leapt back into her throat in fright. A summons from the Vice-

Chancellor? *Immigration?* Practically throwing up with dread, she ripped the envelope open.

She read:

BOX 356, ZARIA

*Dear Teacher ,*

*Top of the day for you over there . . .*

A student. The paper began to tremble as her hands shook in relief and sweat broke out all over her body – her skin tingled with it.

*Hope there is no trouble. How is your work hope it is go on smoothly if so? Glory be to God.*

*The theme of this letter to you is that I want you to be my College Mother. I will be very grateful if you can consider my letter Ma. Please Ma, do not surprise how I known your address. Then I known your address when as I am one of your student and have visited you at your house.*

She glanced down at the signature: Jimoh Igwe. One of her most appalling first-year students. She read on in growing amazement,

*Then as your performance and the way you behave to me and embrase me made me to know your loving hart and made me writting you as my college Mother.*

*I will be wait for your reply because of my resons you will consider me your college son.*

*I drop my biro here.*

*Yours faithfully*

*Jimoh Igwe*

*PPS I apreciate the way you are looking so sexy in your African wrapper.*

Jan's fury at this ill-timed missive knew no bounds. Teacher-like, she was horrified at the atrocious standard of the English – to say nothing of the way her friendly attitude had been misinterpreted. She had no idea what a College Mother was but she had no doubt it would involve copious amounts of sex and/or money in the long run. Whatever it might be, it was not the hapless Jimoh's lucky day. She crumpled up the letter and threw it across the room in disappointment and frustration. To expect a note from Anow and have that piece of cheek inflicted on her!

The lump of fury that had lodged intermittently in her throat since the potato fight with that ungrateful bastard Bassett was back again.

She hauled the gear out to the car. Then, as she took a last glance around the house, she spotted the letter screwed up in a ball on the living-room floor and a thought struck her. She knew the place for it: immortalised in Simon's scrapbook. She picked it up, smoothed it out and shoved it in her shoulder bag. She set out for Zaria.

Ned was startled awake by an urgent rapping at his door. He groped for his glasses, knocking over his large alarm clock. Then he pulled the glasses on, grabbed up the alarm and gaped blearily at its plain round old-fashioned face. *Six o'clock.* He was outraged. Not that an early-bird like him didn't often rise at six but it sure as buggery was too early for some sod to be beating at his door.

He climbed out of bed in his red-and-white striped pyjamas, shoving his feet automatically into worn purple slippers, fumbled his keys off their nail on the wall and picked up the machete he kept for emergencies. It was hardly likely to be robbers at that hour but, after all, he did have that bride-price in cash under his mattress. He cautiously tiptoed out into the small square hall and rammed his face against one of the glass door-panes, brandishing the machete threateningly.

*"Chirr-ist!"* He leapt back in alarm, finding himself almost nose to nose with a robed Tuareg figure.

The Tuareg in question pulled the veil down to his chin with a long finger and with mischievous irony widened his eyes so the whites gleamed at Ned. Then his face creased in a lovely smile that made little long dents in his lean cheeks.

It took Ned another few moments to get his bearings.

"Ah! Cous-Cous!" A sugary smile replaced the goggling look. He stuck the machete behind his pyjama'd bottom, dropped it to the floor with a thud and then shoved it aside with his foot, all the time keeping up eye contact.

What's the silly sod doing here at this time of the morning, he thought, as he fumbled for the right keys on the key ring and unlocked the indoor chain. Finally getting the door open, he thrust his head out. "What's the problem, mate?" he asked. "I'd invite you in but I'm in my pyjamas. It *is* only six in the morning, you know!" Aggrieved and accusatory.

Ikus-Ikoos raised a long-boned wrist on which a heavy gold watch hung loosely and indicated it with a quick movement of the lips. "It's nine o'clock, Ned."

"Eh? Nine o'clock! Don't tell me that, you silly sod!"

"Well, it is," said Ikus-Ikoos calmly.

"Eh . . . I must have looked at my alarm-clock the wrong way round," said Ned. "Six – nine, you see. They *are* similar, let's face it!"

Ikus-Ikoos smiled. "May I come in?"

"Oh! Yes, do come in."

Ikus-Ikoos stepped into Ned's living-room. He was robed entirely in spotless white. Even his turban – the eight-foot-long *tagilmoust* – was the creamy-white version rather than the everyday dark-blue indigo-steeped one or the coveted, expensive *ilisham* with its bronzed glittery purple hue. His skin therefore had no tinge of dusky blue and, darker than the Tuareg norm, was its natural light coffee-bean brown. His eyes were dark to blackness under fine eyebrows and he wore a delicate moustache. Heavy silver rings hung loosely on his slim fingers.

He stood in all his glory, confronting Ned in his red-and-white striped pyjamas with the gaping fly where the button was missing and his purple slippers.

"What a silly sod he is," thought Ned. "Why *does* he insist on wearing that idiotic costume? It's OK for the other buggers – but for an educated man, a lecturer in the French Department! What was wrong with the sensible tropical suit he used to wear before he got daft! Eh, wonder does he wear any underpants under that lot? I'll bet he doesn't, the dirty bugger!" Ned's mind boggled at the thought of standing in front of a hundred students with his dangly parts dangling.

Ned wasn't alone in this attitude to Ikus-Ikoos's overnight decision to revert to traditional gear. Tuareg costume seemed eccentric even with gorgeously robed Hausamen stalking the campus. The truth was, everyone was covertly astonished that a Tuareg should be educated at all, to say nothing of being a university lecturer; and so Ikus-Ikoos was making a political point while pretending wide-eyed innocence. Why should he not wear his traditional costume, he asked if ever questioned, when everyone else was wearing theirs – Hausa, Yoruba, Ibo, Fulani, European?

But his people were considered an eccentric minority in their own country – the fate of nomads the world over – having proudly and fatally passed up on the offer of European education. Self-sufficient from time immemorial, they simply couldn't see the point of sending their children to the French schools. So they sent the sons of their slaves instead. Which left them now like a flock of chickens before a pack of hungry foxes in a chicken-run which had no fences – the Sahara. And left Ikus-Ikoos like a lone proud cockerel heroically confronting the enemy.

The previous day Ned had seized on Ikus-Ikoos like a man dying of thirst in the desert would seize on a miraculously passing camel. Why hadn't he thought of Cous-Cous before? The perfect interpreter! And a man – which meant he wouldn't have Jan Prendergast's silly scruples about women's rights and suchlike rubbish. Not that Ned didn't believe in women's rights but . . .

Ikus-Ikoos had called round to collect the copy of his doctoral thesis on Tuareg poetry which he had lent Ned to read (Ned hadn't got round to it). As luck would have it, he knew exactly where Fati's family could be found – quite close by on campus, in fact, at the workplace of a watchman called Bashir whom he knew quite well. He and Ned had gone there in Ned's old pea-green Lada and negotiations had been resumed.

Bashir worked at the house of an American lecturer, sleeping on a mat at the door and being paid a pittance for the service – the done thing on campus. Ned had cowered in his car across the road, unable to trespass and afraid that the

Americans would think him a Peeping Tom or suspect him of trying to procure a whore. He watched anxiously while Ikus-Ikoos stalked back and forth impressively between the car and the house. He could see the shrivelled old bag glowering at him, from where she sat on a mat in front of the garage, and almost expected to see her make the sign against the evil eye – or perhaps begin to sharpen a stake . . .

Fatty was there, cross-legged on the mat, great buttocks curving behind her, great naked breasts swinging to and fro as she attended to various small tasks – leaning forward, twisting back – the great discs of her nipples beckoning to him.

"Oh dear, oh dear, oh dear, oh Christ!" Ned moaned distractedly.

At one point she clambered to her feet and fetched some charcoal in a brazier. Then, to his consternation, she bent forward at the waist, knees straight, to tend to it – strewing some straw on top the better to light it. As she did so her boobs swung almost to the ground, bringing to Ned's mind the image of a Jersey cow swaying down a country road on her way for milking.

He made a supreme effort and concentrated on the men.

Watching all the lazy posturing, Ned again had that lost feeling: they could have been discussing the current prices for goats in the market for all he knew. As Ikus-Ikoos stepped aside for the umpteenth time with Fati's uncle and offered him tobacco, Ned thought he would burst a blood-vessel in frustration. He watched as they launched into the ritual which involved tilting their heads back, poising the leaves on their lower lips, chewing them, spitting copiously, adding tiny amounts of potash, grinding it with their teeth and chewing it in, then poising the finished product back on the lower lip – throughout which whole maddening procedure they continued to talk in mutters with multiple lengthy pauses and spectacular spitting.

Silly sods, thought Ned in rage and frustration, for Christ's sake why can't they do something civilised like smoke a pipe? It should be banned – all that spitting – disgusting! Spreading all their germs about!

He raged to no effect. Ikus-Ikoos and Fati's uncle continued to mutter – at times reminding Ned of a pair of Shakespearean assassins (enter two murderers stage left) and at other times of a pair of gardeners pleasurably discussing the best way to pot on shrubs.

But the final results were impressive. When Ikus-Ikoos came slowly across to the car, face impassive, scanning the sky like an Englishman checking out the weather, Ned thought all was lost.

But no.

Ten minutes later they were back at the house collecting the bride-price from under the mattress and ten minutes after that Ikus-Ikoos was dismounting from the Lada to make the last stately crossing of the road bearing the bride-price to Fati's assembled relatives.

Ned watched and waited, breath rasping in the stress of anticipation. Within the hour he'd be playing hide-and-go-seek in Fatty's breasts.

Ikus-Ikoos arrived back quite shortly after and got in the car. Various male relatives gathered in fine fettle to see them off.

Ned sat there running his tongue around a dry mouth. "Where's Fatty, Cous-cous? *Is she not coming?*"

"Well, no – they must prepare for the wedding now."

"*The wedding! You daft sod!* Wait a minute!" He glared at Ikus-Ikoos. "I'm not leaving here until I get the girl, you silly bugger! D'you take me for a fool?"

Ikus-Ikoos was at pains to explain that this was a marriage agreement, that the bride-price was always paid up front before a wedding could proceed and that the very basis of a marriage agreement was trust between the parties. "It's not the same as paying for an animal at the market, you see," he said straightfaced and Ned couldn't figure out whether he was being sarcastic or not.

Ned grudgingly bade farewell to his now enthusiastic new relatives who were thanking him profusely and wearing his hand out with countless handshakes.

Well might they be cheerful, he thought, having pocketed his cash.

Facing Ikus-Ikoos now the following morning in his living-room Ned berated himself silently for not giving him a dash of some few naira the day before. Now here was the bugger again – no doubt to ask for a reward for his services, perhaps euphemistically calling it a loan.

He jerked himself back from this meditation to realise that Ikus-Ikoos was gazing at him silently and had pulled the folds of his *tagilmoust* back up over his mouth and nose. A bad sign, that, thought Ned. As if the bastard has something to hide.

Above the creamy-white folds of the cloth Ikus-Ikoos's black-olive eyes were looking at him – apprehensively?

"Eh?" said Ned.

"I'm afraid I have some bad news, Ned," he said gravely, voice somewhat muffled.

Ned paled and his face went blotchy. "Wot? Wot? Fatty?" He should have guessed! "She's trying to back out?"

Alarming hesitation from Ikus-Ikoos. "Worse than that. She's gone. With all her family. Back to Niger."

*"Back to Niger? Gone? But why?"* Ned wailed, Fati's gigantic boobs swinging out of his reach. "It was all settled! They gave their word! How can she be gone?"

"I don't know. I didn't actually see them. Bashir just came to me in a panic, scared the police will consider him an accomplice."

"An accomplice?" Ned goggled. "What d'you mean, an accomplice?"

"Well, the deal was hammered out at his place and the police will certainly take him in for questioning – if you report it, that is." The dark eyes regarded him quizzically.

"But . . ." Ned was at sea. "Well, they broke their word – but – well, they haven't committed a *crime*, have they? Or is it a crime in Islamic law or suchlike – to break a marriage arrangement?"

"Well, no . . . of course not . . . but the money . . ."

"The money," said Ned blankly.

"Well, that's fraud."

"*Frau-ud!* What d'you *mean*, *fraud?*" Ned exploded. He goggled at Ikus-Ikoos in horror. *"You do have my money?"*

"No," said Ikus-Ikoos. "No – as I said – I haven't seen them since yesterday. They have gone with the money."

*"They've gone with the money? You mean they've taken my money? Run off with my money?"* Hopping about in violent agitation he popped another button on his pyjama fly and now his dangly parts were bobbing about like a parrot in a red-barred cage.

101

"Yes," said Ikus-Ikoos, averting his gaze. "I'm very sorry, Ned. I feel responsible. I should have realised they weren't genuine."

"It was that stupid old bag's fault!" Ned exploded. "She got her way in the end! Why didn't someone just sit on her? I thought that's what men do with women in this part of the world? Squash them!"

"Not Tuareg women," stated Ikus-Ikoos firmly.

"Evidently not! The old cunt! It wasn't Fatty, you know, who had a problem – I think she was quite taken with me, in fact. It was that old bag with her theatricals! Pretending to be shocked!" He stormed out to the little hall. "I shall call the police! I'll see they get their just desserts!"

Ikus-Ikoos said, "Ned! You're forgetting –"

"What? My car keys? Have them here, mate . . ." reaching into his bedroom and taking them off their hook.

"No – your pyjamas."

"Eh?" Ned looked down at himself, then stalked off into the bedroom to change,

His money! His Fatty! *Oh my ducats, oh my daughter* indeed, he thought with a whole new insight into the character of Shylock. Those fuckers! But he would get his money back! He visualised himself confronting the police, truculently slamming his fist in his palm, demanding his rights.

Eh?

That brought a whole train of somewhat humiliating memories to mind. Fresh in his memory were the ironic glances and partisan reactions when he had driven the whore from Samaru around to the police post. And his ending up having to pay *extra* to get the greedy bitch out of his car! When had the Nigerian police been of any use to him? How many of the robberies that nightly hit the campus had they solved? Did he really think for a minute that they would stop and search every Tuareg on the road – the several different roads – between Zaria and the border?

He stopped and goggled in the act of pulling on a sock. How would they even recognise Fatty's family? Who probably didn't even have National Identity Cards.

His chin dropped further. *How would they recognise his money?* One veiled Tuareg might look exactly like another but not as alike as two naira notes! All Fatty's family had to do was split up the cash between them and it would look like legitimate paltry earnings being taken home to the bush. It was hopeless. And he wouldn't put it past the police to get their wires crossed – deliberately – and find that *he* had committed some crime: like encouraging illegal immigration.

Christ! The frying-pan and the fire!

He emerged into the living-room a few minutes later.

Ikus-Ikoos was still standing in the centre of the room.

"I have made up my mind," said Ned, thrusting his chin forward.

"Wait, Ned, I've been thinking – it's not such a good idea to involve the police –"

"No! Forget the police! Fuck the police!" A wave of the hand dismissed the entire Nigerian police force. "I will find them myself!" He pounded his chest with the heel of his fist.

"How –"

"The only way, you silly sod! I will go to Niger and as *you're* responsible you must accompany me."

Ikus-Ikoos stared. "I'm sorry, Ned, but I can't just –"

"No!" He held a hand up, palm heading off any protest. "I won't take no for an answer."

"But, Ned –"

"No! You're off work so you've no excuse! And don't forget that if I take this matter to the police *you'll* be the first suspect!"

Ikus-Ikoos glared but was silent.

"We must leave immediately. Oh, *mark my words*, I'll get my money back or my name isn't Ned Bassett!"

His money – or Fatty. He had purchased her after all – she was his property in Nigerian terms. He flushed at the thought and then realised that, more than his money, the notion of bedroom games with the succulent boobs was luring him on.

## Chapter 7

Simon woke to a sense of great loss. He groaned aloud in misery as he realised the ghastly feeling wasn't just the aftermath of a nightmare.

Had he just heard a car pulling out of the driveway? Or was that the echo of a dream? Maybe Kola had taken the car to go buy bean-cakes.

It was nine thirty. Normally Simon would be up some three hours before. He wound his wrapper, female-fashion, under his arms and dazedly shuffled to the window. No, the car was still there. He dragged himself off to the shower. Thank God for the Easter break, he thought. Thank God I don't have to face a lecture or seminar this morning. I couldn't do it. In the bathroom mirror he looked hollow-eyed and gaunt. He needed to shave and that upset him further. Sick at heart, he forced himself to get rid of the stubble.

Showered and feeling marginally better but desperately

in need of a coffee, he made for the kitchen. Should he make some breakfast for Kola too? As he normally would? All his newly awakened insecurities made him hesitate. Perhaps he should check first.

Cautiously, he pushed down Kola's door-handle and opened the door a crack. The bed was empty, the sheet pulled neatly up. He pushed open the door. There was no one there. Startled, he went to check the bathroom.

Hand raised to rap on the bathroom door, he stopped and stood stock-still. He lowered his hand and wiped a sudden burst of sweat off his palms onto his wrapper.

When he went back, it was there all right – he hadn't imagined it. A piece of blue-lined writing paper pinned to Kola's pillow.

He was afraid to pick it up. Trembling now, he eyed it.

He unpinned the paper. It was written in a scribble, obviously in a great hurry.

*Dear Simon,*

*Please forgive me. I must go to Niger. I cannot abandon my child. I am so sorry. I know this is painful for you. But I do not have any choice.*

*Take it easy, See you soon,*

*Your friend Kolawole*

Simon sank down on the side of the bed, letter in hand, and considered the ruins of all his dreams.

Jan was driving back from Zaria with her passengers, pondering on whether to turn off up the Kano road, entering Niger north of Katsina, or to go back through Samaru and make for Sokoto and the border-post at Illela. Luckily, she had a three-trip visa on her passport so she didn't have to go by the Niger Embassy in Kano this time.

She was loaded to the gunwales with people and gear, and feeling rather demented and put upon – a sensation that had set in when confronted with the eight-member family of four adults, one teenager and three children she had unwittingly agreed to carry.

Things were at an all-time low. Langley was probably sitting somewhere stubbing out cigarettes and vengefully plotting her downfall; and now at last the full tide of disappointment and hurt about Anow's no-show was flooding over her.

Fantasies about revenge against Ned Bassett weren't helping either. The lump of fury was back in her throat again. The miserly ungrateful bastard! The whole campus despised him and no wonder!

She was nearing the Kano roundabout, remembering the night it had sprung into existence like a mushroom and she had driven right over the kerb and into the centre of it – *crash, bang, wallop* – no lights or warning signs, of course, nor would there have been even if a trench had been dug across the road.

She started. Just before the roundabout a friend of Anow's called Aghali was on the grass verge, trying to flag down a taxi. She braked and indicated, in that order, and swung in to the side of the road, causing a cacophony of horn-protest behind her.

Aghali ran to the car and squeezed into the passenger seat beside the father and teenage son. She just hoped to Christ he wouldn't take the notion to travel with them to Niger.

"*Madame!*" he greeted her and shook her hand in the

stroking repetitive Tuarag way. He then went through lengthier greetings with Aberfekil and Daud – the father and son – and even more prolonged and stylised exchanges with the old man in the back, all accomplished through the most awkward gyrations in the confined space of the car. A barrage of greetings from the women in the back then followed.

"Samaru?" Jan cut in.

"*Oui, Madame!*" answered Aghali.

And no further than Samaru, she vowed.

She drove on, listening to the loud good-humoured exchanges in a fever of impatience, waiting for him to turn his attention back to her. At last, he switched back to Hausa.

"*Madame!*" Pulling his veil down to grin at her. He was only Anow's age and casual about the veil which he hadn't been wearing long. "You're going to Niger?"

"Yes!" Oh-oh.

"God protect you on the road!"

"Amen!" she breathed in relief.

"Greet Niger for me!"

"Without doubt!" she said fervently. Then, "Aghali? Have you news of Anow?"

"Yes." A pause. "He has gone to Niger."

She glanced at him. "No. He has not gone yet. It was with us he was to go. When did you see him?"

"I saw him yesterday at sunset. He said he was leaving today."

"Yes! That was his intention! But where is he?"

"I think he has already gone."

"Gone! How can he be gone?" she asked in agitation.

"What do you mean? On his own? How? By bus?" Oh, God, no! The minibuses were death-traps on wheels, all of them.

Aghali had tugged his veil up again over his mouth and his eyes had shifted away. When he spoke again his voice was muffled. "No."

"I also saw him yesterday," Aberfekil spoke up.

It hadn't even occurred to her to ask him.

"He said he was going with his *Madame*," he continued.

"Yes," said Jan. "But he didn't come to my house!"

"Not you," said Aberfekil. "The French *Madame*."

She nearly crashed the car. *The French Madame! Marie! Going with Marie!*

"The French *Madame*?" she said, voice quavering. "Was her name Marie?"

"I don't know her name," said Aberfekil.

"She with the Yoruba husband," muttered Aghali, voice expressionless.

She glanced at him sharply. Was he just embarrassed because Anow had defected or nervous because he knew what was afoot?

"But, Aghali, I didn't think he even knew her!"

"He met her on top of the rock."

"Kufena!"

Oh Christ. After she had turned Marie down, Marie had moved on to Anow.

After she had turned Anow down, he had moved on to Marie. Moved on? Had they both found what they were looking for?

The flood of jealousy that swept over her made her dizzy.

Oh, but God! What if he were caught? Apparently running off with a Nigerian's wife! What was the prison sentence for that, she wondered. Prison sentence! He'd be lucky not to have his balls cut off! Jesus!

"Which road were they going to follow?"

They didn't know. He hadn't said.

She pulled up to let Aghali out at the Police Gate, the first gate of the university.

Which road would they have taken? The Kano road if Marie needed a visa from the Embassy. But she might have had a multiple pass . . .

Hang on, Marie was a French national – she wouldn't need a visa at all to get into the former French colony.

That settled it: Sokoto and Illela it was.

She revved up the engine and tore off up the road to Samaru past the university. Seconds after she passed, Simon's daffodil-yellow VW shot out the main campus gate and turned right, making for the Kano roundabout.

Heading up the Kano road Ikus-Ikoos was nervously surveying Ned as he goggled over the steering wheel, chin practically on the rim, hands gripping the wheel on either side of his jowls. He was wondering about the wisdom of travelling in Ned's decrepit pea-green Lada when they could be tearing up the road in a yellow Nigerian taxi – with luck, one in good condition with the driver on nothing more potent than kola nuts.

One problem was that Ned drove at a steady thirty-five miles an hour, a rate which would get them to Tahoua in about three days barring punctures and accidents.

The second problem was – well, everything else. As they swerved wildly to avoid yet another goat, he was remembering one of the rare occasions he had driven with Ned in the past.

It had been at night and, after an embarrassed hesitation, he had remarked, "Ned, your light is on."

Ned had goggled at him. "Eh? Of course it is!"

"No – I mean your interior light. It's on."

"Well, of course it is. What d'you mean 'it's on'? Why wouldn't it be?"

"But it isn't supposed to be on!"

"What? Not supposed to be *on*?" Irate. "So how am I supposed to see the controls then? You are a silly sod!"

Ikus-Ikoos was now belatedly wondering whether Ned had any notion at all of how to drive a car.

"Watch that bicycle!" he said sharply, closing his eyes.

He felt the car swerve again.

"Silly old fart! They haven't a grain of sense, have they? Not an iota! Ah-hah-hah-hah! Look at that!" Ahead of them the rider of another bicycle was steaming along with a huge tin trunk on his head. "Ah-hah-hah-hah!" Narrowly missing the side of the trunk. "No sense and no consideration for other road users!"

Ikus-Ikoos turned his head to watch the bicycle wobble wildly in Ned's wake and almost end in the ditch, the rider's lips drawn back in a grimace of fright and effort and the whites of his eyes glaring around the pupils.

*"Espèce de maladroit!"* muttered Ikus-Ikoos.

"What does that mean? French, wasn't it? What did you call him?"

"It means 'you clumsy fool'." And I meant *you*, you old idiot.

"I must remember that: *"Es-pace!"*

"No – *espèce de* just means 'a kind of a' something."

"So you called him 'a kind of a clumsy fool'? Why didn't

you just call him a clumsy fool?" Ned was baring his teeth in a grin against the glare as he struggled to understand.

"The French always say *espèce de*."

"Christ, but they're rum buggers, those French! Imagine calling someone a *kind* of a fool when you could call him a fool! Why do they do that, then?"

Ikus-Ikoos was ready to strangle him. "I don't know. They just do." He searched for something to get the conversation away from *espèce* but Ned beat him to it.

"So French is your first language rather than English then?"

"No – Tamajegh is my first language. French and English are my – well, sixth and seventh languages actually."

"What? *Sixth and seventh?* What d'you mean, sixth and seventh?"

"Well: Tamajegh, Hausa, Djerma, Fulfulde, Arabic."

"What? You can't count *those*!"

"Why not?"

"Well, they're not *first* languages! They can be *mother* tongues but not *first* languages!"

"You mean that only European languages can be first languages?"

"Well . . . yes!"

Ikus-Ikoos gave up – he couldn't deal with it. He scrabbled around for another subject of conversation.

"How long have you been driving, Ned?"

"Oh, six years now. But I only got my licence three years ago. Ah-hah-hah-hah! *Eight* times I did the test! Failed every time but the last! The first two times he didn't even get in the car! Made me do that reversing between the barrels!" He leant towards Ikus-Ikoos in one of his moments of hilarious self-mockery. "I knocked *all eight of 'em* first time! Ah-hah-hah-hah-*hah*!"

"Ned!"

The car swerved. "Don't care, do they, about their children! Let 'em run naked around the road like goats! Easy come, easy go, wot? Lose one, produce another! Half of 'em have four wives – let the women do the work, wot? But if I knocked one of those kids down there'd be hell to pay. Oh, they'd care then! We'd hear about it then. But you wouldn't see me stopping! Not to have them set about me with machetes! Oh, there've been cases!"

Ikus-Ikoos frowned. It was true. There had been cases.

"Oh, yes, there have! There was that American on the road to Kaduna. Stopped to pick up an accident victim when every other car was passing by. Good Samaritan, ah-hah-hah-hah! Took the man into Kaduna – found himself arrested for manslaughter – and the victim wasn't even dead! Luckily, he recovered. Oh, never stop – that's the golden rule! I mean, I'd be sorry to leave some poor sod bleeding to death on the road but there it is!"

"Well . . ."

"'Ere, my driving tests. Y'see, I refused to dash 'em, that was the trouble. So third time the bastard does get in the car at least! But I had only changed into first gear – it did catch a bit – when the bastard jumped out and stalked away! Oh, a nasty piece of goods, that Inspector! On a power-trip, the bollocks. Never anything but a scowl on his face. No manners! Imagine! Not a word – just stalked off – left me gaping after him. Anyway, the *eighth* time I arrived at the office, the bollocks turned to his assistant and said, "I think we must let Mr Bassett pass his test this time – he has tried!""

And he started to giggle! And that was it! Gave me the licence! What do you think of that?"

Ikus-Ikoos didn't think much of that. He pinched the bridge of hs nose hard. He could feel a bad headache coming on.

Jan was making good time. She swung into the market area of Funtua, some seventy miles up the road. She slid out, pulled her sticky cotton wrapper away from her thighs and bum – thank God she was wearing underwear – and looked about for any bar or shop on the perimeter that looked as if it might sell cold drinks. She looked back and the Land-Cruiser had emptied itself of passengers: they were all making for the gaudy market stalls. Damn! It would be the devil to get them back in.

When some kids approached her, trays on heads, hawking tepid Coke kept cool under soaked sacking, thirst drove her into buying a bottle. It was warmly fizzy and sickly sweet. But it was wet and wetness was everything.

As she sucked the fizzy stuff down, small thick bottle raised, she noticed a man standing nearby outside one of the stalls. He had his back to her, with a dark-brown leather drawstring bag hanging from his left shoulder. He was wearing a broad-brimmed hat tightly woven in honey-coloured straw, with a weave of dark red and black around the crown and rim. Few northern Nigerians wore straw hats – they were almost exclusively worn by the cattle Fulani – but this wasn't the Fulani conical hat and this was no bush Fulani. He was too well dressed, for one thing, in his short brown and gold African shirt, blue jeans fresh and pressed. Something about the graceful, rather sexy stance seemed familiar. He shifted his weight as he studied something the stall-owner had handed to him and the movement made him thrust out his right buttock. She had it in a flash.

She walked up behind him and said, "Hi, there!"

He turned his head and, sure enough, it was Kolawole Aboyade.

A broad smile lit up the dark-chocolate face, and yellow-brown eyes looked down at her from under the rim of the hat. She was startled. Considering that the last time she had seen him he had a face like a thunderstorm and looked ready to gut her. He was buying a torch.

"Ah, Jan! How are you?"

He has lion's eyes, she thought. "Oh, I'm fine! And you?"

"Fine," he smiled. "You have come to the market? You should come on Sunday – the Sunday market's best."

"I know. I've often been. But I'm on my way to Niger."

"Oh, yes. The Buzu lady." The smile in his eyes took the possible insult out of it. 'Buzu' had originally been the Hausa term for a Tuareg slave.

Hell, he was teasing her.

"So where are your Buzus? Wait, let me make this man's day and pay him 'first price' – I won't waste time haggling, now that I have met you." He turned back to the stall-owner and thrust some money at him, with the usual expression of agreement. *To . . . shi ke nan!*"

"*Yawwa!*" the stall-owner exclaimed in delight at the easy sale.

A long hand was laid on the small of Jan's back and, again distinctly surprised, she felt herself being propelled quite firmly back in the direction of the car. "So," Kola repeated, "where are they, your Buzus?"

"Oh, God only knows – in the market somewhere. They all scattered as soon as the car stopped."

He hadn't taken his hand away from her back. "How many are there?"

She laughed ruefully. "Oh, too many!"

They reached the car and he unslung his bag and put it on the bonnet. He turned to face her, moving in up close – so close his hat-brim was touching the top of her head – and smiled down into her face.

It was stimulating, the closeness. He was a beautiful man. No wonder Simon was cross-eyed with lust.

"You wouldn't have room to squeeze me in?" he asked softly.

Jesus. He was flirting with her. She felt faint. What the hell was going on?

She had to step back a little – not so far as to make it seem like recoil – to breathe. "Oh, only if you're willing to hold your breath all the way!"

"And tell me –" he glanced over her shoulder, "will I be sandwiched between those two women I see approaching? Oh, what a pity – one of them is quite old!"

Her tribe of Tuareg were mustering, right enough, thank heaven. The women – Takowilt and Semama – reached the car, their hands full of little brown-paper packages of peppered meat and bean-cakes. The small naked boy was hanging onto his mother's wrapper. Kola put his two hands under Semama's withered forearms and lifted her bodily into the back of the car and then, with a wicked grin, placed his palms under the ample curves of Takowilt's buttocks as she clambered up and heaved her in too.

Suddenly Jan liked him a lot. And liked him even more

when he gently handed up the little boy and, in response to the women's shrieking at the other children, he laughingly swung the two slender little girls round and about and lobbed them in, their long braids flying.

Jan thought of Simon with a pang. Kola would make a great daddy. She bit her lip, suddenly almost on the point of crying.

She went round the car and climbed into the driver's seat, to find Kola already settling into the passenger seat. Where the hell was he going? Sokoto?

When Aberfekil arrived a moment later with his son he was visibly put out at his seat being taken. He stared at the usurper a long moment before remembering his manners and greeting him half-heartedly. The boy, Daud, went sulkily round to get in the back but not without protest and a gentle cuff in the ear from his father. Jan made a mental note to make sure the boy got his seat in front again when Kola got out.

"So," she asked Kola, hand on gear-stick, "where can we drop you?"

The mischievous flutter of his eyelashes was pure Eddie Murphy.

"Niger," he answered.

"Blimey! Look at that daft bugger!"

"Ned!"

"Well, now I've seen everything! Riding a bicycle with a goat on his head! But you have to give it to 'em! Marvellous control!"

"*Va apprendre à conduire, espèce d'imbecile!*" muttered Ikus-Ikoos.

"What did you say there?"

"I told him go learn to drive – a bike," said Ikus-Ikoos distractedly, turning his head to see the goat-bearer sail into the grass verge in their wake, hit an anthill and collapse in a heap of dried mud, goat and bicycle. He watched in trepidation to see if the rider recovered. To his relief he saw him get to his feet and check his goat for injuries. The anthill must have been abandoned by the troops. Luckily.

"Though, in fairness, he must have phenomenal balance really! But so have circus dogs! Ah-hah-hah-hah!"

"*Espèce de porc à la manque!*" muttered Ikus-Ikoos.

His head was pounding but his muttered imprecations in French were relieving the stress a little – despite the fact that he had to translate every time.

"'Ere, what does that one mean?"

"Kind of a worthless pig."

"Oh, very good! *Es-pace!*"

Ikus-Ikoos now fell silent, cowering inside the folds of his *tagilmoust*, hoping to discourage Ned from further speech.

And indeed, for a few blessed minutes Ned trundled up the centre of the Kano road in silence.

It was getting very hot and Ikus-Ikoos was horribly sleepy – he had hardly slept the night before. A faint smile touched his lips as he remembered a night spent naked and enfolded in the black-blue of his Maryam's veil, drunk with the odour of oil-based perfume and indigo on her skin – whispering praise-poems in her ear, making full sure she would long for the hour when he held her in his arms again. God grant it would not be too long! Could he trust her to wait if it happened she must?

He began to nod off, each time starting awake in fear

that if he took his eyes off the road Ned would hit the next goat or bicycle or child or calabash-bearing Fulani milkwoman or minibus without fail.

But as Ned's silence stretched miraculously Ikus-Ikoos was overcome with drowsiness. He leant his head back gingerly and closed his eyes, praying that, if it be the Will of God, death should not come for him in a heap of nasty pea-green metal on the Kano road that day.

"*Waltzing Matilda, Waltzing Matilda!*"

He started awake, heart pounding, at Ned's raucous blast of melody.

"Oh, sorry, mate! Were you dropping off?"

Ikus-Ikoos closed his eyes again, heartbeat steadying.

Another short spell of silence followed. It made him uneasy. After a minute or two he realised that all his muscles were contracted in tension. His eyes were actually darting back and forth beneath the closed lids. The impulse was irresistible: he opened one eye and squinted at Ned.

Ned was grinning hugely at some private joke as he battled on, sweat standing out on his mottled face and staining his pink shirt red under the arms and down his back.

Ikus-Ikoos cautiously closed the eye and tried to relax.

"Ah-hah-hah-*hah*!"

Opening his eyes this time into the glare of the burgeoning sun was painful.

"'Ere! Cous-cous! I *am* a daft sod! Here I am, driving up the road to God knows where, and I could have stayed home. Y'see, I was worried that there was no way of identifying the bastards who took my money as all you effing Blue Men look alike. But think of this! I could have issued an identikit for Fatty – an artist's impression: two enormous boobs! *Wanted! Has anyone seen this woman?* Ah-hah-hah-hah-*hah*! Last seen wearing, wot?" He leant across and nudged Ikus-Ikoos in the ribs. The car swerved. "They could have used her vital statistics as a yardstick! Can you imagine it? The Nigerian police checking every boob that went through the border-post for size! With their rulers and tape measures! Throw that one back in the water, Sergeant, *not big enough! Not by a long shot!* Ah-*hah*-hah-hah-hah! 'Ere! What do you feed 'em to grow breasts like that? Whatever it is we should give it to the gals back home!"

"Milk," muttered Ikus-Ikoos.

"Oh, yes-s-s-s! Force-feed 'em, don't you? The little girls? Jan told me about that – holding their noses and pouring kettles of camel's milk down 'em till they almost burst."

That straw broke the camel's back.

"Ned," said Ikus-Ikoos in desperation, "I really have to stop. I have a terrible headache and I need to –"

"Oh, Jan was furious about that! Very upset, she was! Very self-righteous is our Jan. Full of pity for the underdog and all that – bit of a feminist –"

"Ned – I must stop!"

"What?"

"I must drink tea – my head is pounding."

"Oh! A cuppa, eh? Wouldn't say no m'self."

Simon was driving gaily up the Kano road in his yellow VW, fantasising about his child-to-be. As the mother was Hausa, she might with luck be quite light-skinned – milk-chocolate brown, dark honey or even golden-brown. Golden-brown would be wonderful, he thought with a sigh – that would produce a dark-honey baby who could pass as a "half-and-half" as they called mixed-race children in this part of the world.

He couldn't understand why it hadn't hit him instantly, when he heard about the baby, that this was the God-given answer to his prayers. Oh, well, he had to go through the Trough of Despair first before he emerged into the – his memory failed him – onto the Sunny Uplands, he substituted. Like a bolt from the blue, like a starburst of joy, like the closing chorus to *Hello Dolly*! it had hit him as he sat on the side of Kola's bed. And when it had, action followed on concept like the African night clanged down abruptly on the day. Or like a dose of the runs after pepper stew.

It would be a boy, he was sure of that. He was vague about why he wanted it to be a boy, when a girl would be so lovely. I guess I just like boys, he giggled. But a girl . . . he slid into a pleasant fantasy where he was dressing his little honey-dark girl for a birthday party . . . *her* birthday party . . . she was three, no, four years old and he was tying little pink ribbons in her bunches of fluffy black hair while she squirmed about giggling in her new pink and white cotton party dress. Her brown eyes slanted up at him in mirth and her cute smile dimpled her cheeks . . . his heart melted . . . she was perfection . . . and he would be wearing –

"*Blaaaaaaaaaahhhhhhh!*" The blare of a monstrous horn blasted him out of his daydream and he swerved onto the hard shoulder as a huge petrol-truck thundered by.

Heart pounding, hands sweating and slipping on the wheel, he turned the car onto the road again. He must concentrate. He couldn't afford even a minor accident. He must get to Tahoua before Kola made any decisions.

He dared not think about what those fatal decisions might be if he didn't arrive in time to save the day. He slid into another daydream where Kola stood defeated and despairing and the Hausa parents wrung their hands at their disgrace – then the upright graceful figure of a striking Bature stepped through the mud entrance. A kind of nobility shone on his (her?) face as he (she?) calmly glided towards the pregnant girl. "I will take the baby," s/he said. And at the words, hope dawned on all their faces. "Thank you!" they collectively sighed, stretching out their hands towards him/her. And with a profound humility and wisdom – a hard-won wisdom – s/he folded the weeping young girl to his/her breast.

Simon did a re-run on that last scene to accommodate the girl's bump which he had forgotten about – so now when s/he folded the girl to his/her (flat) breasts s/he was pressing a large pliant swollen belly against his/her own belly – well, groin actually, as s/he was much taller than the little Hausa girl. Would he wear his wrapper for this scene? Why not? And dare he sketch in a little bosom on the Bature's slender figure? Oh, just a little wouldn't do any harm . . . he allowed the flat chest to swell and curve just a little. *Lovely.* But now the Bature was speaking in low, vibrant tones: "Come with me until the baby is born. I will devote myself to your welfare. Think of yourself as my daughter. Your grief is my grief, your pain is my pain . . . *whither thou goest I will go . . .*" Oh, oh, how did it go? "*Thy people shall be my people and thy God my God.*" Oh, excellent! If he hadn't been driving, he would have hugged himself in delight. Was it perhaps too much? No . . . not really . . . that's what s/he would say . . . But now the declaration of devotion shifted to the Hausa girl without Simon's much noticing. *"Thy people shall be my people,"* she was saying, *"and thy God my God."* While a certain well-hung Yoruba, father of the baby, looked on – lost in admiration of the Bature's heroic generosity, to say nothing of his/her slender graceful figure with its nicely curving buttocks.

Wriggling in his seat, smiling, Simon sped towards Niger.

"Tea! You call that tea? I shan't be drinking any of that." Ned had been watching Ikus-Ikoos's tea ritual with smug amusement.

Ikus-Ikoos was sitting on a mat under a broadly spreading tree. Ned had sneered at the idea of sitting on a mat ("Not bloody likely! Call that comfort?") and had opted to perch unsteadily on a fallen branch instead.

Now he was contentedly digging at his pipe, sweating away in the pleasant shade. He squinted up through the thickly leaved branches where the glaring sunlight glimmered through.

"This is the life, eh? To think I could be stuck in a cubby-hole of an office in Manchester or Birmingham! 'Ere! What's that big white cone?"

Ikus-Ikoos was chipping away with a little silver hammer at a huge cone of white sugar, almost as long as his forearm and thicker at the base. Its top was rounded and its texture very dense. "Sugar, is it? A bit phallic, isn't it? Bet your ladies find that useful nights when you're off shagging the sheep! 'Pastoralists', aren't you? Ah-hah-hah-hah-hah!"

Ikus-Ikoos winced at the blast of laughter. 'Shagging' – that would be like shearing, he supposed. His headache was lifting a bit – like all Tuaregs he was addicted to tea, from the first powerfully bitter glass to the third golden honey-sweet one, and needed frequent hits of it. As Ned was refusing to partake, there was more than the usual for him. He tossed back the last glass of the first brew. It had gone almost cold as it sat on his little brass tray while he went through preparations for the second brew. But it still had that kick that would wake the dead, He put the glass down with a sigh of relief. What was the old man saying now?

Ned was goggling at him expectantly. "I said – have you ever tried it?"

What was he talking about? Some kind of tea? Jasmine maybe? Or was he still talking about sheep-shearing? "Em, yes . . ."

"You *have*! Jesus, you're a rum bugger!"

Ikus-Ikoos smiled deprecatingly, understanding the tone – one of amazed approval – rather than the words. He didn't know what 'rum' meant used as an adjective like that and he was vague about 'bugger' but knew it was a term of abuse. But Ned used terms of abuse as compliments.

Ned shook his head at the tea and continued to gaze at Ikus-Ikoos with a strange open-mouthed expression. "Often?" he asked.

Ikus-Ikoos hesitated. "Quite often." It was easier to blunder on than to try to recap.

"And what's it like, mate? I've often wondered."

Ikus-Ikoos frowned, as he searched for an innocuous answer. *Was* he talking about tea? "Well . . . it wouldn't be to everyone's taste . . ." he said cautiously.

"*Ah-hah-hah-hah-hah!*"

The explosion startled him enough to make him drop a

large lump of sugar into the tea-pot with a splash that lost him a quarter of the little pot.

"You *are* a rum bugger!" In great good humour Ned started the attempt to light up his pipe. After a period of strenuous sucking and the loss of five matches, he suddenly exploded in mirth and asthmatic coughing. He had to take off his glasses to wipe the tears from his eyes with the back of his hand.

Ikus-Ikoos was alarmed and perplexed.

"Tell me," Ned coughed out at last, "did the earth move?"

Ikus-Ikoos stared, at a loss. Was 'did the earth move' a colloquial expression of some sort? Or was Ned talking neither about jasmine tea nor sheep-shearing but astrology? But what was so funny about it?

Luckily, Ned was so taken with his joke he went into further paroxysms and that kept him occupied for a while. Finally, he calmed down and proceeded to wipe his eyes again, sighing after his excess of laughter. When he could speak again, he said raspingly, "Christ, Cous-Cous, my mouth is as dry as a gravel-pit. I'm nearly tempted to drink that molten tar of yours."

Ikus-Ikoos sighed inwardly and reached into his leather tea-satchel, a complete small goatskin. He pulled out a little tin of sweetened condensed milk and a tin mug. Taking a decorated knife from inside his robes he punched two little holes on opposite sides of the milk-tin.

Ned had attempted to light up again and it had brought on another bout of asthmatic heaving.

Ikus-Ikoos poured one little glass for himself and then, with another heartfelt inward sigh, poured all the rest of the tea into the tin mug. He then held the tin over it, letting a steady rope of condensed milk, thick and sticky as syrup, pour into it from one of the little holes. Then he stirred it with his knife and handed it to Ned.

"What's this, mate?" asked Ned suspiciously but he didn't hesitate to take a great sucking sip of the tea. He smacked his lips, nodded with a "Not bad, not bad at all!" and soon was slurping it down with every appearance of enjoyment.

Ikus-Ikoos took off his *tagilmoust* wearily and stretched out, bundling the soft loops of cloth under his head. He longed hungrily for sleep – a long, long sleep – but, as that was impossible, ten delicious minutes would be a wonderful thing . . . he closed his eyes and slid into his Maryam's arms . . .

"*Ta-ra-ra-boom-de-ay!*" sang Simon as he flew northward, tapping on the wheel.

He was well over half the way to Kano. A village – probably Kabo – hove into sight.

"Hove into sight!" he giggled as the phrase occurred to him. And in that moment wished he had a companion. Then he remembered: wasn't Jan travelling to Niger too – and wasn't it *today*? And wasn't it through *Tahoua*, the very place he wanted to go? Oh, fuck! How could he have forgotten? Ruefully, he admitted that he'd been tossed up there onto Cloud Nine by the lightning bolt of the Great Solution. He'd been in an alternative world ever since. Now he came down just a few degrees to earth.

In any case, Jan would be off into the desert and would probably not emerge until the full three weeks of the vacation were up – if then. But at least they could have travelled in convoy.

Kabo was a sizeable roadside village. He decided to stop and get a cold drink. If such a thing existed. The sun was high now and well into its sadistic stride. Just his luck all this should happen in the hot season, the cruellest period of the year.

He pulled up and got out. The sun blasted down on him. His wrap-around shades were slithering down his nose and his hair was dripping with sweat behind his ears. The African shirt he was wearing, a fabulous mix of violets, purples and dark blues, was stuck to his back and his jeans had chafed the cleft of his buttocks unpleasantly. And he'd only been on the road for a couple of hours with the hottest part of the day yet to come. Oh, for a private room with a shower and a tube of vaseline!

He locked the car, wishing he could at least leave a window open – but that, of course, was out of the question if he wanted to find the steering wheel still in place when he got back.

A small market stretched back from the road with the usual ramshackle straw- and tin-roofed stalls. It was surrounded by sturdier mud-walled constructions, one of which, he fervently hoped, would house a fridge or at least a huge earthenware pot full of cold water with bottles of Coca-Cola nestling in its depths.

He spotted a Coca-Cola sign on a mud building across the market so he plunged in and, a few minutes later, was sitting on a wooden bench outside the hut under a corrugated-iron awning, with a bottle of reasonably cool Coke in his hand. Little girls in myriad colours came hawking their wares as he sat, even the six-year-olds looking like little pint-sized adults in their headscarves and long cotton dresses with brightly coloured sashes tied round their waists. He always delighted in watching the unconscious skill of such little girls – and boys – the way they could chew on a sugar-cane, twirling around on their bare feet and joking with their friends, all with a large tray of tiny tins of peanuts or bottles of Coke or heaps of bean-cakes on their heads. Would his little girl inherit that skill from her Hausa mother? Oh dear, it had become a girl! What had happened to his little boy? A glorious thought struck him: what if she had *twins*?

He was so taken with this notion that he didn't at first notice the commotion in the market. In fact, it took a tug at his shirt from one of the kids to get his attention. The child was saying something to him, a look half of glee half of fear on her face. "*Abokinka! Abokinka!*"

'*Aboki*' – friend. '*Abokinka*' – your friend.

Shrieks and laughter reached his ears. His eyes followed her pointing finger. There was some kind of rumpus afoot. Children were scampering off and hiding behind stalls, women were darting off, hands over mouths, then turning and staring back, men were backing off. It was chaos but it had a pattern – as if he were looking through a kaleidoscope. Something at the centre of the chaos was acting as magnet and moving back through the market to the side nearest the road.

*His friend?* What did that mean? Maybe he'd misheard. Maybe the child was speaking about his *car*. Was there something wrong with the car? Alarmed, he drank off the remainder of his Coke and apprehensively skirted the market at a rapid pace, visions of the blank space he would find instead of his car filling his head.

But the yellow VW was sitting there intact. He almost kissed it.

Renewed howls of laughter burst on his ears and he swung around to behold the extraordinary spectacle of Tom Purthill bursting out of the market in stork-impersonation mode.

Simon experienced the same sensation that had afflicted Jan at the university: wanting to laugh, wanting to cry, wanting to run away – while being utterly dumbfounded.

Tom hadn't seen Simon yet. The trouble was, the presence of man, woman or child to his right or left, fore or aft, sent him veering off in a panic in the opposite direction. Meanwhile, the inhabitants of Kabo were trying to stay out of his high-stepping way and his sudden about-turns and changes of direction were sending them veering as crazily as him and scattering every which way as they screamed *"Mahaukaci! Mahaukaci!"* hysterically. *Madman! Madman!*

Tom was clutching a green canvas satchel to his chest and had a small tartan zip-lock bag in his left hand. He was wearing his usual long khaki shorts and shirt. As Simon watched, he high-stepped madly towards a small group of brightly robed Hausamen who up to now had been keeping their dignity as the kids, women and market boys yelped and shrieked and ran and convulsed in laughter. *"Mahaukaci! Mahaukaci!"* Now, seeing Tom – limbs flailing wildly, face contorted, head thrown back – bearing down on them like a car whose brakes had failed, the robed men scattered in all directions revealing what they had been shielding: a man with two hyenas on chains. Seconds later, the two spotted animals were rampaging through the market dragging their chains behind them while Tom ploughed on, now like a kamikaze pilot on a roll, straight into a cowskin which was stretched on a frame to dry. This acted like a trampoline and Tom bounced back spectacularly, both bags flying from his hands, to lie stunned and at last motionless on the dusty ground.

The inhabitants of Kabo were now distracted by the mayhem the hyenas were inflicting on their market – in fact, most of them were barricaded behind closed doors by this time – and Tom's trampoline finale went unfortunately unobserved, which was a great shame as it would have served to amuse generations to come.

Simon knew he should go and see if Tom was OK. But he still stood motionless by the VW. He'd better get him up off the ground before the hyenas came ravaging back and ate him alive. If he was alive. But . . .

At that moment a familiar voice boomed on his ears. "Tom! Tom Purthill! Get up, man!"

One of the hyenas bounded forward from nowhere and landed on Tom's chest. The breath went out of him with an audible *whumph* and Simon's heart almost flew out of his mouth with fright – then he saw that it was not a hyena at all but a great big German Shepherd.

Hetty Coleman came striding forward on her strong brown feet in their leather sandals.

That was enough for Simon. Now identifying the latter stages of his paralysis as a simple reluctance to have anything to do with Tom Purthill, he waited only to see Tom raise his head, then leapt into his beetle and was on the road to Kano faster than a stripper would have flipped off his G-string. He only hoped that his car hadn't been noticed by either Tom or Hetty. It was such an indiscreet colour – normally it stuck out like a sore thumb (a *really* bad colour for cruising) but with all that commotion . . .

Well, it didn't matter. The incident would have faded from all their minds before he saw Tom or Hetty Coleman again. And he had more important things to deal with.

## Chapter 8

"Takes everything too seriously, does Jan. Don't you think so? Oh, she was furious with me about arranging this marriage. Oh, she didn't like that! Wouldn't have anything to do with it! I tell you: she'd have stopped me if she could – especially after I pelted her with potatoes –"

Ikus-Ikoos opened his eyes from blissful visions of his Maryam to this stream of babble. Potatoes? And then, as he blearily returned to consciousness, a sudden silence startled him. He raised his head in alarm. Ned was still sitting on his tree-branch, goggling vacantly, wattles quivering.

"'Ere . . . 'ere, mate . . ." he said at last, in a ghost of a voice.

"Yes?"

"Oh, the bitch!"

"What?"

"Oh, now I see what she's done!" said Ned, in a voice that gathered steam and outrage with every word. "She's stolen Fatty! That's what she's done! She and that fancy toy boy of hers! That's why he didn't turn up later yesterday!"

"Em, I don't think –"

"Don't you see?" Ned turned on him, glaring savagely. "Don't you see what she's done! She's sabotaged my wedding – because I threw a few potatoes at her!" High dudgeon.

"Potatoes? Why –"

"She left this morning, didn't she? She must be ahead of us on the road – but I shouldn't think she's crossed the border yet. I shall report her at the next town and get them to phone the Embassy in Kano and the border-post!"

Ikus-Ikoos couldn't bear another moment of Ned's ravings. "Ned, that's crazy. It doesn't make any sense!"

"Don't you see, you silly sod? She told me herself that she was taking a Tuareg family with her!"

"But, Ned, her trip was planned weeks ago – *and* the arrangement to take those people! It's not Fati's family, I assure you! Jan's passengers were staying in Zaria!"

"That's what she told you, mate! But how d'you know where she picked them up? *You* weren't there, *were* you?"

This last was said so aggressively and with so violent a shaking of his scraggy neck that Ikus-Ikoos felt quite nervous. He wound his *tagilmoust* on again. "Well, we had better be on our way. There's a long road ahead of us." He began to pack his tea-making equipment into the goatskin bag.

"Christ, but you're rum buggers!"

Ikus-Ikoos paused, startled, then realised that Ned had been distracted from his wrath by seeing him wind on his *tagilmoust*.

"So that's how it's done, eh? The quickness of the hand deceives the eye, wot? But tell me, why do you buggers veil your men and not your women?"

Ikus-Ikoos laughed. "We think our women are too beautiful to be veiled."

"Well, that's a rum answer! That's why the Arabs *do* it, you silly sod! To stop other men lusting after them!"

Ikus-Ikoos smiled, pleased. This was a subject dear to his heart. And had formed no small part of his doctoral thesis. "We are very different from the Arabs. We are a matriarchal society. Traditionally, inheritance and succession passed through the female line. Our women are revered."

"But not as much as your camels! Ah-hah-hah-hah!"

"You're right! Our poetry is about camels, women and raiding, in that order!"

"And sheep, I gather! Ah-hah-hah-hah-hah!"

Ikus-Ikoos stood up. 'Well, no. Camels are very desirable – sheep less so. Camels and goats would be the Tuareg thing – and the occasional donkey. Though of course we don't write poetry about donkeys! We just use them but don't desire them much."

Ned was open-mouthed. "Donkeys? Camels?"

"Yes. Camels are the most desirable thing on earth. We adore our women – so you can imagine how we feel about our camels!" Shouldering his mat and his goatskin bag.

"But, Cous-Cous –" He followed Ikus-Ikoos to the car. "If you don't mind me asking a delicate question . . . how do you *do* it with a *camel*?

"Do what?" asked Ikus-Ikoos.

"Well . . . how shall I put it? Eh, mount them?"

"Oh, they kneel. They are trained to kneel."

"Blimey!" Ned opened the boot and Ikus-Ikoos put his mat, brazier and charcoal inside. "So that's why they kneel! But, 'ere, mate! Isn't a camel . . . a little too *roomy*?"

Ikus-Ikoos was at a loss again. What did the old bastard mean? He pinched the bridge of his nose. "Um . . . no, we don't find them roomy at all . . . we find them a perfect . . . fit."

Ned looked amazed.

Ikus-Ikoos hesitated, wondering whether attempts at further communication were worth the effort. "Um . . . it is a bit tricky until you learn how but our fathers teach us really early . . . if you don't have experience you expect to have a better grip . . . better balance . . ." He gave up in the face of Ned's gaping astonishment.

"Chir-rist!" was Ned's comment as they got into the car. "I'd like to see your equipment, mate, if you think a camel is a perfect fit!"

"Oh," said Ikus-Ikoos vaguely, "I'll let you see it when we get to Tahoua."

What was the old bastard goggling at now?

Simon's hope that his yellow VW hadn't been noticed was in vain. Tom Purthill had seen it all right as he burst from the market in galvanised mode. He was almost sure it had been Simon Cullen's car with Simon Cullen standing in its vicinity. He was puzzled by this as the car had disappeared by the time he had properly come to.

Apart from this, Tom was pleased with how things had turned out. Here he was, sitting in the passenger-seat of a Land-Rover instead of a lethally speeding taxi or one of those deadly 'buses'. And Jan Prendergast hopefully was not too far up the road ahead of him.

Ah, Jan! Yes, this was the necessary touch, this would clinch it! He knew about her obsession with the desert! Happily, he imagined their encounter: desert sand, palm-trees, full moon – Jan seeing him in a new light as a daring, dashing, desert adventurer! Yes!

Thank God she hadn't witnessed the scene back at Kabo. He had bumps and bruises a-plenty; that had been a terrifying experience after those children and hawkers had started to pursue him, seemingly without cause. But – all's well that ends well and this had certainly ended as well as one could have hoped for. A villager had even rushed forward with Tom's tartan bag when Hetty had revved up her Land-Rover. Who would have believed or expected such honesty?

Tom had dropped the tartan bag when trampolined and hadn't even noticed its absence, his attention being entirely focused on his green satchel. As long as that was safe, all was well.

He only knew Hetty by sight, but of course fellow-feeling was strong under such circumstances. She had been patently amazed when he told her that he had been travelling to Kano by bus – or minibus, to be precise, with several dozen others squeezed in like sardines in a can – and even more amazed, eyebrows disappearing up underneath her straight greying fringe, when he explained that the bus had driven off without him while he was buying a drink in the market. He had no idea why.

"Thank you again," he said now, simpering and aware of it. "I'm most grateful." He sounded effete and ridiculous. His efforts to communicate with people grew ever more hopeless. He invariably chose the wrong expression or the wrong words or the wrong tone of voice or the wrong body language – at best one of those – at worst all four which was ghastly when it happened. Somewhere in the gap between himself and other human beings he floundered every time. While every other soul bridged it with ease. Didn't even notice it was there.

"Nonsense, man," snorted Hetty. "I was hardly supposed to leave a fellow-countryman in the lurch. Besides, it was excellent exercise and practice for Ajax."

It had been spectacular. And would probably live longer in the annals of the village of Kabo than his unfortunate performance. Yes, Hetty and Ajax had eclipsed him.

Hetty had set Ajax on the hyenas and, as she directed him with a series of ear-splitting whistles, he had rounded them up in two flicks of a ram's tail and sent them cowering back to their master for protection. Ajax was then rewarded by Hetty with a roll on the dusty ground, to the astonishment of the villagers who had then feted mistress and dog with drinks and peppered meat while giving Tom Purthill a wide berth,

"Another strange thing," he said and laughed lightly, then was appalled to hear the laugh emerge as a snigger, "I imagined I saw Simon Cullen standing beside his yellow VW at the edge –"

"You didn't imagine it," she interrupted brusquely. "He was there. I saw him too. Drove off. Deserted you. Lily-livered, of course. Tell me, is he queer?"

"Oh. Well, yes, Simon is homosexual. H-h-h-he has a N-n-n-nigerian boyfriend." Oh, God, his stutter. Always under stress.

Proved how intimidating he found her.

"Have I not seen him wearing women's clothing around the university?"

"Y-y-y-yes."

"Humph. A common syndrome. Denied social interaction and sexual play with siblings and others, affection and sexual feelings are transferred to an inanimate object. Hence an object such as a high heel may trigger sexual responses. Psychology is my sideline, you know. I have a number of diplomas and have been involved in many cases as a consultant and observer. I intend to do a doctorate and eventually become a 'shrink'."

"Delightful, I'm sure." His legs seemed to cross themselves of their own accord and his hand made a flapping gesture. 'Delightful'! Wrong word, wrong word!

Hetty didn't seem to notice. "I remember one case where sexual attention was lavished on a large teddy bear. Several times a day the bear was thrown to the ground and ravished. Torn to shreds it was eventually and horribly sullied – he wouldn't let anyone wash the bear, of course."

Tom stared out at the baked landscape, clutching his bag, wondering if he had misheard. Afraid to respond in case he had.

"And there was the case involving an umbrella."

Tom's Adam's apple bobbed up and down painfully. This was frightful. Was he now suffering from aural hallucinations? The experience with Jan Prendergast – at the thought of her his right leg went into a spasmodic jerking – had left him wondering. She was adamant that there had been no vows or promises between them, not even implied.

Hetty glanced at him. "Very painful, as you may imagine.

We had to be firm in the end. It might have done permanent and severe damage."

"Quite," said Tom faintly. He had begun to find 'quite' a very useful noncommital word. His right shin was banging off the metal of the car. He clutched it with both hands and stilled it by main force, chin lowered on his green canvas bag. He twisted his head in Hetty's direction.

If Hetty thought his posture peculiar she didn't betray the thought. She continued cheerfully. "So your friend has simply been deprived of the necessary social and sexual interaction at a significant age and has therefore transferred his instincts to women's clothing and the penis. Initially, his mother's and his own respectively, probably. And I would have no doubt that some early sexual encounter with a black man will have provided further conditioning. Australian, is he?"

"Quite."

"Well, there are blacks in Australia."

"Quite."

"Is his boyfriend aggressive?"

"I d-d-d-don't know – I d-d-d-don't im-m-magine –"

"I expect he would be," said Hetty firmly. "As Simon Cullen has chosen a submissive female role it is inevitable. I well remember a case – which arose in a personal relationship of my own, as it happened. I cured such aggressive tendencies very effectively by a simple technique of *standing* in his bed and trampling it around and around. That demonstrated dominance – mine. I recommend the method. Most people have never heard of it. But it is *the* treatment for aggression which is usually caused by a failure to put the patient in his place."

Tom was mouthing like a codfish. He was attempting to express a safe degree of scepticism – just in case he had misheard or was aurally hallucinating. He hoped he had chosen the right expression. He had not.

Fortunately, Hetty didn't seem to notice.

"Sometimes aggression springs from abusive behaviour in the early years but often it may simply arise when, out of mistaken affection, the patient is allowed to sleep in one's bed. Dominant behaviour is sure to follow as night follows day. Allow him to sleep in your bed and he will automatically assume he rules the roost. Though he is not a cock, never forget he has one!"

Tom laughed nervously at the joke and then abruptly stopped as he realised she wasn't laughing.

"Not that I practise what I preach," she added, smiling coyly.

Was that a joke? Was it safe to laugh? It appeared it might be OK to chuckle. He did. It emerged as a snigger,

Hetty didn't seem to notice.

Anow awoke and stretched his aching limbs. His clothes were drenched in sweat and he felt as if he had a fever. The shuddering and grinding of the lorry as it hauled its load of grain and passengers was torture. As was the sun that beat down on them as they lay on the full, rock-hard sacks of grain with no shelter other than their own cotton veils and a single straw mat.

And he could be travelling in comfort in Jan's Land-Cruiser instead of in this metal monster. In his mind's eye he saw himself: bareheaded, with his *tagilmoust* looped around his neck, sitting in the passenger-seat next to Jan, leading the others in song, hands clapping, his voice splitting the very sky as it soared. And Jan would have that happy little smile curving her lips, as if this was her idea of Paradise and she would keep driving forever if he kept singing forever.

Why hadn't he fixed things up? That was not difficult with Jan – all he had to do was throw an arm around her, smile in her face, call her 'my *Madame*' or 'Mama' and beg her to have patience with her boy. No matter what kind of a black mood she was in, he could always get her to smile.

And she was right to be angry with him about what happened on Kufena. She still loved his brother, he knew that – she had given him her heart and she was loyal, though Moussa was not – well, in truth, Moussa had no choice – the family had arranged the marriage many years ago. And he, Anow, had been her little brother for some years now – for five years, since he was twelve years old. He had broken trust. Without doubt. She was his sister, his mother, and he had done a shameful thing. And it was not her fault, the thing that she had done with him in the rock-pool – a woman needed a man and she had been faithful to Moussa for many long months.

The lorry shuddered and he groaned aloud. Well, thank God that at least they could lie down, though the sacks of guinea-corn they were lying on felt like the rocks of Kufena under his bones by this time. Kufena – he couldn't get it out of his mind. At the thought, the memory, his penis had risen and was now pushing against the heavy folds of his baggy drawstring trousers – the precious jeans and underpants that belonged to his life in Zaria were tucked away carefully in his bag.

He twisted to look at his companion and that didn't help at all.

She was sitting up, staring at the small naked child sleeping on her lap, holding her veil out to make a tent to shelter him; the mat was propped up against her shoulder to shelter the little girl who lay sleeping by her side. She looked up at him from under her veil, her brow furrowed in discomfort and worry. Then she smiled at him, despite all. He smiled back and sat up, squatting before her to provide some more shade for the child, conscious of his penis harder then ever between his legs at her closeness.

There was something strongly disturbing about seeing an Infidel woman dressed as a Tuareg. Jan, of course, wore Tuareg clothes and he had seen her sometimes with her hair braided properly and indigo dye smeared on her skin – and, *kai*, it was beautiful how Jan's white skin shone through the blue – but Marie had become a Tuareg absolutely.

Her hair had been too short so he had got them to plait it in tiny plaits and scoop it up behind, where under the blue-black veil it couldn't be seen.

He thanked God that Aminatu and Raechitu had agreed so wholeheartedly to help. They had plaited and dressed her and smeared her with indigo and perfume and hung beads and bracelets on her. They had laughed as they took off her European clothes and underwear – he was chased outside for that part – and fallen into wide-eyed silence when they realised that she was leaving everything with them: even her watch and gold bracelets and earrings and necklace – even the gold ring from her finger and the one with the glittering stone. He had been forced to take the jewellery from them and refuse to hand it over until they finished their task. Their eyes alight with avarice, they had continued with even more vigour. They had tied plastic bags full of ground henna around her hands and feet to dye them a beautiful red-brown. They had made fine henna decorations on her face, a lovely straight line down her nose making it look longer and little circles and lines on her face.

She looked beautiful – indeed he had feared that they had gone too far and made her look like a Tuareg beauty on her way to a festival instead of a weary travelling mother. But the black robes were patched and dusty and the sweat which stood out on her skin and the worry-lines between her eyebrows had taken that shine away.

The earrings had been a big problem. Every Tuareg woman wore huge heavy hoops of silver, thick as a finger at their thickest end and thick as a baby's finger at the point where they entered the earlobe. So every Tuareg woman had huge enlarged holes through her ears, and elongated earlobes from which swung these hefty pieces. There was no way Marie's tiny ear-piercings could take proper women's earrings. The women had tried, with vaseline and patience, to force the earrings painfully through. When Aminatu had joked that it was like trying to force a virgin Anow had suffered a violent erection and he had rushed outside the shelter for fear he would come in his trousers in front of the women. He had come, in fact, outside behind the fence, where he had squatted pretending to urinate. After that, he had wiped the sweat from his face and shakily returned to supervise the final stages of the operation.

Remembering now, he feared he might have to fake urination again – but with nowhere to pretend to piss except on the sacks of grain he was forced to pray instead that the lorry might stop at some village soon.

She was too thin, of course, and her breasts too small — like a young girl's. Her lips were too thin also and her nose not noble enough.

Jan wasn't fat enough either and had the same thin lips — even thinner lips. But Jan — Jan's beauty was in her voice and in her smile and in her laugh and in her sparkling blue eyes. It didn't matter that her hair was an ugly colour — though it did glitter wonderfully in the sun — and her skin burned an ugly red. He knew that under her clothes where the sun hadn't reached it was an amazing white and, though he knew that extreme white was an ugly colour, it drew his hand like a magnet. But Marie's skin was a truly beautiful gold and her eyes were a truly beautiful glowing brown.

He longed to touch her and then, to his utter shock, he did. Like one possessed, he observed his own hand take leave of its senses and cup one of her breasts. She started but didn't recoil. His trembling thumb settled on her nipple and he was amazed to feel it harden and point under his touch.

The fact that behind him and on either side were fellow-travellers, their view blocked by her sheltering veil, made him dizzy. Her eyes were fixed on his face and astonishingly she didn't pull away.

Suddenly terrified that he might throw himself on her in front of all these people, he abruptly twisted away and lay back down again, his back to her, veil pulled over his face, nursing his penis in agony.

"H-h-h-hetty?"

"Um?"

They were bowling along the highway at a cracking pace that Tom found intimidating. He was further intimidated by the fact that Hetty had seemed deliberately to hitch up her cotton dress so that her knicker-encased thighs were on view. He had, nevertheless, over the space of the last ten miles been working up the nerve to ask his question. "As you are a psychologist . . . could I ask you . . . a friend of mine has been under stress and . . . well, he finds that the f-f-f-full moon has an adverse effect on his c-c-c-condition."

"Ah!"

"Yes," he said, encouraged. "He even on occasion has taken to *h-h-h-howling* at the moon."

"Not common but nevertheless a well-known syndrome – well documented in 19th century lunatic asylums where the patients became agitated and restless at full moon, some of them even howling at it. Hence the word 'lunatic' – derived from the Latin *luna* meaning moon."

"Yes, I had heard of –"

"The gravitational pull of the moon," Hetty overrode him relentlessly, "has a profound effect on our biorhythms – notably on the female cycle of menstruation which corresponds exactly to the twenty-eight days of the lunar cycle – indeed, the blood from the uterus may have originally ebbed and flowed in synchronisation with the lunar cycle and the swing of the tides in a mighty liquid pulse – waxing and waning, waxing and waning."

"Yes," said Tom timidly, viewing her strong brown thighs encased in their beige knicker-legs. "Very nice, I'm sure. B-b-b-but about my friend's problem . . ."

"It is my opinion that the female cycle can easily be re-adjusted to coincide with the moon's phases. The menstrual cycle is, of course, extremely sensitive to outside influences – for example, women who live together frequently find that their cycles coincide – which creates a problem in Muslim polygamous households." She glanced at Tom and smiled broadly. "A thought that pleases me mightily."

"Quite. B-b-but –"

"Contact with menstrual blood being anathema to a Muslim man."

"I –"

"Are you not feeling well, Tom? You're looking awfully waxy all of a sudden! Should I stop?" She began to brake.

"No – no," he said faintly, "it's just the h-h-heat. But about my friend's p-p-problem with the moon –"

"I have only come across a single case. Bertha, her name was – no – Bessy. She used to stare at the moon in a trance for hours at a time. I began to believe she might be a werewolf!"

Tom gulped, his Adam's apple bouncing like a yo-yo or a trampoline artist. "Did Bessy have any other symptoms?" he asked, hoping it sounded like a light and frivolous query.

"Of moongazing?" She frowned at him and he quailed.

"N-n-no . . . I meant . . . of being a werewolf." He quailed further back in his seat and clutched his bag tighter to his chest. Now, instead of sounding frivolous, the query sounded – lunatic.

"Like having a hairy coat, fangs and running through woods like a wolf pouncing on any small animal she might have the luck to catch?" Hetty chuckled.

"Um . . . yes . . ." He gave a short laugh which sounded utterly false to his ears.

Hetty glanced at him. "Oh, she had all those symptoms all right!" She chuckled heartily.

Tom was aghast.

"And you know what?" She gripped his lean thigh through his long-legged shorts and squeezed cruelly. "She was never cured!" She burst into laughter.

Why on earth was she laughing? "W-w-w-what methods did you try?"

"Oh, I didn't."

"W-w-why not?"

"Well, she wasn't actually harming anyone by her activities so why bother?"

Tom shrank even further against the passenger door as she turned a beaming smile on him.

"I'll let you into a little secret. I sometimes moongaze myself, especially when my ovulation phase coincides with the full moon. And I sometimes do howl."

For some reason, rather than finding relief and comfort in this confession from a fellow 'lunatic', Tom found himself absolutely terrified by it.

Hetty was staring in her rear-view mirror. He glanced behind and realised she was making eye contact with the dog in the back. "Ajax," she said, "I like this man. He seems to have a sense of humour. We may have found ourselves a new playmate." And she grinned.

Wolfishly, thought Tom. That was a grin that could be described as wolfish.

He found himself very much wanting to get out of the car.

## Chapter 9

Having battled through the dusty city of Kano – where petrol stations, Coca-Cola, bicycles, white-painted mud buildings, high-rise hotels, mosques, ghetto-blasters, donkeys, limousines, prostitutes and purdah whirled in a mad kaleidoscope of assorted cultures – Simon was glad to reach the Niger Embassy in its leafy suburbs.

He switched off the ignition, threw his head back and closed his eyes. When he opened them a few minutes later it was to behold the grimacing face of Tom Purthill pressed flat against his windscreen.

He shrank back in inevitable recoil at such an unexpected and quite horrible sight, the likes of which he hadn't seen since childhood when he used to press his open mouth against that of his Aborigine friend outside, through the glass of his bedroom window. Though that had been far from horrible – visually grotesque, yes, but . . .

When he got his breath back he got out of the car and

greeted Tom who had withdrawn from the windscreen and stood, simpering, clutching the green canvas bag to his chest with both arms. At his feet was the small tartan zipped case.

"I'm going to Niger, you know," said Tom, slyly smiling, "and Hetty Coleman thinks you have a fetish – for black men – *oomph!*" This last sound effect being caused by his slapping a hand across his mouth.

Simon perceived, with chilling effect, that Tom's mouth seemed to continue to emit sentences behind his gagging hand. Pure Stephen King, he thought, with a *frisson*.

"Umm, looking for a visa, are we?" he said brightly. Good God, Purthill must be pursuing Jan into Niger! Was he safe?

Tom nodded, eyes wide, and then took away his hand. "Y-y-y-yes," he said, "and H-h-h-hetty – *arrrgh!*" A hand clamped itself about his lean throat, just under his prominent Adam's apple.

Simon decided to ignore this very odd behaviour. "Shall we go in, then?" As if speaking to a small child.

Tom nodded and then gazed, agonised, at his tartan case. He couldn't pick it up – he had no spare hand.

Simon, perceiving his difficulty, picked up the case. Then he said, "Don't you have a car?"

Tom's clamping hand seemed to shake his head.

"Maybe we should put these bags in the boot until we come out, then?" said Simon.

He opened the boot and put the tartan case inside, then reached for the canvas bag. He had already caught it by the strap when Tom began the tug of war.

"No, let me take it," said Simon. "It will be fine in the boot."

Tom, while continuing to throttle himself with one hand, pulled away from Simon in great jerking tugs.

Inexplicably exasperated, Simon found himself clinging on to the strap and was forced to tug in retaliation if he wanted to avoid being shaken about like a rag-doll.

"*Ikon Allah!*"

Fortunately, an exclamation in Hausa close by brought Simon to his senses. A huge splendidly robed Hausaman, ten feet away, was staring pop-eyed at them, head thrust forward.

Simon let go, horribly embarrassed.

And Tom staggered backwards, fell to the ground and lay there, knees drawn up, whimpering, clutching the canvas bag to his chest once again with both arms.

Simon guessed that the damask-robed man, with his embroidered Hausa pill-box hat, was an embassy official. He was behaving like a village idiot however, thought Simon, as the Hausaman continued to gaze goggle-eyed, open-mouthed, neck out-thrust, at the whimpering Tom.

"Um, we're here about visas," Simon said politely.

The Hausaman made no response beyond a glower, then turned and strode into the embassy.

"Well, thank you *very much*!" said Simon and struck a momentary camp posture.

Tom had got to his feet and was looking slightly abashed. But was clutching the canvas bag to his chest again.

They made their way into the embassy. None too grand, it occupied a shaded dark-furnitured building.

"The Consul is ready to see you now," announced a young male secretary some minutes later.

And, of course, the Consul was the damask-robed Hausaman.

Oh dear, thought Simon, aware that on occasion or whim visas were denied to expatriates.

The man was unpleasant-looking – round-faced, very black, lower lip out-thrust, eyes small, pill-box hat set on a round head. He looked like a sulky child.

Simon smiled his brightest smile.

"You are under suspicion," said the Consul in a thick staccato voice.

Simon's smile went out like a light, a hundred sexual misdemeanours thundering through his head. "Oh, I'm sorry, I'm sure," he said and then cringed at the inanity of it.

By his side, Tom was cringing big-time, practically seeking shelter in his canvas bag.

The Consul continued to glower, his petulant infant's mouth set.

Simon was at a loss.

Tom began to whimper again.

It seemed to be stalemate and Simon didn't even know what the game was.

"Your car has a Zaria licence-plate," accused the Consul.

"Why, yes," said Simon. "We are working in Zaria – at the university."

The Consul raised a pudgy hand and brought it down on an electric bell set in the desk.

At the harsh buzz another berobed man entered.

"Give the police permission to search them, their belongings and the car," said the Consul.

"*To,*" said the man and exited.

Simon stared in consternation after him. He swung back to the Consul. "The police? Search? For what?"

The Consul glowered – it seemed to be almost his entire repertoire. "Give me your passports."

They handed over their passports.

"Go!" the Consul then said – a man of few words, obviously. "Outside!"

To Simon's astonishment a small slender Nigerian police officer with a hostile look in his eye was waiting outside. "De keys," he said.

What was a Nigerian policeman doing in the Niger Embassy?

Simon handed over the car keys and made to follow.

"Dis way!" Another Nigerian policeman waved them into a small room where two others stood waiting.

They're like clones, thought Simon. Small, lean, solemn, scowling beneath their berets, prominent buttocks encased in navy-blue uniform trousers. What are they doing here? This is supposed to be Niger territory.

They rapidly searched through his shoulder bag and laid it aside.

"Strip!" said the second policeman.

"Don't mind if I do," said Simon out of habit. But he did mind, because he was wearing his favourite gold silk panties with the strips of lace that went so delicately over his hip-bones.

Simon glanced at Tom for support – which was rather a silly thing to do. Tom stood there, mouthing away. Apart from the grimacing, Simon's addled brain noted that there was something strange or out of place about Tom but he was too rattled to figure out what.

"Strip!" snarled the policeman, eyes intense.

Simon closed his eyes and did. Would they use a probe? Would they be gentle? Batons seemed to be the only instruments to hand.

Batons! Would the sight of the gold knickers enrage them? *Enflame* them?

The answer to his question came in a raucous explosion, a tidal wave of laughter from all round.

Simon's eyes sprang open. He stared as the three policemen fell around the place in their hilarity, slapping each other on the backs, slapping hands together in African high-five style, throwing words he well recognised from one to the other: *dan daudu*, *dan tada*, and *dan kushili*. They were in no doubt that they were looking at an effeminate homosexual transvestite – not someone who had just pulled on his wife's knickers by mistake. Someone behind him was also convulsed. He turned to see the Consul in the doorway, tears running down his pudgy cheeks, massive chest heaving.

Simon thought it best to laugh with them.

Tom, for once, was wearing a roughly appropriate expression as he stood, head turned away from Simon but eyes twisted back, looking sly and amused and mischievous.

Finally the Consul, face still wreathed in mirth, said to the policemen: "Do not be so stupid. The things are too big to fit in his women's panties! Search their bags!" With that and an ironic smirking glance he went back out and closed the door behind him.

The third policeman exited and, while the second amused himself by flirtatiously prodding Simon's testicles gently with his baton through the golden silk panties (in his dreams Simon would have been orgasming at this point but the reality was highly unpleasant), the other one set about Tom, prodding and probing around his groin, giggling.

Simon heard the words *dan daudu* again and realised they

must be discussing whether Tom was also wearing lacy underwear. The temptation proved too much – the policeman thrust a hand up the loose leg of Tom's shorts – presumably to check for lace panties – and after a startled hesitation began to rummage about in earnest. "The Bature is naked," he announced to his mates. "He has no underwear at all!"

"*Aooow!*" squealed Tom as the foreign hand tossed his genitals about.

I should be so lucky, thought Simon to himself glumly. And then, remembering the tug of war, wondered why Tom didn't go absolutely berserk at this invasion of his privacy.

Just then the third policeman entered carrying Simon's travel-bag and the tartan one.

The cases were laid on the desk, unzipped and searched fairly casually. As the Consul had said, whatever they were looking for was pretty big – no mere sniff of cocaine, wad of hash, no diamonds hidden in toothpaste.

The discovery of more women's clothing in Simon's bag led to sly grins from the searchers, whose faces now were uniformly wreathed in smiles. "You are going to visit your girlfriend?" said one, either kindly or cruelly – Simon couldn't figure out which – holding up one of Simon's wrappers. "She will be happy!"

Simon smiled politely, nodding, and then was seized with dismay. Of course! He *must* take some gifts to the mother of his baby. How could he have considered going empty-handed! That was *so* un-African! He must get to a market immediately! In his agitation he could suddenly think of nothing else. How lucky that the policeman had made the remark! His whole beautiful scenario would have been devastated beyond repair! Of *course* he must step into that Hausa compound *laden* with gifts – for the girl, for her mother, for the baby . . .

He found himself back sitting in the Consul's office and the Consul seemed to be apologising. He glanced at Tom who still had that rather cute little sly smiley expression which he was trying to cover with his left hand while his right was wrapped tightly across his breast. The find-the-odd-man-out sensation that had vaguely made itself felt earlier during the search gripped Simon again – but now at once he had the answer: where was the green canvas bag? The bag he had the life-and-death tug of war with Tom about? Tom wasn't clutching it, it wasn't at his feet and it hadn't been with the bags that were searched.

The Consul was pushing their passports across the desk to them and wishing them a pleasant stay in Niger.

But just as Simon was heaving an enormous sigh of relief Tom began to hum. His fingers being tightly over his lips, the buzzing effect was something like that of playing a comb through tissue paper.

The Consul stopped, his fingers in the act of pushing the passports across the desk to where Simon's fingers were poised to grab them.

Simon could have wept. He turned a beseeching look at Tom who had now begun to accompany his buzzing with a rhythmic backwards and forwards motion.

"What is the matter with this man?" asked the Consul with more staccato emphasis than ever.

"Nothing," said Simon.

"Is he sick?"

"No – not at all!" said Simon gaily.

"Why is he moving like that?" He was scowling again.

"He – has a-a-a nervous condition,"

"He is a madman?"

"Oh, no, no, no! He's a university lecturer!"

The Consul shifted his gaze to stare at Simon. "Is he a mad university lecturer?"

"No! He – it's not a *mental* condition. It's his nerves – it's a *physical* condition – um – he needs to take his medication."

The Consul chewed his infantile lip. "Why does he not take it?"

"Well, he's forgotten to take it – he's forgotten it back in Zaria."

Tom's swaying had become so extreme he was now beating his head lightly on the desk.

Simon began to sweat. He desperately tried to make eye contact with the Consul but the Consul was back to staring pop-eyed at Tom as the rhythmic *bump-bump-bump* of his head on the desk continued.

"So how can he travel like this?" asked the Consul at last.

"Um – we must go now to collect his medicine at the pharmacy. Then he'll be a new man!" Simon smiled blindingly at the Consul who scowled suspiciously back.

*Oh, stop, stop, stop, Tom!* Simon prayed despairingly.

There was a prolonged pause. Then, out of the corner of his eye he saw the advance of the passports across the desk. He waited until they came to a halt and the pudgy black fingers were removed.

Then he reached out a sweating hand and took them.

"You must take care of your friend," said the Consul.

Outside at last, they climbed shakily into the car. Tom was

now shaking so hard his teeth were rattling. Simon wasn't much better, As he turned on the ignition he grimaced. If it weren't for Tom's fit of the jitters, he would have asked the Consul what in Heaven's name they had thought they would find in the bags – well, besides lace briefs.

"Well, that was a lark!" he said ironically to his companion.

And there was an odd thing.

Tom was clutching the green canvas bag again.

Ned strode into the Niger Embassy, unlit pipe in hand. He was very much put out. He had expected some support from Cous-Cous in this matter of a visa. After all, it was his native consulate! However, Ikus-Ikoos had frivolously told him that there was no cause for anxiety and that, actually, his presence might even hinder the speedy acquirement of a visa. In fact, Ned would be better not to mention that he was travelling with a Tuareg at all.

He had spewed out huge screeds of gobbledy-gook about the political situation in Niger and the prejudice against his tribe – and while that would have been fascinating conversation over a cup of tea, Ned thought it nothing but an aggravation in the circumstances. He didn't need a potted history of the Tuareg, for God's sake! He needed a visa!

But Ikus-Ikoos had fucked off with his baggage, saying he had friends to see in Kano and arranging to meet Ned at the Grand Hotel later.

Selfish bugger! They were all the same. No loyalty.

An hour of agitated pipe-smoking later, Ned was surrounded by a match-strewn area which looked like an Amazonian logging camp. He had been forced to nip out twice to replenish his match-supply from the little trading table under a tree outside the embassy.

Then at last he was admitted to The Presence.

An enormous berobed figure filled the chair across the desk from him.

"What is your business in Niger?" The voice was flat, evenly accented, almost staccato. The muscles in the pudgy face were almost motionless.

"Eh?" Ned made a number of jerky movements of the neck, for all the world like a wary and alerted cock suspiciously spying out his territory in the farmyard.

"I said: what is your business in Niger?"

Ned remembered that Cous-Cous had warned him emphatically *not* to mention his business in Niger. He smiled in his smarmiest way. "I'm going to see your beautiful country as a tourist," he said, his breath heaving asthmatically. "I have been told that the capital, Niamey, is wonderful!" Then, belatedly remembering another snippet of information from Cous-Cous, he added, "Oh, and Maradi too!" Maradi was a Hausa city while Niamey was Djerma. He didn't know which the Consul was, so it was safer to hedge his bets.

The muscles of the Consul's face relaxed a little.

Obviously, one of his bets had paid off.

"And you are travelling on your own?" asked the Consul.

"Aahh . . . no! I am meeting a friend in – at the border."

"Who is this friend?"

Ned searched wildly for a suitable answer. "Tom – Tom Purthill. A French teacher."

"Ah!" There was a significant pause. Then, "You say he is a French?"

"No, no," said Ned, his tongue clumsy in a mouth that

felt bone-dry. "Not *a* French. He *teaches* French. At Zaria. The university."

The Consul stared impassively. "So you have no objection to being searched?"

Ned blinked and gaped. "S-s-s-searched? What for?"

In answer, a pudgy hand descended with a thump like a bag of flour falling and a bell rang. It might have been a trick of the light but it seemed to Ned that the Consul had a slight smirk on his face.

Minutes later, a spluttering Ned was undergoing a search of his belongings and the indignity of having his person probed with batons. By the Nigerian police, what's more, who had no right to be operating in a Niger Embassy. His outrage reached an explosive peak when they appeared to be investigating his underwear with great hilarity – but he thought of Fatty and suppressed his rage, his chest heaving like a rumbling volcano, breath rasping asthmatically through his teeth.

The Consul appeared at the door and asked a question in Hausa, then burst into massive laughter and, as if on a signal, the others launched into a further fit of hilarity. Ned had never been so insulted in his life and the fact he hadn't a clue what they were saying heightened his sense of outrage.

But, unlike Simon and the hapless Tom, when he at last faced the Consul again in his office he was strutting like an irate cock, chest out-thrust, and demanding an explanation for the search and the hilarity – and the presence of the Nigerian police in a foreign embassy.

To his extreme surprise, it was immediately forthcoming.

Anow, in a state akin to agony yet keen with pleasure, was lying on the grain-sacks behind Marie as the lorry trundled north. She lay in a stupor of sweat with both whimpering children sheltered beneath her veil against her breasts, the straw mat on top of them for shelter, as the sun glared cruelly down. Through the narrow slit of his *tagilmoust* he squinted down at the black folds of his trousers which were actually touching the soft cotton of Marie's buttocks. Her buttocks were small and slight, certainly, and he was thankful for that – because if she had richer curves he would surely be unable to control himself. His breath came harshly. Inside the thickly gathered folds of the trousers his penis lay in rigid agony, no more than the length of a little tea-glass from her bottom. Less, he thought, as he pressed closer.

He thought feverishly of what the men said: that with a sweetheart you entered from the front – if she'd allow you – but with a wife, in the darkness of a tent, with other sleepers around, you entered from behind and how the curve of her buttocks against your belly spurred you on and better still if you placed her beneath you face down – then your weight plus the weight of her buttocks and the firmness of the ridge at the back of her cunt – all bearing down on your penis . . .

Anow shuddered and groaned and pulled away. With a huge effort he turned his thoughts to the ordeal ahead.

He had reason to be pleased with himself.

His first thought had been to steal across the border under cover of darkness. Then he had decided that no, they would cross at the hottest part of the day – when senses were dulled by the searing heat and the horse-guards were likely to be resting under the merciful shade of a tree rather than searching the scorching grasses for a few poor Tuareg.

But then he had the clever plan – well, to speak the

truth, the grace of God had presented it – of travelling in this lumbering lorry full of sacks of guinea-corn. Marie and the children had already been sitting in a taxi when he noticed the transport and the fact that it had a Niger licence-plate. Straight through to Niger! It was like a finger pointing his way! He had felt so strongly that the lorry had been sent by God that he'd insisted on Marie dismounting from the taxi and joining the other few passengers on top of the grain-sacks which filled the back of the lorry to within a yard of the top of its rail.

He felt in his heart that, in this heat, at midday, the police would not go to the trouble of getting passengers to dismount from the top of a loaded lorry – passengers so poor they had to travel in such gruelling torment would surely not be worth the bother. Better stay in one's customs office or mud guard-hut close to the fridge or the God-given coolness of an earthenware pot.

Yes, he was sure.

And, if the police at the border made him dismount, he was sure – yes, he *was* sure – they would not force a woman to climb down with the two poor feverish children sheltering in the sweaty shade of her veil. And what was a woman, after all, in their way of thinking?

He was sure. And yet it took heart to do it. And he must have the heart of a lion to do this.

He *would* have the heart of a lion.

Jan would see that he was a man.

For Ikus-Ikoos it was more of a relief than otherwise when Ned's car shuddered, coughed, stalled and died outside a village called Yashi, north of Kano.

He could only wish that the car's owner did likewise. Since Kano there had been an unrelenting stream of loud talk – veering dizzily from reproach to gratitude to boasting to hilarity – as Ned let off steam after his ordeal. Then, as Ned once again began to recount the man-to-man talk he'd had with the Consul ('a nice, intelligent chap – great sense of humour') and the business about the women's underwear, the car had mercifully died.

Thank you, God, Ikus-Ikoos prayed silently.

Cheerfully, shouldering his tea-equipment bag – he would expire if that was pinched from the car in his absence – he set off to walk the half-mile or so into the village.

As it happened, a taxi slowed down to see if he wanted a ride and when they heard of the plight of Ned's car they carried him into the village for free.

A quarter of an hour later he was back with assorted small boys and a few young men and they pushed Ned and his car into Yashi.

There, Ikus-Ikoos persuaded a mottled and goggling Ned to leave his car at the police station until his return from Niger. A mechanic would look it over in the meantime. It was probably just the battery but if they delayed they would lose the scent of Fatty and family.

Ned's greed for money, revenge and Fatty's boobs swung the situation. Though in his normal senses he would no more think of abandoning his car at a bush police station than he would think of wearing beads, a giant impulse drove him forward. He left the car to the tender mercies of the Yashi police, praying that he would even remember the *name* of the village on their return, and turned his face northwards.

Or rather, turned his face southwards as they took up the classic position at the side of the road and began to wave down a lift.

Several loaded-to-the-seams minibuses tore by, swaying alarmingly, and several full-to-the-brim yellow taxis, leaning on their horns in arrogance.

Ned squinted down the long white-grey road curving south, sweat blurring his eyes. He heard Cous-Cous's start as another flash of bright yellow came tearing up the road.

It wasn't until the yellow VW pulled up alongside that he realised it wasn't a taxi and that maybe this was his lucky day after all.

"Oooh, *ladies*!" was his grinning greeting. "Got your lacy knickers in place, then?"

## Chapter 10

A now climbed shakily down from the lorry. Now that the moment had come he was very much afraid.

With the small bunch of men and boys he made his way into the border-post building. Outside, in the lorry, there remained two bush Fulani women, one with two infants, the other withered with elongated breasts that hung to her belly – and Marie with her children.

He was sick in his stomach and sorry, very sorry, he had agreed to this madness. His hands were shaking. He felt like a very small boy masquerading in his father's *tagilmoust*. He wanted Jan – and now suddenly she was his mother again. Maybe he was not a man after all.

He pushed forward to the front of the group as they approached the desk of the police official and, with a trembling hand, proffered his ID Card cautiously, the one with the ugly photo. He wanted this trouble to pass swiftly.

The policeman glanced at his card and handed it back.

No questions, nothing – Anow stepped back in relief. The others were showing their cards. Anow cursed as a complication arose. Two of the men had no ID. The policeman let rip with aggressive questioning.

Meanwhile Anow and the other men were ordered to empty their pockets and wallets and place the contents on a table. Among the handkerchiefs full of tobacco, the dog-eared photographs, the decorated key-rings, were wads of money. The policemen's eyes lit up. Anow was allowed to collect his small bunch of notes and was ordered outside.

Sweating with relief he looked over at the lorry. A single policeman was standing next to it, looking up at its load.

Anow wavered. Should he keep away or rush to the rescue? By the time he had walked to the lorry at a casual pace, the policeman had climbed up the metal ladder at the back and was prodding the grain-sacks with a pen-knife. Then he swung over the top rail and Anow climbed the ladder rapidly.

Marie was seated midway down the lorry, the small boy on her lap, the little girl lying against her. To his alarm, Anow saw that the children were awake – drowsy but awake. The policeman was squatting beyond them, investigating the sacks.

"*Sannunku!*" the policeman greeted the Fulani women.

"*Yawwa, sannu!*" they responded.

"*Ina wuni?*"

"*Lafiya kalau!*"

He began to run through a string of conventional greetings with them as he probed and prodded and, as he did so, his eyes darted a few times to Marie who hadn't responded in any way.

Anow swung over the rail and moved across the sacks to

squat in a friendly fashion near the policeman, partially blocking his view of Marie. He pulled his *tagilmoust* down to his chin, swallowed painfully, then indicated Marie dismissively over his shoulder with a quick movement of his head and lips. "She doesn't hear Hausa," he said and smiled.

So now, if the policeman spoke to her in Tamajegh they were fucked. Or if the children began to spout French, which no bush children would know. Why hadn't they gone with the notion of saying she was deaf and dumb?

The policeman raised his eyebrows in surprise. "A true bush woman!" he said with an expression somewhere between good humour and contempt.

"Yes – I'm taking her back to her bush!" Anow joked.

"She is your sistah?" asked the policeman in English, now pausing in his work to stare at Marie.

Anow had done the wrong thing, Now the policeman was interested. "My – *cousin*," he answered, pronouncing it the French way. He didn't know the word in English.

The policeman nodded, seeming to understand.

Anow glanced back at Marie whose eyes were big as they stared. Then she lowered them and busied herself with settling the children more comfortably, her mouth tight with tension.

"*Babu Hausa, mata?*" asked the policeman smilingly. *No Hausa, woman?*

Marie smiled and ducked her head as if in embarrassment. "*Babu*," she murmured. *None*.

Anow's heart was pounding against his ribs. This was where the policeman would shift to Tamajegh, if he knew any – which fortunately, on this side of the border, was unlikely. He forced himself to look away from Marie and back at the policeman. And then he heard Marie's little boy say *"Maman!"* and Marie's immediate, urgent *"Shhhh!"*

The policeman rose and stepped past Anow who, petrified, didn't turn his head.

*"Allah kiyaye hanya!" God protect you on the road.*

Anow looked round. The Nigerian was casually swinging himself over the heavy metal tailgate. He descended the ladder.

Marie and Anow stared silently at each other, faces beaded in sweat.

The thick wads of cash they had inserted between the grain-sacks under Marie's bottom were safe for the moment – her personal savings, she had said, but Anow suspected from her demeanour that some of it must be her husband's.

Now relief rushed through his veins like a rainy-season flood.

They were going to make it. He would end up making his way home with his payment, not in a Nigerian prison.

The Niger police lay ahead.

But this time he would say she was deaf and dumb.

Jan drew into the large open area in front of the border-post building. As she did so, she looked eagerly around, hoping to see some buses or taxis or maybe Anow himself emerging from the police-post. But all she saw was an elderly couple climbing into a Land-Rover with a British registration and a large dark-red transport-lorry loaded with grain-sacks pulling grindingly out onto the road leading north to the Niger frontier.

She had made terrific time on the road itself but had lost it all and more in the countless stops demanded by her passengers to buy bean-cakes and dried peppered meat, to get water, to urinate. At one point she walked a few steps into the bush with Takowilt to urinate. While she struggled with her panties, trying to keep balance, trying not to wet them, Takowilt simply pushed her layers of black wrapper behind her like a train and squatted with enviable ease. Practical, simple. Sexy. Hmmm. Back to square one in the underwear debate.

And at one point they had to stop for Kola to drink a Star beer at a roadside bar, which he did while scribbling something very intently on a sheet of notepaper. She was intrigued to see him shove it hastily into his bag on her approach. Oh-ho. Simon would be interested in knowing who he was writing to.

And then, after the beer, they had to stop for Kola to urinate. Which he did in a great flashy fountain, standing European-style at the side of the road, instead of discreetly squatting as a civilised African would. The Tuareg women pointed and roared with laughter while the men muttered disapprovingly. As for Jan, the glimpse of a sizeable penis set her blood-pressure up a few points. She was almost sure he had deliberately turned so she could see it. They had also been delayed by the necessary scouting of taxi and bus parks, scanning vehicles, futilely asking, asking, asking for a young Buzu accompanied by a woman and two small children – as if anyone would remember such a thing. She was beginning to despair. It had somehow seemed easy enough from the vantage point of Zaria. Easy to overtake and find them. But in practice needles and haystacks came to mind.

She detested going through border-posts. Anything could happen. The police could find or invent irregularities to do with passports and visas, car insurance and tax, work permits, re-entrance permits, currency, etc etc. For her, it was doubly difficult because she was always lugging bush people who had no identification at all and no legal right to cross. And so, in Nigeria she was under suspicion as some kind of people-smuggler and in Niger as an undesirable researcher or journalist. Which said everything about the status of the Tuareg; they were considered a suspect and dangerous minority in both countries.

But this time would be different. She had Kolawole Aboyade at her side, a bona fide black educated Nigerian – a guarantee of her good faith and good taste. With him she was at last respectable – instead of something between an offence and a joke, with her loadful of ignorant bush men of the wrong skin-colour.

Kola was casualness and confidence itself as he strolled into the building with the muscled grace of a panther. At last she was beginning to understand what Simon saw in him. He really was something else.

It was therefore a bit of a shock to her when the official in charge, dapper in his well-pressed beige uniform, had no sooner glanced at Kola's passport when he barked at him to step into a side room to be searched.

She moved nervously from the passport check to the car-papers check to the currency check. Everything was in order, for a wonder. She moved on to security where a hefty policewoman took her into a private room and did a more than cursory search of her person, prodding conscientiously at her bra and even between her legs. This was most unusual. She was definitely searching for something specific – but not so small it would fit in any body cavities.

Back at the security desk there was a casual but even more embarrassing search through the dozens of items she always carried in her shoulder bag.

She was then given a chair to sit on – that was certainly a courtesy. Minutes passed. She had begun to relax a little when a glance behind her through the window revealed that the Tuareg women and children had been heaved out of the car and a search was afoot. She watched anxiously. In dismay she saw the police probing tins of powdered milk and jerrycans. This was extreme. She felt disaster looming. She turned away and concentrated on biting her nails. Minutes dragged by. She didn't look outside again.

"Well, let's be off!"

She looked up, startled.

It was Kola, smiling down at her cheerfully. She swung around and looked out the window. All the gear was safely back in the Land-Cruiser again and the women were climbing in.

Relief flooded through her. "Did they strip-search you? Are you all right?" she muttered, getting up.

He put an arm about her shoulders and steered her firmly outside.

"Let us not outstay our welcome," he giggled. "Simon taught me that expression. A good one, I think." He looked animated and amused.

"Was that fun?" she asked, only half-joking. "The search? I had an Amazon search me. Did they use a body probe?"

"These are the Nigerian police," he grinned, "not little green men from space."

"Um. Simon has you well educated." Why was she suddenly sounding so sour?

"Simon has not been my only educator, you know. I can read, for instance."

He was still smiling but she was embarrassed. "Sorry," she mumbled and flushed. "I'm becoming too accustomed to illiterates."

He laughed again at this and squeezed her shoulder.

Jesus. She was beginning to really like this guy. It was unexpected. And unwelcome, considering.

"Let's go," he said. "I have something *very* interesting to tell you."

"What?"

"Let's get your 'illiterates' on board first."

Semama and Takowilt had already climbed back into the Land-Cruiser and were screaming at the children, who were racing around wildly outside. Kola did the honours again, swinging them round and up into the car. She had the impression, from the way they were glancing at him from their Bambi eyes, that being swung by him was the object of the whole exercise.

"I'm so glad I don't have to swing their mother into the car," murmured Kola, lips quirking, eyeing the bulk of Takowilt.

The men had arrived, full of vituperative and over-excited talk about the indignities they had suffered at the hands of the police.

"May God repay them, the bastards!" shouted Aberfekil as Jan drove off cautiously down the road joining the two border-posts. He had been relieved of some of his naira as a fine for having an outdated ID Card and had been fined for the rest of the family who had no cards at all.

Jan thought he had got off lightly. But it had bitten into his meagre savings.

They were almost at the Niger frontier before she remembered. "So what's the interesting thing you have to tell me?"

"Mmmm. It's such a delicious secret. Maybe I should tease you a little with it . . ."

"Oh, God! Tell me! Just tell me! My nerves are in shreds already! Don't tease!"

"But we're already at the police-post! Let's hope these don't decide to sieve your powdered milk or drain your petrol."

"Did you see all that? A bit extreme, wasn't it? And the body-search!"

"Oh, but they had a reason. A very good one." He was gazing ahead, looking smug, long forefinger on his generous lips.

She imagined the cushiony feel of those lips.

The barrier was before them. It rose. They went through. They were in Niger. The place she loved most in the world.

She got out.

The Niger post was a modest mud hut at the side of the road.

The military police there always looked fearsome. Dressed in dark-green fatigues and heavy combat boots, carrying serious-looking weapons and wearing scowls, they inspired her with dread.

She stepped inside the small, rather dark hut. The usual little band of Tuareg were lined up against the wall – being held for questioning. Probably simply lacked ID's. It was Catch 22: the police made it hugely difficult for the nomads to acquire ID Cards in the first place. They wanted them to stay put in their desert. It hurt her to see them: any threat to the Tuareg was a threat to herself.

For once, to her surprise, the process was smooth and simple. They took the papers she filled out, checked them over, asked a few perfunctory questions. And that was that.

Kola got off equally lightly. Perhaps because, to her further surprise, he proved to have a nice turn of French.

Even Aberfekil and family went through painlessly.

Well, you never could tell, thought Jan. The heat had probably a lot to do with it. Levels of energy were low and there was only a small table-fan in the hut.

The relief of being through was tremendous. Her hands shook and sweated on the wheel as she drove off.

"So, now tell me," she said when her hands and heart had steadied. "What were the Nigerians looking for?"

"It is to do with your Head of Department, Langley Forrest."

"Langley!" Her heart nearly stopped. *Langley*! Marie! Anow! When she spoke again her voice sounded thin and high. "What do you mean? How can it have anything to do with *Langley*?"

"He has made a cock-up, a balls-up —"

"Yes?"

"A screw-up, a fuck-up —" he went on, mischievously airing a wonderful vocabulary learnt from Simon.

"Kola! Cut it out! What's Langley done?" Her heart was pounding and she was going to thump him if he teased her any further.

He relented. "You know that collection of museum pieces he got on loan from the States?"

Museum pieces? She immediately began to breathe easier. "The stuff from Boston?"

"Yes. Well, the most important piece has been stolen – a

bronze mask worth millions. And some smaller pieces – two, I think – heads in gold. And they hadn't even been exhibited yet – they were taken from the storeroom."

"Oh, *no!*" Oh, yes! Excellent! Nothing to do with Frenchwomen disguised as Tuaregs or young nomads apparently running off with Nigerian wives! Boston or the police could hang Langley from the nearest baobab tree for negligence for all she cared.

"Oh, yes!" said Kola.

"But – but why did the police tell *you?*"

"Well, you see, I'm actually Head of Nigerian Security working under cover –"

"*Kola!* My nerves can't take it!"

"OK, OK!" He burst out laughing. "Take it easy! I overheard a telephone conversation made to the police in Zaria – checking the facts out against us. Unfortunately for us, the robbery took place last night. Bad timing, eh?" He shot her a serious look, then grinned again. "Though how they expected to find a large bronze African mask up my ass I really don't know."

"They didn't!" she said in amazement.

"They didn't, no," he answered and laughed hugely. "But they had a good probe for the golden heads –"

"*Kola!*"

"OK, OK, I'm kidding!"

"You're always kidding!" she said with some asperity. "I don't remember you being such fun and games in Simon's house."

Silence from Kola.

"Well?" she said.

She glanced at him.

He shook his head. "Simon bothers me," he answered soberly.

Intrigued by his change of mood, she decided to push it. "Aren't you happy with him?"

"I am. Life is good with him. In fact, without him life seems flat, monotonous. I like him very much. He's funny and intelligent and kind. And different. He keeps me . . . alive." There was a long pause. "But – he confuses me. I find myself reacting in strange ways. Losing my sense of humour is one of them . . ." He flashed a look at her and bit that cushiony lip in an apologetic way.

It was a strange confusing moment but Jan, skin still tingling with the relief of getting past the police, just grinned at him. She was feeling euphoric.

The grin was a mistake, she thought, as with a speculative look he laid a long-boned hand along his thigh and the powerful little finger began to trace deliberate circles on hers through the thin cotton of her wrapper. Her crotch contracted instantly like one of those squashy purple sea-anemones do at a touch.

Think of Simon, she said to herself.

## Chapter 11

This is all rather jolly, thought Tom Purthill, as he peered at his three companions in the darkness of the car interior. Ned was a scream really, telling about his experience in Kano and what the Consul had told him about the lacy underwear.

And these were all Jan's friends! Fate had been kind to him indeed! They were bound to link up with her eventually. *Then* she would see the Real Him, the dashing adventurer; after all, he had always modelled himself on Indiana Jones. *All's well that ends well*, he thought and decided to risk saying that aloud, hoping it would come out right.

He took a deep breath. "All's w-w-well that ends w-w-well," he said. In response, Ned Bassett turned and gaped at him and Ikus-Ikoos's eyes widened above the folds of his turban.

Tom bit his lip and drew back in his seat. What *had* he said? Not 'All's well that ends well' apparently. But maybe it was his tone of voice that had been wrong – he never knew. He began to whistle casually, pretending he was at ease. Then even Simon swung his head around to gape at him so he shut up in mid-whistle.

"You OK, mate?" asked Ned Bassett uneasily.

He nodded nonchalantly. In the lights of a passing car he saw Ikus-Ikoos wince at him.

It was safer not to make any sound or movement at all.

His mood spoiled, he covered his face with his hands, keeping his satchel pressed to his belly with his elbows, and let his thoughts drift back to Hetty Coleman. He had managed to lie to her successfully or so it seemed. Said he was going no further than Kano. At least that must have come out right. But then she never listened anyway. Not a great attribute for a psychiatrist, he would have thought. Surely, in that field, listening was paramount. All those case studies she said she'd been involved in – however had she managed? She *must* have listened to Bessy the moongazer, to the fellow with the teddy-bear... he had been tempted to stay with her, wherever she was going, in order to question her further about his own difficulties.

But she had made him feel so *uneasy*. Still, it couldn't be denied: Providence had thrown a psychiatrist – well, a psychologist and aspiring psychiatrist – in his lap and he had let the opportunity slip. And the Chaplain had warned him that God might move in mysterious ways his wonders to perform and that he should be on the alert, open to the possibility of help arriving from unexpected sources.

But he had found the bits of information she had imparted terrifying rather than illuminating. He had found *her* terrifying.

On the other hand, to look on the bright side, his trip

with her had been unusual and entertaining – the kind of experience that one could recount to new acquaintances for years to come: *Oh, dear, I well remember the trip I took to Kano with this outrageously eccentric woman . . .*

Ned and Simon were bickering – they had been almost all the way so far – while Ikus-Ikoos had been doing a lot of wincing all the time. He was doing it again now and, having pushed back his headdress, was putting pressure on his two temples with long beringed fingers.

He seemed to be under terrrible strain. How strange! Tom had always imagined the Tuareg to be serene and philosophical. He admired that quality: it was so important to be able to relax. *Blessed are the serene*, he improvised, *for theirs is the Kingdom of Heaven. Blessed are the calm at heart, for they shall see God.*

"This is bloody ridiculous!" Ned was ranting. "If you hadn't insisted in dragging us all off to that sodding market – miles off the beaten track, for Chrissake – to buy those silly bales of cloth, we'd be over the border long since!"

"But it's still only eight o'clock! It's quite a *reasonable* hour yet! And we're nearly there!"

They were, in fact. A short while after, they rolled up before the impressive single-storey Nigerian border-post building. All four men sat and peered out at it apprehensively, each busy with his own thoughts: Ned goggling, Simon frowning, Ikus-Ikoos wincing, Tom grimacing,

At last, it was Simon who sighed and said, "OK. Let's get it over with."

Perhaps it was only in Africa that one could say 'darkness fell', thought Jan. Compared to Europe and especially the long lingering fading of the summer light in Ireland, fall it did – though in slow motion over the space of half an hour or so, like an extended drum-roll heralding the beautiful, soul-caressing, body-caressing ultimate pleasure of evening.

She was lying on a mat by a small fire outside Birnin Konni in Niger, pillow under her head, warm air massaging her skin, her whole aching sun-beaten, road-beaten body almost screaming in joy at the rest, the relief, the coolness, the stillness. The fact that she wasn't being fried by the sun. The fact that she didn't have to move. That she could close her eyes. That she could lazily listen to the guttural familiar sounds of Tamajegh, sounds that to her spelt home and security. The hard earth pressed upwards from beneath her mat into her bones, into her muscles, in a pleasure that no soft mattress could ever bring. She always found that a strange thing.

Not even the fact that there had been no trace of Anow with his Frenchwoman, and no news of them through the Tuareg grapevine, could disturb her content in that moment. Not even the fact that she had begun to wonder whether Kolawole didn't in fact have a bronze mask up his ass.

What *was* he doing here in Niger?

Kolawole was sitting on the mat at her feet, scribbling again on his pieces of notepaper by the light of a torch. He was forever at it, she had discovered, and it really mystified her. Surely, as an artist he should be sketching not scribbling? Was it a diary? Letters? Or did he have a girlfriend – a boyfriend?

The younger woman, Takowilt, had cooked. Tuareg fare. Pounded guinea-corn with fermented milk they had bought from a passing calabash-bearing Fulani woman. The milk had sizzled almost audibly with active goodness and Jan had scooped it up with relish in the wooden spoon they passed from mouth to mouth. With the blandness of the grey stiff guinea-corn porridge she was thankful for the tang of the fermented milk – fresh milk added to the soft swell of the porridge and she didn't like the mawkish combination much.

She would, in truth, have preferred to go with Kolawole to the market and eaten Nigerian fare – Yoruba fare – pounded yam with pepper sauce which was heaven on earth.

And she would, in truth, have relished Hausa roadside coffee thick with sweetened condensed milk rather than the Tuareg green tea. She normally detested sugar but, in this heat, somehow it was a life-saver.

In this heat, one could go for many things one would not normally have a taste for, she thought, as she peered through slit eyes at the man sitting close by. Really close by, she thought, as he began to caress her feet. She had washed her feet earlier, thank God – or thank Daud, the teenage boy, who had brought a *bidon* full of cool water from a nearby tent to wash her face and hands and who had then poured the remainder over her burning, aching feet.

And, of course, she had inevitably thought of Anow as Daud squatted there and smilingly dribbled the precious water, using his strong young hands to rub her feet clean.

The thought sprang to her mind, as it had a thousand times, of how much she loved this culture – physical, courteous, liberal, open-handed.

But now she looked at this man beside her, this Kola, from another race and culture – and Christ, was he *gay*?

If he was gay, why was he caressing her feet? He wanted to convince her he was straight? That he was, in that ridiculous term, 'bi'? Why?

Was he *leaving* Simon? Did he care for him? And who the hell was he writing to, all the time? Where was he *going*, in God's name? *Tahoua? Why? Did* he have a bronze mask up his ass?

Most Yorubas would never in their lives venture north into the harsh dryness of Hausaland – to say nothing of the Sahara. Well, there were little pockets, little communities of Yoruba traders here and there in the major towns everywhere – but Kola was not a trader. There was nothing to compel him north, away from the tropical rainforest, away from the pounding West Coast ocean, the startling colours and powerful smells, the opulent and pulsing sensuality of the south, the great irresistible flow of the mighty river Niger pacing onwards inevitable as life itself.

Yet here he was, in this parched landscape, caressing her feet.

Think of Simon, she said to herself.

"Oh, thank you!" said Simon and sat on the chair the Nigerian policeman had brought into the room. He crossed his legs in a ladylike fashion and bit his lip in what he hoped was a disarming way.

"That is not for you!" growled the policeman and, as Simon leapt up like a scalded cat, sat himself down on it.

"Oh, sorry, I'm sure!" said Simon. He went back to standing in a line with the others. Or should he say line-up?

Two other policemen entered and stood, almost at attention, behind the large desk.

Simon glanced at his companions: Ned in bulldog stance – pipe in hand, Ikus-Ikoos erect – entirely muffled in his headdress, Tom in a sideways languid pose – arms folded across his breast.

The Chief Immigration Officer strode into the room, looking quite sophisticated in a tailored beige uniform. His skin was an extremely light yellowish shade which Simon thought unattractive. He thought of Kola's luscious dark-chocolate skin with longing.

The Immigration Officer sat and ignored the line-up for a few minutes, making notes on a sheet of paper. Then he looked up so suddenly they all swayed slightly backward.

"Passports?"

They stepped forward in turn and proffered them – Ned awkward, Ikus-Ikoos stately, Tom jittery, himself graceful – then stood back into line.

The officer studied each passport, page by page, breathing deeply through his nose, checking through every entry and exit visa they had, it seemed. This was unusual.

Meanwhile the two policemen behind the desk and the one in the chair fixed unblinking stares on them. Simon felt fresh floods of sweat spring to the surface of his skin. The perusal of the passports seemed to go on forever. What in Heaven's name could he be looking for?

At last he looked up. "Why are you travelling to Niger?" he asked.

The hesitation that followed was unfortunate.

"I am travelling with Mr Bassett," said Ikus-Ikoos, voice muffled inside his headgear.

Oh, dear, thought Simon, why doesn't he speak up clearly? That sounds positively guilty. And why hasn't he just said he's going home on a visit? Ned was also looking rather startled at Ikus-Ikoos's answer.

"You speak English?" the officer asked Ikus-Ikoos with an air of surprise.

"Yes."

The officer's eyes shifted to Ned. "Is this man your nightwatchman?"

The question was so unexpected Ned just gaped at him.

"Is he your –"

"Eh, no – he's a colleague," said Ned in his politest voice, with his best smile.

"He is a Buzu! How can he be your colleague?" He turned his gaze on the policeman in the chair and they shared an unpleasant ironic smile. The two behind the desk took this as permission to sneer at each other.

Whatever is he at? thought Simon. He has Ikus-Ikoos's passport there – he can see he's been abroad to be educated and all the rest. "He's a lecturer in French at the University of Zaria," he said and blushed to sound so ingratiating.

Another prolonged pause, while the officer stared them down. He sat back in his chair, linking his hands together over his groin.

Oh, God, don't do this to me, thought Simon, seeing his dream of getting to Tahoua begin to slip inexorably down the drain.

The officer sat forward again.

"Why are you travelling like this in a troop?" he said aggressively.

A *troop*, thought Simon. As in *military troop*?

"Em, we're not a *troop*," he said in his prissiest voice.

"Yes, we're not even travelling together," said Ned

183

through the strings of spittle suddenly on his dry lips. "You see, my car broke down on the road and these gentlemen were kind enough to give me a lift."

"You and the Buzu?"

"Eh, yes." He sucked at his dry pipe and then automatically damped down the non-existent tobacco in its bowl with his thumb.

"And where are you going?" The officer swung his attention to Simon.

"Em, I'm going to Maradi and Niamey – to see your great cities, you know."

"I am a Nigerian, not a *Nigerien*," said the officer heavily, throwing a God-give-me-patience glance at his colleague in the chair. "Those are not my cities."

In his efforts to ingratiate himself, Simon had forgotten that they were still in Nigeria.

"Well, I have already seen the *greatest* city," he tried to recover lost ground. "Kano is unforgettable."

"I am from Lagos," said the officer.

"Oh, yes – well, I've been there too – Lagos is unsurpassable – Lagos has *international* status after all," he gabbled.

"So why travel all the way to Niamey?"

"Oh – just sightseeing, you know. Just to be able to say I've seen the Niger."

"You can see the Niger here – at Kainji, at Jebba, at Onitsha – why go to Niger where it is but a stream in comparison?"

This was a nightmare. "Oh, but I've already seen it in the south! I'd just like to be also able to say I'd seen it at its origins – nearer its origins, that is."

The officer froze Simon with an ironic stare then turned his attention to Tom.

Four pairs of sceptical and three pairs of concerned eyes fixed on his quaking figure.

Inevitably, he began to jerk and jibber spectacularly, standing there – *without* his green canvas satchel. Simon looked about the room to see if he'd dropped it somewhere but there was no sign of it. Just like at the Kano embassy. How bloody peculiar!

"And where are you going?"

Tom's face contorted and a slight strangling sound began to issue from his throat, while his folded arms appeared to wrestle together in his attempt to keep his body under control. In a moment the armlock would break and he would be prancing around the room, ruining any last chance they might have of getting across the border.

"He is travelling with me," said Simon.

"Why can he not answer for himself?"

"Oh, he can," said Simon.

"So where are you going?" The officer directed his question at Tom again.

Help! thought Simon.

"N-n-n-n-niamey!" uttered Tom in a superhuman effort.

"Ah!" exclaimed the officer, comprehension dawning. He turned his gaze on Simon again. "Your friend has a stammer."

"An extremely bad one," said Simon. "But thankfully it's intermittent." As his head nodded repeatedly he thought how easy it would be to develop Tom's exaggerated nervous tics. He put his hand under his chin, gripping the elbow with the other hand – and thought again how often Tom used that pose.

The officer began to flick through the passports again

and, out of the corner of his eye, Simon saw Tom's state of agitation subside a little.

At last, the officer put one of the passports aside – it was a British one – Ned's.

Then he riffled once more through the other British one – Tom's – the riffling accompanied by a series of little squeaks from Tom. And put it aside.

Simon's pulse started to strum hard and fast as he picked up the Australian one.

Think of Simon, thought Jan to herself, as Kolawole's hand continued its progress beneath her wrapper, sliding up as far as her ass. He was no longer sitting at her feet. He had moved much closer to her and was now sitting cross-legged, the curves of his buttocks against her knees. The fire was dying down but she wondered if there was not still enough light to let the others see his straying left hand. Early though it was, the children were already asleep on the opposite side of the fire and talk became desultory as even the adults grew drowsy after their long gruelling day. His fingers began to probe further, right in the soft hollow to the side of her vagina where the elastic of her underwear ran – and, yes, she was wearing knickers and the manner in which they enhanced this slow titillation was yet another point to add to her list of reasons for considering them the apex of sophisticated civilisation. And, talking of apex . . . she pulled back an infinitesimal distance from the fingers.

Think of Simon, she said to herself.

The Immigration Officer browsed through Simon's passport yet again. Simon could hear Ned's breath rasping in time with his own heartbeat. The passport was put aside.

The Nigerien one remained. The officer went through it again attentively, then closed it. But he still held it by a corner as if it were dirty, as he abruptly raised his eyes and stared at Ikus-Ikoos.

"You are an educated man? So why are you wearing this – this fancy dress?" He waved a hand, utter contempt in the gesture. Ikus-Ikoos hesitated, as if he were wondering whether it would be safer to agree that he was, indeed, on his way to a fancy-dress party.

"This is not fancy dress," he said at last. "This is my traditional costume."

"It is fancy dress," said the officer, glaring at him ferociously. "You are trying to hide your face! Take it off!"

Simon quailed, feeling Ikus-Ikoos's humiliation like his own – for a Tuareg to be asked to bare his head before strangers was the ultimate shame. Much worse than his own stripping down to his lace panties. Ikus-Ikoos, of course, was a modern man and accustomed to being bare-headed but still . . .

Ikus-Ikoos slowly unwound the headdress. It seemed to take forever as the full eight yards of it were unloosed. Unwound, it filled his arms in a soft bouncy bundle.

The officer checked Ikus-Ikoos's face against his passport. Then he said, "And the gown."

"Oh, really . . ." said Ned and his breath began to rasp again.

Ikus-Ikoos handed his *tagilmoust* to Simon, pulled his white gown over his head and stood there in his traditional baggy trousers and a white tunic that came almost to his knees.

A small squeak came from Tom's direction.

"When were you last in Libya?"

Ikus-Ikoos looked unmoved as the question was shot at him, as if he had expected it. "I have never been to Libya."

"I believe you are a spy for Libya! Is your name not Mohamed Baraka and have you not smuggled Buzus into Libya by taking them through Nigeria and north through Chad? Are you not on your way to Libya now?"

Ikus-Ikoos made a slight despairing gesture with his hands at his sides. "No. I am not," he said quietly, almost muttering.

Simon felt fit to faint. This was dreadful. How could Ikus-Ikoos bear that treatment with such steady calm?

"Oh, really, officer, I know this man well," Ned protested. "He isn't a *spy*. And he isn't going to Libya! He has a job in Zaria! A job, you understand! A good job!"

"I'm accompanying Mr Bassett, as I told you," said Ikus-Ikoos. "To act as interpreter and sort out a problem for him in Tahoua."

Ned gaped, startled.

Simon wondered what Ikus-Ikoos was at – he had thought they were keeping quiet about Ned's business.

"Is this true?" the officer asked Ned.

"Eh . . . yes."

"What sort of problem?"

"A very delicate matter –" began Ned in his politest voice.

"He has paid a bride-price for a Tuareg woman but she has run back home to her family," Ikus-Ikoos cut in.

This pleased the Nigerians mightily. Collectively, they burst into laughter, and exchanges in Hausa and Yoruba, presumably ribald, bounced from one to the other.

"Mr Bassett, could you not keep her happy?" asked the Chief at last, still grinning.

"Eh, no," answered Ned.

"I am surprised at you, Mr Bassett. A senior person like you – to marry a bush woman. It is a stupid thing. You cannot trust these bush people. I advise you to retrieve your bride-price as quickly as possible and forget the woman."

"Eh, yes – that is what I intend to do with the help of Mr Cous-Cous here –" He stopped, mystified, as they all broke into laughter again.

"Search them, search the car," said the officer cheerfully, getting up from his chair, "and if there is no problem let Mr Bassett proceed to chase his escaped bride!"

The fire was a glowing red heap of coals now. The murmuring conversation had trailed away and died. Children and adults seemed to be asleep.

But certain parts of Kolawole's anatomy at least were still wide awake. His probing fingers for one thing.

He and Jan were were no longer at the fire. They had withdrawn a little distance, with her mat and couple of blankets. Between the two sleek soft blankets Kolawole's hard muscular body was naked and radiating heat. Beside him, Jan was now wearing only a skimpy version of that extraordinarily practical and erotic human invention: the underpants.

I'm clinging by the skin of my teeth to some last vestige of loyalty to Simon, she thought, and the briefs are a symbol of that loyalty. But it was only a matter of time. She was, in truth, helpless with desire at this point, nipples sizzling with it, muscles slack with it, crotch drenched with it, brain swimming with it. All thanks to that niggling sense of loyalty and a pair of panties which had combined to prolong the delicious agony to the last outpost of eroticism. Kola's fingers had wormed their way past the actual and symbolic little barrier. He was certainly sensitive to the nature of the game since he made no attempt to slide down from above under the waist of the briefs. No, he knew what he was at. At one point he even withdrew his fingers and stroked her clitoris through the fabric which had her soon squirming and then pushed the tops of his fingers actually into her vagina, pushing the barrier of the cloth before him like a little artificial hymen. That almost did for her but he knew better than to stay too long.

He *was* a tease. Just as he had teased her verbally all day with his clever words, he now was teasing her silently with his clever fingers. He did like to tease. He was a master.

And how did he use that mastery on Simon, she wondered feverishly and why didn't he come and how could he have so much control?

She could feel his penis lying heavy and alert against her belly. How could he resist just putting it in? Her mouth pressed against the soft and springy texture of his chocolate-dark skin over the muscles of his chest, its musky dusky taste and smell filling her nostrils, her hand rooted itself in his thick thatch of hair, as his long fingers reached once more into her vagina, sliding over the slick rucked walls, the folds and crevices to touch the sea anemone at the back – earlier, much much earlier she had thought of that image – earlier she had thought of many things.

Like Simon.

Think of Simon, some part of her wailed!

Simon, Ned, Tom and Ikus-Ikoos were sitting, drained, in the VW which had been searched to within an inch of its life. As indeed they had been. For once they all shared a common facial expression: relief. They were free to go, apparently.

And none too soon – they still had to get through the Niger post and Ikus-Ikoos said it closed for the night at a certain time – around nine or ten, he thought. Now, in other words. Simon moved off as rapidly as he dared.

"Christ!" Ned exploded. "What if we get stuck between the border-posts for the night? What if that happens?"

"Oh, we'll just have to sleep in the bush," said Ikus-Ikoos with malicious intent.

"The *bush*! What! What about snakes? And mosquitos? That may be all right for you, mate, but what about me?"

"Relax, Ned, you can sleep in the car."

"In the *car*? You expect me to sleep in the back of a *beetle*?"

Simon suddenly thought of the rolls of cloth he had bought as gifts and had the uneasy feeling that they might have been tampered with or even filched during the police search. He pulled up again and got out.

"Where're you going then, mate?" Ned blinked anxiously, owlishly.

"Oh, just straightening a few things out." He went to the front and lifted the bonnet, The police had made a mess. Tom's tartan bag was still unzipped. Simon zipped it up, at the same time taking the opportunity to peek surreptitiously inside – nothing but a few pairs of shorts, shirts, a comb, a towel . . . a thought struck him. He lowered the bonnet to eye-level and peered over it at Tom in the back seat.

Tom was clutching his satchel again.

Where the fuck had it been in the meantime? While the

police were searching the car? And what the fuck was in it? He vowed he would find out. Whatever it was seemed to be quite rounded and roughly the size of a football – no – about the size of a head, a human head.

Simon froze, still gazing across the raised bonnet. What was that film? *The Postman Always Knocks Twice?* No – *The Dark at the Top of the Stairs* – no, no – *Night Must Fall*, that was it. Where the serial killer had a hatbox he treasured? With a severed head inside? Always clutching and protecting it, while the head slowly festered and rotted.

A nauseating dizziness sizzled through him. What if it were Jan's head?

"I say, mate, there's something –"

"*Aaah!*" Simon let the bonnet drop with a slam.

Ned had leapt back a yard in alarm. "*Chirrrist!* You trying to emasculate me or what? Your sodding bonnet nearly bit off my tackle there!"

Simon sucked in a breath and waited for his heart to stop racing.

"Sorry, Ned, I – um – you startled me."

"Buggering hell, what a way to react!" Ned was hitching up his belt, looking very aggrieved. "Well, anyway – could you come over here a mo'?" He turned, outrage in the stiffness of his movements, and moved some distance away from the car. When Simon unwillingly followed and stood, hands on hips, Ned stepped right up close so that Simon could feel his breath hot on his face. "I just wanted to have a word with you – there's something I was told by the Consul in Kano but he told me to keep it under my hat – and anyway I didn't want to mention it in front of Cous-Cous or Looney Tunes there, especially since I'm convinced that Tom –" He stopped abruptly.

"OK. What is it?" Simon asked peevishly.

"Oh, bugger – Cous-Cous," he muttered.

Ikus-Ikoos was out of the car, leaning over the door, a wide smile on his face, *tagilmoust* wound loosely around his neck.

"We had better move on," he said. "We must still get into Niger."

"We really had," said Simon.

"Oh, hang on, mate – this is really important – what I'm trying to tell you –"

Simon was making for the car.

"Oh, bugger," said Ned in resignation and followed him.

Ikus-Ikoos raised a hand and saluted the police post behind them. "Goodbye, Nigeria!" he said. "*Mun gode Allah!* We thank God."

"Absolutely!" said Simon.

"'Strewth!" said Ned.

Inside the car, Tom gave a little yelp and covered his mouth.

Fuck Simon, said Jan to herself, as Kola at last slid what seemed, to her heightened senses, like a yard of penis into the right place.

## Chapter 12

A now gazed down at the sleeping figure of Marie on the mat beside him.

He really couldn't wake her again. Not after their exhausting nerve-wracking trip. Not after already waking her twice. She had unfortunately fallen into a deep sleep after they had fucked the first two times. He should be equally exhausted but his nerves were tight as the strings of a lute and he couldn't sleep at all.

He suddenly thought of a wonderfully poetic way to wake her. He pressed his lips lightly to her ear and recited – badly – a poem he remembered about a lover comparing himself to a lute that longed to be played by his beautiful noble ladyfriend. Unfortunately the poem was in Tamajegh but he was willing to translate into English as well as he could.

In any case, Marie hardly stirred. She did brush her ear as if shooing away a bothersome fly or mosquito and his heart leapt but then she had snuggled her veil around her head and headed back into sleep.

She deserved it. She had been so brave. She was a wonder at the Nigerian border. At the Niger one they hadn't even had to pretend she was deaf and dumb – the police hadn't even searched the lorry.

So they were through. It had been so easy after all.

But he knew well it could have ended in disaster. Even now his heart thudded when he thought of what might have happened.

He knew it had been madness. He would never have done it, not even for the money, if it hadn't been for the trouble with Jan.

He sighed a sigh that came up from the soles of his feet, then he lay back and closed his eyes. But it was no good. His head felt as if it were full of frisky young goats as images bounded about. And every second image had to do with fucking Marie. He groaned as his penis grew hard as a tent-pole again. How could he sleep with a tent-pole between his legs?

It was truly a wonder that she had agreed to him. In truth, she would never had agreed but for the sweetness and madness that had possessed them after they had safely passed the border. He thanked God. Now he didn't care if she never paid him – he had something more precious. He allowed the image into his mind again, an image with taste and feel and smell – which was the sensation of thrusting into the warm pulsing wet darkness of Marie's cunt. He broke out in a sweat.

The truth was, he had only ever had one woman properly before Jan – that had been a couple of years before when he was home on a rest from work, when a married cousin of his had let him fuck her a few times when her husband was away. It had been wonderful even though it was very rushed – during the day, fully dressed, in a tent where she had to keep watch under the tent-flap in case anyone was coming. He had been nervous and clumsy and it was necessary to finish very quickly. But he had thought of that warmth and sweetness many times since.

Apart from that, he had played with a lot of the young girls and even come many times against the black cotton swathing their soft, bouncy buttocks but they wouldn't let him fuck them, of course, because they were afraid of getting pregnant. And that didn't count.

Oh, God forbid that he should have to use his hand – a terrible thing to do with a real live beautiful woman beside him. As she lay on her side with her knees raised, her smallest child cuddled up to her belly, her buttocks seemed to be begging him to come to them.

He turned and pressed himself against them, small and firm like a boy's as they were but she was no boy and he well knew now about the sweetness between her legs.

In desperation, he did the only thing he could; he lifted her wrapper from behind and, finding the sweet hole there, he let her sleep while he went inside.

Marie slept on.

Simon jerked awake to the ghastly blare of a horn, the dazzle of glaring lights and the concerted cries of his three companions. Ned, in the passenger seat, was clinging to the dashboard, face clammed against the windscreen.

Heart thumping violently, Simon swung the VW off the

road and it lumbered to a halt in the sand. He cut the ignition, embraced the wheel and allowed his head to flop down on his arms.

Bliss.

"'Strewth!" came Ned's voice weakly. "You nearly killed us there, mate. Nearly hit that minibus."

"Must sleep," groaned Simon. He settled himself more comfortably against the wheel and silence reigned. When he woke again, drooling against the wheel with an ache in his jaw and a bursting bladder, the others were still unconscious. Ned was snoring open-mouthed, head thrown back against the seat, and the other two were sleeping in the back like Siamese twins joined at the head, each clutching a bag to his chest: goatskin bag and green canvas satchel.

He peered out. Bright moonlight on sand and scrub. A narrow strip of tarmacadam running northwards.

They were north of the border on the road to Tahoua. Some hours earlier, on an adrenalin high, having successfully negotiated the Niger frontier post, he had decided to keep on driving rather than look for accommodation in Birnin Konni. He was lit up like candles at the thought that if he kept going they could be in Tahoua for breakfast. It had seemed like a good idea at the time.

Now, after his shut-eye – he had no idea how long he had slept – he felt refreshed enough to continue. Sun-arise-early-in-the-morning he could still be confronting Kola in Tahoua over cappuccino and baguette.

He swung the door open, stepped out and watered a thorn-bush with a surprisingly copious amount of urine, considering the arid conditions. Lucky little thorn-bush. An unexpected morning treat.

Zip up. Tahoua, here I come!

Then he turned back to the car and saw that the front left tyre was flat as his own bustline and the back left subsiding stealthily. Belatedly he remembered Ikus-Ikoos warning him about the six-inch thorns embedded in this sand.

He leapt for the bonnet, yelling at the others.

Jan woke to the mother-of-all 'what-in-Jesus'-name-have-I-done' scenarios. Oh, Jesus! Simon! Anow! Moussa! Oh, my God! Her sense of horror was so great that she covered her face with her hands and rocked back and forth – she would have been slamming her face on the sleeping-mat if her back had been just a bit more supple. Christ Almighty! What a cock-up! What a shambles! What a bleeding fucking disaster!

She turned her head and peeped through her fingers to see a beautiful black muscular back beside her. Her immediate and almost overpowering impulse was to clamp herself onto it like a barnacle.

Oh, Christ! She lay back down and stuffed the corner of her blanket in her mouth and bit down on it as she screamed through her teeth, "Oh, Christ!"

She popped up again, blanket still in her mouth. She must get him up off her mat and away before the others awoke. She squinted over at the other mercifully sleeping figures in the rosy dawn light. Yes! All still asleep! Thank you, God – at least for that much!

But no amount of shaking could rouse Kolawole Aboyade.

The bastard! He was faking it, deliberately teasing her! No one could sleep like that unless drunk or stoned!

Oh, *fuck*!

In the end she had to get up, get cleaned up using the sparse and precious water in the *bidon*, and move into the back of the car. Nobody was going to believe she had chosen to sleep scrunched up on one of the short and narrow side-seats there. But, if she went through the motions, she could at least argue a case.

A couple of hours later she awoke again, cramped and sore. She gazed out at the already bright morning. The Tuaregs were up, the women busying themselves about the camp. And Kolawole was sitting there on the mat, head bent, straw hat in place, writing on his blasted bits of notepaper.

Simon drove his yellow VW slowly through the streets of Tahoua, eyes peeled for the sight of a sexy Yoruba – probably in a straw hat. But there were many straw hats here, though conical ones unlike Kola's, as the town was full of nomadic cattle Fulani in from the bush. And because it was basically a Hausa town, full of sharp young men in European-style clothes, Kola's black skin and style of dress would not stand out in a crowd either.

This was dreadful. How had he ever thought he would find him? He had imagined Tahoua to be a little mud village but it was a sizeable town in fact. The few main streets were tarred and geometrically laid out, the rest sandy winding alleys. It seemed extremely busy; there was a lot of bustle and traffic – camel and donkey mostly – perhaps it was a market day.

They dropped the spare tyre off at a petrol station for repair. Simon shuddered as he remembered his frantic early-morning efforts to pitch the others, stupid with sleep, out of the beetle and get the jack on before the second wheel subsided completely.

And then the ghastly discovery that he had no tyre-repair kit, the flagging down of a passing Land-Rover, the embarrassing begging for help from a supercilious Frenchman who scoffed at the idea of travelling over such terrain in a VW beetle: "It is not serious," he said with a shrug and a grimace, making Simon feel about two feet tall.

Humiliating.

Simon pulled up at the market and looked out at the milling crowds of Hausa, Fulani and Tuareg in despair.

A sweating Ned in the back, mouthing and squinting out at the glare, was equally nonplussed. "I say, Cous-Cous? How are we supposed to find Fatty in all this?"

Ikus-Ikoos had an answer at the ready. "When in Rome, Ned, do as the Romans do. We settle and stay put and let her find us."

Simon took heart. Would that work for him too?

"You mean, news will travel and they'll hear we've arrived?" asked Ned. "Why, you silly sod, they're bleedin' thieves – they'll take to their heels! Why should they come to us?"

Ikus-Ikoos laughed. "But news of them will. I guarantee that. Before the day is out we'll have news of where they are."

Simon spoke up timidly. "Em, Ikus-Ikoos . . . do you think you could put out a couple of feelers for me too?" He arched an eyebrow and then wished he hadn't. No need to pretend to be taking this lightly.

"Certainly," said Ikus-Ikoos. "What do you want me to ask?"

Simon was now sorry that he hadn't recounted his woes in detail to Ikus-Ikoos somewhere along the way. "I'll tell you . . . later . . . in fact, I need your advice . . ."

"OK. Well, let's settle you people in the *campement*. They have cold drinks there and the food is good. And if it's full they'll let you sleep on the tennis court for a charge."

"On the tennis court!" Ned was mystified. "Charge us for sleeping on the tennis court? Why should we pay for sleeping on the tennis court? Is there a sodding floor-show or what? One of those frilly-knickered Wimbledon ladies prancing around showing off her arse? Perhaps the local version! Oh, I'll pay for that! Ah-hah-hah-hah!"

With Ikus-Ikoos navigating from the back seat, Simon drove out of the market area and along a tree-lined street to where the *campement* sprawled on a hill. He pulled up in front of the building, nosing the bonnet of the VW into the shade of a tree. Instead of gratefully tumbling out of the sweaty interior of the beetle, all four of them sat and gazed out, exhausted, hardly able to credit that only a few steps would lead them to blissful shade, cold water from a fridge, beds, fans, beer!

They climbed out and, following Ikus-Ikoos' lead, wandered into a small shady inner court where they thankfully plonked themselves down at small green-painted metal tables. Ikus-Ikoos told Simon to order cold drinks – Flag, he said, was the beer available – while he went to enquire about the rooms.

The beer came in small green bottles.

"A little bit of heaven, eh?" said Ned, guzzling it down.

Half an hour later, having downed more beers than were good for them at that time of the day, they were luxuriating in the simple fact of being out of the sun in spartan rooms where there was an extra charge for using the electric fans. *En suite* was not a term one would think of applying but there were adjoining stone-floored bathrooms with proper toilets and simple showers. It was heaven.

But not for everyone, it seemed.

"Look at that daft bugger," said Ned to himself, peering out through the wicker window-blind. Ikus-Ikoos was sitting on his mat in the courtyard, busily making tea and chewing tobacco. "He actually *prefers* to crouch on a mat in the sodding heat! Blimey! You can take a man out of Essex but you can't take sodding Essex out of the man!"

Simon was having a rapid shower in the bathroom he was sharing with Tom, resisting the urge to stand under the blessedly cold, deliciously *wet* water for the rest of the day. He must brief Ikus-Ikoos.

As he stepped out of the shower, modestly covering himself with his wrapper, he saw that Tom was on standby ready to step in: wearing the miniscule threadbare towel he had seen in the tartan bag, the green canvas satchel tucked under his arm. Simon was quite disturbed to notice that Tom had rather a nice body undressed – smooth-skinned, sallow and lean – and that the miniscule threadbare towel was bulging impressively in the front and outlining appendages of interesting dimensions. If he were Jan he might be tempted to investigate. But Tom's masculinity seemed inappropriate and somehow shocking. As for a green canvas bag that must follow its master into the shower . . . enough was bloody enough. He vowed to find out what it contained before the night was out.

He dressed quickly, combed his wet hair perfunctorily and stepped out into the corridor.

*"Psst! Psst!"*

Ned was grinning at him through the half-opened door of his room and beckoning to him.

Fuck! thought Simon.

"I've always wanted to say *'Psst!'* to someone," said Ned, gurgling with laughter. "People always seem to do it in books but never in real life."

Simon didn't give a fuck at that point about what people did in books. He had a large slice of reality on his plate and thought it was time to be assertive. "Ned, I really need to see Ikus-Ikoos —"

"But I want to tell you something!" Very aggrieved. "I've been trying to tell you since you picked me up and you won't ever listen — what the Consul told me in Kano —"

The mention of the Consul, reminding him as it did of Ned's baiting him about the lacy-underwear episode, lent Simon a bit of extra backbone. "We've heard the lacy-knickers story already," he said severely, "and, if there's something else, you'd better keep it for later. Ikus-Ikoos is anxious to get into town about *your* business and I need to fill him in on mine —"

"Oh, piss off, then!" Ned waved a hand and shook his wattles, turning back into the room in a huff.

"Oh, don't be like that, Ned!" sighed Simon. "I'll be right back to you." Then he thought: Oh, do be like that then — what the fuck do I care? He hurried outside.

Ikus-Ikoos had made short work of his tea-drinking — he really was anxious to get into town. It struck Simon that he was, in fact, greatly excited at being back in Niger despite his outer calm. Perhaps he had a girlfriend lurking about.

He came to meet Simon, leather bag slung over his

shoulder, wad of tobacco poised on his lower lip. They sat down at a metal table in the courtyard and Simon crossed his legs and arms and prepared, rather nervously, to tell his story. What the Tuareg take on homosexuality was, he had no idea. Jan was either vague or wary on the subject. But he had long ago discovered, to his chagrin and embarrassment, that the kohl eyeliner, braided hair and perfume didn't necessarily make them fellow-travellers.

"So you're off to the town?" he began lamely.

"Yes," Ikus-Ikoos smiled, tobacco poised with practised ease on his lower lip.

What a gorgeous smile he had, tobacco notwithstanding! With those little long dents in his cheeks! Cutting across Simon's agitation came a sudden curiosity about this lovely man. And the stray thought that – well, was there the *faintest* possibility he could be gay? "Going to visit a girlfriend then?" he found himself asking archly.

Ikus-Ikoos's tobacco disappeared inside his cheek and his olive-black eyes glinted. He looked down shyly. A long forefinger stroked the table. "No." His smile gleamed even more as he looked up at Simon again. "I'm in love." He laughed at himself. "But I've left her in Zaria."

Oh, well, thought Simon – shame. "So will you marry her?"

"Well, she's said yes," Ikus-Ikoos smiled, eyes dancing.

Simon felt a pang. The other man's joy filled him with envy. He sighed aloud, breaking eye contact, and combing a hand through his wet hair plunged abruptly into his own sorry tale. "I need your help. I've come all this way to find my friend, Kolawole –"

"Do I know this guy?" Ikus-Ikoos interrupted, tobacco making an appearance on his lip again.

"You may have seen him on campus."

"So what does he look like?"

"Well, he's a Yoruba – quite tall, slim but muscular, dark-chocolate-colour skin, beautiful teeth, a big smile, gold-brown eyes – let's see . . . he often wears a straw hat –"

"Well, you don't need me to find him," said Ikus-Ikoos decisively, standing up and spitting a dark stream of tobacco-juice practically at Simon's feet.

Simon's mouth dropped open at what seemed like a gross insult.

"He's there," said Ikus-Ikoos.

"Where? In Zaria?"

"No, he's *there*. Look at him." He gestured by bobbing the wad of tobacco on his lower lip towards the door behind Simon.

Hardly daring to believe, Simon turned his head.

Kola was standing poised at the door leading into the courtyard, fingers lightly hooked onto the doorframe on either side, wearing his straw hat and a rueful smile.

"Ikus-Ikoos! Simon!" came Jan's delighted voice as she appeared, ducking under one of Kola's arms. She then stopped short as if embarrassed, smile fading perceptibly.

"You see?" grinned Ikus-Ikoos with his lean, dimpled smile. "I told you we should stay put!"

Jan sat at one of the small metal tables, drinking Flag beer by the neck. This was just ghastly. The only way she could possibly cope was by getting as drunk as she could as fast as she could.

God bless the Danes, she thought, as the cold bite of the beer hit her taste-buds, or whoever it was first got enthusiastic about this stuff. In this dryness the beer, with its coldness and wetness, was like bottled gold. And she suddenly hungered for a soft Irish day with the sun glancing through the rain and the skin sucking that merciful moisture up.

She was sorely tempted to light out of the *campement* and go stay with Aberfekil and family. They had begged her to stay when she had unloaded them at an encampment far north of the town; she had only come back to Tahoua because Kola was making bedroom eyes about real rooms and showers.

This was bloody awful. She couldn't look at Simon without blushing, Ned without glowering and Kola without getting palpitations. And at Tom Purthill without wanting to wring his neck – if he ever stayed still enough for her to get her hands on him: since she arrived he had been behaving like a skittish horse, shying away from her every glance and movement. Potato-fights, teasing fingers, Vice-Chancellors, bronze masks and betrayal swirled in her head.

Ikus-Ikoos? Ikus-Ikoos was an old and trusted friend. But he had shagged off into town.

Simon and Kola seemed to be circling each other warily. What was that about? Had Kola been running away from Simon? But why the hell would a Yoruba run north? It was only a matter of time before they had a colossal row. No doubt they would set to during the *sieste* – Simon had already prepared the battle-ground by dumping Tom out of his room and into Ned's. Then, with the row, would come the revelation: Kola was sure to throw the fact he had sex with her at Simon's head. Without a doubt. Married people were famous for it. If they didn't tell out of guilt, they did it out of spite. Somehow – and this was interesting – Kola qualified as 'married'.

She glugged down the rest of the bottle and started on another.

But, in fact, Simon had not been preparing a battleground. A love-fest was more what he had in mind. He was high again on the adrenalin surge that had catapulted him out of Zaria. He was now in the bathroom, attired in his *Bottom Power* wrapper, shakily applying mascara and making a mess of it. Oh, Christ! That looked ghastly. He grabbed his facecloth and rubbed soap on it. Oh, hurry, hurry! Kola had taken the car to buy some stuff he needed at a stall down the road – he'd be along soon. He scrubbed at his eyes. Oh, God! That stung! In pain, he peered at the mirror – the mascara was smeared all over the place. Oh, God! He scrabbled in his toilet-bag. Thank God, there was his cold cream. In a panic, he applied great globs of the cream to his eyes. The stinging subsided but now he couldn't see. He groped for the loo-roll. A sploshing sound told him he'd knocked it into the loo. He groped for the facecloth and rinsed it out, eyes closed tight, then started swabbing the cream off.

He heard the outside door open. Kola. Oh, Christ! He swabbed furiously. He opened his eyes and looked in the mirror. The mascara was gone but his eyes looked red and raw, as if he'd been indulging in a crying jag. Oh, it was too much! Just when he'd wanted to look terrific! He slammed the facecloth into the sink and went into the other room.

"Simon!" Kola was sitting on the bed, his leather drawstring bag open beside him. He had a new writing-pad and some biros in his hands. "I thought you were still downstairs!" He rose and peered at Simon more closely. "Simon! You've been crying!"

"Oh, no, actually, I –"

"Oh, Simon!" said Kola, in a voice so thick with emotion it stopped Simon in his tracks. "I'm so sorry!" He threw the pad and pens on the bed, reached out and drew Simon into his arms. "I'm *so sorry!*"

Oh, this is a good start, thought Simon, as he let himself be embraced and then seated on the bed. Standing had been better, actually – full-frontal contact.

"I'm *so sorry!*" Kola took both of Simon's hands and grasping them between his, bowed his head over them. "I must have been crazy!"

Simon thought he must be dreaming. This was the very height of romance. Wasn't kneeling on the floor and proposing marriage the next step?

"I'm so sorry for everything! I've been so stupid!" He looked up and Simon was moved to see tears in his eyes. "Simon –" his lips trembled, "I . . . you really confuse me . . . you make me react in crazy ways. When you confronted me about that letter and told me about wanting a baby, I just lost my head . . . God, to cause you all this pain!" He began to kiss Simon's hands, nipping the knuckles between his white teeth as if mere kissing wasn't enough.

Simon's heart was lifting by the second, about to take off like a burgeoning beautiful balloon. "But, Kola, everything's OK! After you left I thought of a wonderful solution!"

Kola stopped nipping and looked up, this time a shade apprehensively.

Simon took a deep trembling breath. "I want to take the

baby. I want it to be mine – maybe adopt it if I can. But the mother can come too, to take care of it if she wishes."

Kola stared, speechless, and Simon was gratified to see tears well up in his eyes again. But then Kola let go of his hands. Not so gratifying.

Simon stared as Kola bowed his head and, elbows on knees, gazed at the floor. He waited in consternation. Where was the relief, the joy, the gratitude, the admiration?

Kola at last raised his head and looked at him. "You're too good for me, you know," he said, lips trembling, voice thick again. He shifted his gaze back to the floor. "That's – so wonderful. You're a wonderful person, my friend. There's no doubt about that. Unfortunately . . ."

*Unfortunately.* "What?" breathed Simon, now waiting for the moment his heart would be crushed.

"Unfortunately – your generosity is the only genuine thing in this situation."

"What do you mean?" said Simon faintly. *He didn't love him! He wasn't even gay! He was married with children! He was a professional con man!*

Kola wiped his face with the palm of his hand and heaved a huge sigh. He looked at Simon again, eyes swimming with regret. "Simon . . . there isn't any baby. I'm sorry."

It was like receiving a reprieve and a blow in the belly in the same moment. "She isn't pregnant after all?" he said at last.

"There isn't any Aminatu," said Kola thickly.

Simon laughed – a short painful bark. "What do you mean?"

"Well . . . I just panicked. About you wanting a baby. I

just wanted to scare you off in that moment. So I came out with that stuff . . ."

"You made it all up?"

"Yes."

"But . . . that's crazy, Kola."

"I know."

"There is no girlfriend?"

"No."

"But – but what about the letter?"

"Oh . . . I feel so stupid. It would have been so easy to explain. It was a letter I was helping my friend Sule to write. He is the one with the pregnant girlfriend."

Simon's mind felt dry and grey as ashes. No baby. No young mother. Just Kola, so terrified of commitment to him that he had concocted a bizarre lie. And taken off up the road like a bat out of hell.

Kola was now looking at him apprehensively over the back of his hand.

If he's waiting for a reaction from me, thought Simon, he'll be waiting. He felt nothing but a desolate blankness. He'd just had a miscarriage.

Around eight in the evening, they were all seated together at dinner in the courtyard. Hunger had ruled a temporary truce and the staff, despite mild protests, had obligingly (they thought) constructed one long metal table from the little square ones, thereby unwittingly throwing all the warring parties into one jolly bunch.

The food and beer cheered the Zarians despite themselves and a kind of cat's-cradle of fairly amiable conversation started up about innocuous things: Jan never addressing Ned or Tom, Simon never addressing Kola, Ned still in a huff with Simon, Tom never addressing anyone – and so on. They were eating brochettes and baguettes with salad – the entire repertoire of the kitchen that evening despite there being a whole list of other things, from couscous to roast chicken, on the menu. The brochettes were tender, though, and the French bread a scrumptiously delicious change from the Nigerian doughy, sweet, British-type loaves.

Then the roar of a vehicle pulling up outside alerted them to another arrival and promised fresh blood and a welcome diversion. They craned their necks to see who might be joining them.

But when a large German Shepherd bounded through the door more than one diner prayed that he was hallucinating. In vain.

"Ajax!" boomed Hetty Coleman. "Heel!"

A moment later she was standing flat-footed in the doorway, bending a stern and disapproving gaze on the company.

They gazed back in dismay, brochettes and baguettes raised to mouths smeared with French dressing – somewhat like a pack of shamefaced dogs caught devouring a slaughtered sheep.

The woman inspired guilt and apprehension.

What followed was worse than any of them could have anticipated. Hetty moved to stand at the end of the table, Ajax at her side like her henchman, his teeth bared. Hands on cotton-clad hips, she launched into booming speech without more ado.

"Tom Purthill – you lied to me about staying in Kano.

Pursuing Prendergast, were you? I'd neuter my dogs if they behaved as you do."

Tom squealed, crossed his eyes, sucked in his lips and then hid the ghastly expression that resulted behind his canvas bag.

"Simon Cullen – you deserted us in Yashi, ran off lily-livered – but I would expect no better from a degenerate."

Simon made a flouncing movement which he cut short.

"Ned Bassett –" she was systematically working her way around the table, "my nightwatchman told me how you are making a fool of yourself about that bush woman – no fool like an old impotent fool."

"Impotent!" spluttered Ned, bits of lettuce flying from his mouth.

"Jan Prendergast – you *silly* girl. Have you been so stupid as to smuggle that deranged Frenchwoman over the border?"

Oh, Christ, no, thought Jan in alarm as all eyes swung to her at news that fell like manna from Gossip Heaven. How the fuck did Hetty know? Langley? Or no – the fucking nightwatchman again! Jesus, she must be sleeping with the man! "No, I –"

"Probably. You're a foolish romantic – see yourself as something out of a bad musical like *The Desert Song*. Ikus-Ikoos – are you still prancing around in that ridiculous get-up, imagining you're making some political point?" Her eyes came to rest on Kola. There was a long pause. She eyed him speculatively. Ajax growled. Kola gazed back, at ease, where a lesser man would have hidden under the table. "Kolawole Aboyade – you need therapy."

That damning conclusion seemed to give her great satisfaction, She chuckled.

"Hello, Hetty!" they all found themselves saying then, almost in chorus, like dutiful schoolchildren at a refectory table on a headmistress's arrival. They then hid again behind their brochettes, baguettes and bottles of beer.

She swung a metal chair in to the table with a flick of the wrist and sat down. She looked at them sternly.

"Now I have something to say."

"We thought you had said it," said Simon smartly with great temerity.

She glared at him. "I have said nothing of moment yet, merely commented on your sad vagaries."

Simon giggled. "Sad vagaries!"

She quelled him with a crushing glare as Ajax snarled. Simon hid behind his hand.

"Now," she said. "I want your full attention. I want you all to understand that I *know* who is guilty and I intend to bring that person and that person's accomplices to book. They will not get away with their crime, believe you me. I have *inside* information. We will say no more now. But the guilty parties should beware!"

None of them needed to be guilty to find this quite terrifying. Then, before anyone could do much more than cringe, Hetty yelled for the boy to bring beer for all the table and turned her attention to Tom.

"Tom!" she grinned. "To be honest, I am pleased to see you. I was planning to contact you on my return to Zaria. But now, happily, we have met. What I would like to discuss with you is this: when I return to England – shortly – I intend to set up a clinic where I can practise behavioural psychology in my own backyard, while completing my studies in psychiatry. I would like you to attend. I find you very sympathetic. I feel we have a lot in common and can help each other. Scratch each other's backs, so to speak."

Tom squirmed at having his dirty linen aired so flauntingly in public by the heavy hand of Hetty. But he was also flattered. The expression which resulted suggested acute indigestion.

Hetty didn't seem to notice.

Ned was determined to get his oar in – enough of letting the old basket-case dominate the table. "But, really," he huffed, "do you have enough experience in behavioural psychology to set up a clinic?"

"Masses, man. Some very fascinating cases."

The young lad arrived with the beer on a tray.

"*Merci, garçon.*" Hetty passed the bottles around the table.

"Give us an example then – an interesting one," said Ned.

"Right." She guzzled down the larger part of her beer and wiped her mouth with the back of her hand. "Well – there was the case where the young patient couldn't control his bladder. Whenever his mother arrived home – she always brought him a treat – he would automatically urinate in his excitement – couldn't hold it. I think I will order some brochettes. *Garçon!* Where is he? Oh, there he is! *Garçon*, more brochettes and bread – and beer." She gestured around the table to include everyone and noticed Ikus-Ikoos was drinking Coke. "With a Coke – a couple of Cokes. And make it snappy."

The *garçon* went off, grinning, to report to the kitchen staff on her larger-than-life attitude.

"You were saying? About the incontinent youngster," said Simon, smirking over his brochette.

"Yes – then there was the adolescent –"

"But did you cure the other one?" interrupted Jan.

"Yes, indeed. Very simply. The mother was instructed to behave very calmly on her arrival home, bring no treat and make no eye contact. Only after he had calmed down was she allowed to acknowledge his presence in any way. It worked. That is the beauty of behavioural psychology. The solutions can be so elegantly simple. Like handing your clients a key. *Merci, garçon!*" She passed the beer around.

"And the adolescent?" asked Simon. "Do tell us about the adolescent."

"Yes. He habitually greeted his family with a highly visible erection –"

Ikus-Ikoos gasped in horror and Hetty looked highly gratified. She nodded her head in his direction in a rudimentary bow. "Yes, the mother all but had a nervous breakdown – a weak woman, couldn't cope. He also had the habit of standing in the middle of the front garden at all times of the day or night thrusting his erection into thin air! A very alarming sight for the postman who began to refuse to bring the post into the house – and who would blame him?"

"Who indeed?" sniggered Ned. "Ah-hah-hah-hah-hah!"

"And y-y-y-you cured him, H-h-hetty?" Tom spoke up, startling them all.

"Alas, no, one of my rare failures. Castration was the only answer. Such a shame in an adolescent. He might have grown out of the habit – but his family insisted and, well, what could I do but comply?"

Tom's legs tied themselves in a knobbly knot on the instant of this pronouncement. "C-c-comply? Y-y-you mean you –"

"You don't mean you performed the operation yourself, do you?" Ned asked.

"I did indeed. I've done dozens! Simple enough – you'd be amazed. Do one and it holds no fears. Just snip-snap! Doesn't even need an anaesthetic! But, Tom," she leant towards him, leering, "uncross your legs and don't worry! Despite my earlier remark, I have no interest in performing that operation on *you*! Which reminds me . . ." She got to her feet. "I need my scissors – I'll go fetch my things from the car. Be back in a moment . . . Ajax!"

He sprang to attention.

They watched her go.

"Crikey, I'm glad I'm not sharing a room with her," said Ned. "She might get an itchy finger on her scissors in the night!"

Simon leant forward and asked, "What was she on about when she first came in? About guilty parties? What does she think we've done?"

"I don't know," said Jan. But she thought she did know, in fact. "I was afraid to ask her in case it might start her off again."

"Oh, I need therapy, Simon's a degenerate," said Kola, "Jan's a romantic, Ikus-Ikoos is a freak, Tom's a liar and Ned's impotent!"

"Are you sure?" said Jan, giggling. "Wasn't it Ikus-Ikoos is a degenerate, Simon's a liar, Tom's a romantic, I'm a freak and you're impotent?"

"You know it wasn't," said Kola, with his laziest and widest grin.

Simon threw him an odd look. "She used the word 'crime'. I don't think impotence qualifies, as least not in legal terms."

Ned folded his brawny arms on the table and leant forward portentously with a smug smile. "I know what she meant." He prepared to milk the most he could out of his big disclosure. Unfortunately, this preparation involved excavation in his pipe and while he was fiddling at it, luxuriating in keeping them on tenterhooks, something happened which stole his thunder.

"You know," said Tom chattily, "I've decided that I will take her up on that offer and attend her clinic for treatment in England."

All heads swung towards him and they gazed, amazed that he had made a fluent statement and afraid to respond at all in case he might clam up.

"Yes, I find what she says is very sound, very sound. I'm sure she can help me with m-m-m-my slight nervousness around people."

Simon risked saying: "She's very sound indeed."

"I think so – G-g-god m-m-moves in m-m-mysterious ways, you know. I think he sent her to c-c-cure me," said Tom, looking both pleased and embarrassed – appropriate expressions for once. Then embarrassment won out. He scrambled to his feet, grimacing, clutching his bag. "G-g-goodnight!"

They hailed goodnights on him from every direction like well-wishers scattering confetti.

There was a long silence after he left.

"He seems a lot better," said Ikus-Ikoos to break the odd silence. "The idea of this clinic seems to have cheered him up. Do you think she can help him? She seems very experienced."

"Um," said Simon then.

"Eh . . ." said Jan.

"'Ere," said Ned, ignoring Ikus-Ikoos, "d'you think we should tell the poor sod?"

"Tell him what?" asked Ikus-Ikoos.

Simon pulled a face and hunched his shoulders. "Well, you see . . ."

"The poor bastard's got it completely wrong," said Ned.

"Got what wrong?" Kola's lazy voice butted in.

"Well," said Simon, "you see, Hetty's an *animal* behavioural psychologist."

There was a soft low giggle from Kola.

Ikus-Ikoos stared blankly when asked to take this idea on board. At last he said slowly, "But the clinic – she said she was setting up a psychiatric clinic . . ."

"Oh, there will be a clinic all right," answered Simon. "*Dog* psychiatry, you see. When she said she wanted to practise in her own backyard, that's what she literally meant."

"A *dog psychiatric clinic?*" This was well beyond Ikus-Ikoos's ken. "Is there such a thing?"

"Oh, there is," said Ned. "And if there wasn't Hetty would invent it. Ah-hah-hah-hah-*hah*!"

"Well, you know," mused Jan, "Tom might fit in quite happily,"

"So – should we tell him?" asked Simon.

"Well, don't tell him now, for Christ's sake," blustered Ned. "The shock might be the final straw and we'd have to chain him up."

"Very appropriate," said Kola dryly. "Hetty could begin treatment immediately."

"Here she comes," whispered Jan. "Not a word!"

"Not a woof!" muttered Simon.

Ikus-Ikoos departed soon after to spend the night on the town, Tuareg-fashion, and eventually Simon and Kola went off to bed – but not at the same time. Kola went first, Simon soon after.

Their departure left Jan biting her nails. It seemed they hadn't had their row yet. They were very cool with one another but she hadn't heard any blow-up in the afternoon, though she'd stayed awake waiting to hear raised voices. That meant it would happen now. Oh, God.

She excused herself, leaving Hetty, Ajax and Ned carousing. She was now sharing with Hetty – to say nothing of Ajax – and hoped she wouldn't be raped in the night. She would put on four pairs of knickers. Hey, maybe she'd filch one of Hetty's beige pairs with the elastic around the legs. Knickers as chastity-belt. She sat on the bed and bit her nails. She could hear no sounds at all from the other rooms.

God, by some miracle, were they peaceably settled down for the night?

She tiptoed out into the corridor and along to Simon's room. The door was very slightly ajar. Had they gone out? Forgotten to lock the door? She rapped softly. No answer. She pushed the door open tentatively with the tip of a finger. It swung back a little. And, as if on cue, Simon stepped out of the little bathroom.

"Oh!" she said, startled. "I didn't realise you were here –

I thought you'd gone out and forgotten to lock the door . . ."

"Kola's gone out looking for Tom. He's not in his room and we were worried."

From the way he said it, she was confident that he wasn't looking on her as a traitorous bitch – yet.

"But now Kola's been gone ages," Simon went on. "Let's go and have a look, shall we?"

"Sure!" she said supportively, traitorous bitch that she was.

Maybe she could grab Kola and threaten him with something or other to keep his mouth shut. She couldn't imagine what.

Outside, the low hill inclined gently down to a sandy area dotted with bushes and palm-trees. Beyond were small sand-dunes.

They trotted down the hill. And came upon Kola, kneeling under a palm-tree, in the very act of laying Tom's famous green canvas bag on the ground before him.

"Where is he?" said Simon in fright. Then, leaping back five yards, "You got it!"

"What are you doing with his bag?" asked Jan, dismayed.

"You got the bag!" Simon backed off further. "Open it up! Open it up!"

Fingers very intent on getting the job done, Kola needed no encouragement. He had already opened the little brass-tipped straps of the satchel.

"But where *is* he?" cried Jan. "And why are you at his bag?"

"Relax and be quiet," said Kola softly. "He's over there on the sand-dune in some kind of trance – staring at the moon. I sneaked up behind him and grabbed the bag." He started to giggle quietly as he flipped back the green canvas flap and plunged his hand in.

Jan drew back slightly – Simon's alarm was contagious. Kola's dark-brown hand emerged clutching something round and yellowish and hairy.

Jan recoiled while Simon's shriek, as he skittered off into the dark in panic, was his best qualification to date for female status.

Kola held the balding trophy up. Its dark eyes and the slash of red around its neck gleamed bright in the moonlight.

"Come back, Simon!" called Kola softly. "Come back! It's a teddy bear!"

But Simon was convulsed behind a bush at a distance.

"He's getting sick, I think," said Jan as they strained their eyes to see.

And then they heard rather than saw the sudden flurry of flailing limbs as Tom Purthill came galloping to the rescue and snatched his bear from Kola's still upraised hand.

"Shit!" cried Kola.

They watched as Tom flailed his way into the distance, wending through the palm-trees like a lanky little boy playing at being an aeroplane.

Jan was bewildered. "But – but how did you know there was anything odd in the bag?"

"Oh, Simon says he's been clutching it all the time! Even takes it into the shower with him! So he got the idea that it was a severed head! Possibly yours, he thought before you turned up."

"Oh, God, Simon's imagination will be the death of him!"

Kola nodded. "Yeah, I had to check before he got too obsessed about it." He shook the bag out – there was nothing else in it.

Simon was making his way back.

"Did you hear, Simon?" called Jan. "It was only a teddy bear and he's galloped off with it into the sand-dunes."

Kola was still staring into the darkness.

"Kola?" said Simon.

Kola looked up, shamefaced. "I feel bad about this – I think I should go after him – in case he comes to any harm or gets lost tearing around like that." Picking up the canvas bag, he got up. "And I'll have to apologise to him." He set off in pursuit of Tom.

"A teddy bear," said Simon softly. "Poor man. It's funny but one feels one should have guessed. What else?"

Jan shook her head, grinning. "A severed head possibly?"

Simon glowered.

Back in Simon's room, she lay down on Kola's bed. Unpleasant thoughts involving probing fingers and cushiony lips beset her. She shook them off.

Simon yawned, stretching himself out on the other bed. "We never did find out what Hetty was on about," he said sleepily. "And I wonder what Ned was going to say? You know, he's been on at me since Kano about something the Consul told him."

"The Consul?" Jan was wide awake again, the word 'Consul' being a bit too close to 'Vice-Chancellor' and even closer to 'Immigration Officer'.

"Yes," said Simon. "But I didn't give him the chance to tell me. It's probably something silly and scandalous and Ned-like. As for Hetty, she's always spouting some aggressive rubbish, sounding off like a brass cannon. Like on Kufena she had a bee in her bonnet about the museum pieces coming from Boston –"

Jan's ears pricked up. "About the museum pieces?"

"Yes, she was saying the security arrangements were hopeless – that the stuff would be stolen . . . Oh, my God, *that's it!*" He shot up in the bed.

Jan sat up too. "Yeah," she said soberly. "That *is* it. Kola overheard a phone conversation about it at the border-post. There was a robbery from the storeroom – the very night before we left – the most important piece, a bronze mask, and a couple of small gold heads."

"And Hetty's in pursuit!"

"Yes, and she thinks we've done it."

"She *knows* we've done it!" said Simon delightedly. "She said she has inside information."

"She must have," said Jan. "She'd hardly come bolting up the road like a bat out of hell otherwise – though, mind you, all those hasty exits from Zaria the very morning of the robbery must look really suspicious."

"But where would she have got 'inside information'?"

"The Tuareg grapevine, I expect," said Jan. "That sly old watchman of hers again. But, who knows? She'd terrify admissions out of anyone."

Simon started. "So that's what the Consul told Ned! And why the police were at the Kano Embassy and put us through such a rigorous search!"

"Down to our lacy knickers, I believe – I must add that to my list of the uses of underwear: disarming policemen and Immigration officials."

"As if any thief in his right mind, about to flee the

country," Simon scoffed, "would wait to get a visa until *after* he'd done the dirty deed!"

"Oh, it was probably an exercise in cross-border co-operation – or half-assed payment for some kind of services rendered. What puzzles me is this: why didn't they put up police barricades outside Samaru and Zaria? Or, in fact, at the university gates?"

Simon shrugged. "There weren't any. I suppose they assumed – rightly, I daresay – that the thieves would have fled the area in the night – if they weren't just small-time locals. No doubt they raided the premises of the usual suspects."

"And concentrated on the borders and airports."

"Oh, God!" Simon clutched his head theatrically. "We're Bonnie and Clyde and didn't even know it!"

"Reckon we're going to die in a hail of bullets?"

"Don't even *say* that!" Simon shuddered.

"Oh, come on! Our fifteen minutes of fame! Riddled with bullets in your yellow beetle!"

"I want to die tragically with Kola, not you! He must be the robber anyway. His reason for crossing the border doesn't even exist."

*What?* "What do you mean?" she said carefully.

Simon was silent for a moment. When he spoke his voice was dry and unemotional. "The day I last saw you, I found a letter to a girl in his wastepaper basket. He told me she was a Hausa girl from Tahoua and that she was pregnant with his child."

"Oh, Simon!"

"Please. Don't waste your sympathy. It was all a lie. Then he took off, left a note saying he was off to rescue his baby. This afternoon he tells me she doesn't exist. No girl. No baby. Just Kola on the run from me."

Jan started at a sudden thought. "Simon," she said reluctantly, "maybe – maybe she does exist after all. He was writing to someone furiously all the way from Zaria – at every opportunity."

"Well . . ." said Simon slowly, "I spy with my little eye . . ."

"What?"

"Something beginning with . . ."

"B!" she said immediately. Her eyes followed Simon's to where the leather drawstring of Kola's bag protruded from under the bed. It was there! The first time Kola had left it out of his hands!

Simon knelt and pulled it out.

"Oh, Simon, I don't know . . ." God knows what he might find. A bronze mask? Jesus! A diary! Oh, Christ!

But he was already opening it and plunging his hand in.

"Here!" He pulled out a bunch of papers and thrust them at her. "You look! Tell me what they say!"

She took them reluctantly, remembering her previous mad desire to see these scribblings.

"Go on!" said Simon. "Hurry! I can't bear this!" He stayed there kneeling, head turned away from her and the letters.

At first she couldn't make any sense of what she was reading. Because they weren't letters from Kola – it seemed to be correspondence between two people, a man and a woman – Richard and Julia. But all heavily scored and corrected – a right mess, actually, like the original manuscript of a much over-worked poem. What? Was he correcting somebody's letters? Proof-reading? But . . . then she noticed . . . they were all in the same handwriting.

"Simon?"

"Yes?"

"Simon! Look at this!" She held out one of Richard's letters. "Is this Kola's handwriting?"

"Just tell me what it says!" he cried.

"Please! Is it his writing?"

He glanced at it. "Yes, of course!"

"And this?" She showed him a letter signed 'Julia'.

"Yes, of course! Can't you see it's the same?" He stared at her, perplexed.

Then she noticed other names, on other pages. "I can't make this out . . ." Still at sea, she turned to another page: *Angelina decided to reply pretending she did not love Peter in order to test his love*. And she suddenly knew what she was looking at. She quickly scanned the other pages again. Yes! "Oh, my God, Simon! You won't believe this!"

"What *is* it?"

The pain in his voice made her look up.

"Oh, love, sorry! Just hang on a minute . . ."

She scanned the pages again. Yes. Without a doubt. *Another negative reply to a letter proposing marriage – A positive reply to a letter proposing marriage* .

She looked at Simon, biting her lip, not knowing whether to laugh or cry.

"What's so funny?" he asked in anguish.

"Oh, Simon . . . I don't know how to tell you this, love . . . but your Kola seems to be Sunshine Boy!"

He gazed at her, bemused.

"These are – sample letters. Kola is writing some stuff like those *Sunshine Boy Advises* pamphlets – though a damned sight classier and more sophisticated. Look!" She pushed them into his reluctant hands.

Simon bowed his head over the pieces of notepaper. Minutes passed. Jan waited.

She waited for it to dawn on him.

When he lifted his head she could see it had.

"The letters I found in the wastepaper basket about his pregnant girlfriend..."

She nodded, grimacing. "Samples."

"Fakes. Like him." His voice was bleak.

## Chapter 13

Ned was savagely excavating in his pipe-bowl. "The bloody cow! She's like a steam-roller! No resisting her! We were bloody fine in the *campement*!"

He was referring to Hetty who had risen on the morrow and, on her flat sandalled feet, had shepherded them all – with the expert help of Ajax – into her Land-Rover and out of the town into the surrounding desert. They had reacted like a timid flock of sheep and allowed it all to happen, partly attracted to the idea, vaguely feeling that they might more easily get news through the Tuareg grapevine outside the town.

"Authenticity!" she had boomed. "Authenticity!" And had lobbed them out at a Tuareg bush encampment she was familiar with – very familiar with, they realised, as they watched her commandeer a bunch of the low goatskin tents with no regard whatsoever for the owners she was evicting. The owners, of course, allowed themselves to be herded sheep-like into the remaining few tents.

Evening was now approaching and they were all feeling massively frustrated. The impulses that had driven them so energetically up the road had become dissipated like water in sand. Simon had deflated like a punctured balloon and Ned and Jan found themselves helpless in Ikus-Ikoos's hands.

And Ikus-Ikoos had slid inevitably into Tuareg mode and pace. His graceful leisurely walk became almost languorous, tea-making took hours, tobacco-chewing even longer.

Jan could see him now, sprawled on a mat by a neighbouring tent, foot supported by the raised knee of the other leg.

She was peeved with him, vaguely feeling that he should be actively helping her. How *was* she to find out what had happened to Anow? She would have to go to his encampment which was far far north beyond Tchin Tabaraden and she couldn't do that without a guide. But when she had spoken to Ikus-Ikoos about it – unable of course to explain about Marie – he had told her to relax. He would get news of Anow soon. Not by sprawling there on your butt, she thought! And why wasn't he urgently seeking Ned's money? Ned's Fati?

Ned was raving on. "Water! Showers! Fans! Beer! Food! We had it all at the *campement*! Why the *fuck* did we not resist her? Why can't we do something about her now? United we stand, divided we fall! Christ! I could willingly slit her throat – and how is Cous-Cous to find Fatty out here – though I must say the silly sod doesn't seem too perturbed – eh!"

Jan followed his goggling gaze. Two giggling girls were

passing by, bouncing their buttocks, obviously already well practised in teasing Ned.

"Ummmmm! Delicious!" said Ned, kissing his fingers to them. "Oh, I could rummage about in *their* nether regions! No beige bloomers on them!"

The girls had turned and now were approaching again, their high young breasts jiggling. Jan would have sworn they were jiggling them deliberately. If so – at that moment before Jan finished her thought, one of the girls caught the other's breast in her hand and squeezed it so the nipple pointed invitingly at Ned.

"Ah-hah-hah-hah! Look at that! They want me!"

Jan's unfinished thought was confirmed: they had in the space of a day learned something about Western culture from Ned's leerings – normally they were as unselfconscious about their breasts as they were about their noses or chins.

"Nay-ed! Nay-ed!" they called.

"Oh, look at them," said Ned, sighing like one viewing a basket of puppies. "'Ere, Jan?" He turned a spittle-flecked smile on her. "D'you think I should forget about Fatty and make an offer for one of these little beauties?"

"Um – I don't think so – and there's your money – you must get that back at least –"

"What is that sly bastard up to?" Suddenly enraged.

"Wh-who?" said Jan, startled.

"Cous-Cous! *I don't trust him!*"

"Oh. God, Ned! Don't start!"

*"Nayed! Nayed!"*

He grinned at the girls again, distracted from his fury. "Reckon they're up for it, eh Jan?" He gazed at her with a little-boy eagerness in his eye.

"I really don't know." She didn't either. She wished she did know.

"Well," he ran his tongue around his dry mouth and grimaced into the sun, "there's only one way to find out!" He clambered to his feet. Grinning at the girls, he hitched his trousers up at the waist and pulled the band of his underpants further up over his shirt at the back. The girls turned and strolled off, buttocks bouncing, alternating giggles and languorous glances over their shoulders.

Ned strode off hopefully in their wake, grinning, pipe in fist.

Jan joined Simon on a mat outside his tent, just after sunset. She was seething with exasperation about everything. And now the last straw: a bra-strap about to give way. Knickers she might do without, but a bra never. She had no doubt about *its* primary purpose. Burn her bra? Go ask a marathon runner to burn his jockstrap . . .

She plonked herself down and began to rummage in her shoulder bag for her tiny sewing-kit. After two minutes of this she was just about ready to grab the bag in her teeth and savage it like a terrier with a rat.

"Why is it," she asked Simon, "that *always* the thing you're looking for inside a handbag is the very last thing that meets your hand? Is it some law of physics? Vertelheinbacker's Law or something, if we did but know it?"

No reponse from Simon.

Oh-oh. God, she should have begun by inquiring about what had happened when he confronted Kola. Come to think of it, had Simon been keeping out of her way all day?

"And don't tell me that all I need is a little organisation," she continued, fearing the worst. "I know you're going to say that – but you're not a bloody woman and that's further proof!" She gave in and tipped everything out of the bag onto the mat beside her. Right away, there was the bloody sewing-kit.

And among the familiar items was a crumpled-looking page of notepaper she didn't recognise. She unfolded the creased page. It was Jimoh Igwe's letter asking her to be his College Mother. She held it towards the charcoal burner and peered at it but there wasn't enough light to read it from the glowing coals.

"Oh! I had forgotten this – God, I was so angry the day I got it! I kept it for you! For the scrapbook. Here! See if you can read it – I've left my torch in the car –"

She held it out but Simon ignored it.

Oh, God, this was serious.

"Oh, God! You're sulking again!" Keep talking, Jan. "Because I said you're not a bloody woman? Here!" She stuck the letter into the pocket of his shoulder bag. "There it is for later."

No response from Simon.

Oh, Jesus. This was the moment of truth. What had Kola told him?

Panic was fluttering in her throat. "So . . . what happened with Kola?" she forced herself to say. It came out sounding thick and abrupt.

A pause and he spoke at last. "You were right." He wasn't looking at her at all and his voice was cool in the extreme. "He writes for the publishing company in Ibadan that does those Sunshine Boy pamphlets."

"And what about the letter . . . ?"

"To Aminatu? Yes, just another sample. *Sunshine Boy Advises: A Positive Reply to a Letter from your Newly Pregnant Girlfriend.*" His cynicism seemed more deflated than bitter.

After a pause, she took the risk of pressing on. "It *is* extraordinary," she mused, "that he preferred to wound you horribly rather than tell you he's a kind of Agony Aunt. But I suppose, in a perverse – eh," she flushed, "way it shows how much he cares for you. He always thought we were sneering at those letters – he obviously thought that you'd despise him if you knew."

Simon nodded, chin on his upraised knee. "Yes." He still hadn't looked at her. He was studying the mat in front of him, tracing the weave with a finger. The nasty suspicion in her mind suddenly ballooned and made her heart thud.

"So," said Simon, "my soul mate turns out to be an Agony Aunt. Very appropriate."

"Jeez, yes," said Jan. "The man must be gay, despite all."

"What do you mean 'despite all'?"

"Oh, nothing . . ."

"But what do you mean by it? 'Despite all'? Despite what? Don't you believe he's gay?" Simon flicked her a look.

"Oh, I do, I do! I just meant if there ever was any doubt this would prove it," Jan floundered.

"Oh, so you didn't mean that having fucked you so successfully you had concluded he must be straight?"

She could feel her jaw drop. "Oh . . ." she whispered. "Oh, Simon . . ."

Later that night Jan lay on her side on the hard woven mat the Tuareg used as a covering for their wooden bedframes, head on a leather pillow, and tried to keep her mind off the ruins of her long-time friendship with Simon Cullen. Instead, she focused on the conundrum that was Kolawole Aboyade. She got nowhere at all. The man and his motives seemed like some kind of maze without an exit – in fact, forget an exit – it would be nice if she could take two steps forward without banging her head against a brick-wall cul-de-sac. Could a man who had made love to her as he had, with such mastery and ease – could such a man possibly be *gay*? She didn't at all believe in bisexuality – the real drive had to be towards one sex or the other. So where did that leave Kolawole?

Inexplicably running north with Simon in pursuit.

"Make sense of it if you can!" she whispered vehemently to herself, hitting the leather pillow with her fist.

*Did* he have a bronze mask up his ass? Was that the missing piece of the puzzle? But, if the yarn about Aminatu was just a smokescreen for his nefarious exploits why had he now blown his alibi sky-high? Oh, for God's sake, it made no sense! If he were fleeing the country with a bronze mask up his ass, he'd hardly leave a letter in Zaria saying exactly where he was heading!

OK, forget the mask. Funtua. She had met Kola in Funtua. What if . . . what if he had never intended to go any farther? Maybe he had just been going through the motions, laying a false trail for Simon's benefit. But he had met her there and seized on the opportunity – hitched a ride and the perfect means of demonstrating that he had really gone to Tahoua. That had to be it! So . . . that implied he was trying to shake Simon off by pretending he was getting hitched to a woman. But why go *north* where he knew no one? Wouldn't he have dozens of boltholes south in Yorubaland and dozens of girlfriends and distant cousins he could claim to be marrying?

So . . . let's say there was an Aminatu, after all. Maybe he was now simply trying to prevent Simon from bouncing in on her and her family like the cat among the pigeons? But, if so, why didn't he just tell Simon to fuck off? Because he intended to deal with the Aminatu situation and then go back to take up his relationship with Simon.

And now she had completed yet another circuit back to square one which was somehow always Simon.

Maybe, at the end of the day, the man was in shock, had taken fright at Simon's bridge-too-far gender-confusion and didn't know what the hell he was doing.

OK. Leave that one. Another question: why have sex with her? To prove to her, himself, Simon that he wasn't gay? Or because he bloody wasn't gay? Fuck.

It was hopeless.

Why was he living with Simon to begin with? Here again there was a multiple-choice answer: a) for a comfortable rent-free gaff and other perks; b) he was a homophobic sadist into domination; c) he loved him.

One thing was for sure: whatever murky waters he and Simon were swimming in she had no business stirring them and she should never, never, never have had sex with Kolawole. But, he was so rushingly, achingly, manfully, irresistibly sexual.

She had only to think of him and she was squirming.

Which raised the question: why had she slept with him? Multiple choice: a) sheer lust b) sheer lust c) sheer lust.

And, last but not least, d) sheer lust.

She giggled in the darkness, then tried saying his name aloud: "Kola."

A hand touched the bare skin of her arm. She nearly died of fright.

"Kola?" she said softly, turning onto her back.

"Jan?" The voice was soft, tentative.

"Kola?" she whispered.

Silence.

She sat up slowly and peered in the dimness of the tent at the figure squatting beside the bed. She put out her hand and touched the soft hair.

"Oh, it's *you*!" she said, her heart lurching into her throat.

Out under the moon, Tom was kneeling in a hollow in the sand, preparing to wrap Pooh Bear in a nice piece of cotton for better protection and to keep him comfy.

He gave him a little cuddle. "There!" he said, kissing him. "Tommy will keep you safe! Don't you worry! We'll soon be back in England and you can share my bed again like you used to. You deserve it! You're a good little teddy bear!" He laid the bear down on the green and yellow cotton cloth and pulled his legs up as if he were a baby about to be changed.

He pressed Pooh's tummy hard with his fingers and frowned.

"So-rry! Does that hurt? Be a good little bear and it will soon be over. OK?"

He put his finger between the bear's legs and pushed it into a slit in the threadbare fake fur there. He knew he shouldn't – he would have to stitch it up once again.

"Anow!" Jan stumbled out of the tent and after him over the sand. Her voice was anguished.

He kept on going with that swift swinging powerful gait, hair a halo against the moonlight.

"Anow! Anow!"

He was outdistancing her, practised as he was in walking on shifting sands.

"Anow! Please!"

She stumbled on, muscles aching as she pushed and slid against the sand in her flat flip-flops.

He kept walking. She kept on doggedly pursuing.

A group of tents loomed up in the moonlight ahead of his striding figure. He halted at the first one he reached and half-turned and stood waiting for her, a hostile figure.

Her steps faltered. She came up to him, gasping. "Don't do this to me! I've been so worried about you!"

"So worried that you gave me his name!"

Oh, what could she say? What kind of instinct had made him so swiftly and unerringly slice right to the truth on hearing Kola's name whispered in the darkness? But he always had that keen perception of her.

She stood there, trying to select a lie that would comfort him, that would be closer to the true heart of the matter which was that she was wild with joy and relief at seeing him and that he was precious to her.

There was a movement at the tent entrance and a woman emerged with an awkward, shuffling movement that puzzled Jan who was used to the limber fluid way Tuareg people entered and exited their low-slung tents.

"Jan!" came a voice in the wrong accent.

The woman threw back her black veil and smiled up at her. It was Marie.

Simon had been walking round and round the camp in a wide circle, fearful of moving out of earshot of it and getting lost. He kept stumbling over lovers huddled in the sand in the course of his circuit, possibly the same ones repeatedly to judge from their hilarity and the mock-abuse they threw at him as he appeared yet again, gaunt and distraught. Well, he assumed he must be looking gaunt and distraught with the welter of poisonous thoughts coursing through his addled head as he obsessively went over the scene of the violently hissed and whispered and spat and growled quarrel with Kola. Maybe, on the other hand, it was a whole circle of pairs of lovers who had taken up position like the numbers on the face of an imaginary clock whose centre was at the camp. And he, unwittingly, was following the outer perimeter.

At one point he was halted in his tracks by the interesting sight of his erstwhile friend Jan staggering along in pursuit of a young man who looked like Anow, big hand and small hand making for twelve o'clock. So Anow had turned up – having heard about Jan through the Ikus-Ikoos grapevine presumably. And wouldn't he be charmed to hear that Kola had so kindly understudied for him in his absence? He must make it his business to let Anow know. But . . . actually it looked like Anow might know already . . .

He watched them cross his circuit and head out into the sand.

He resumed his course. Walkabout. An Australian Aboriginal tradition.

Much later, now exhausted, he returned to the camp and the tent that, perversely, he was still sharing with Kola. There was a light inside. Torchlight.

He squatted down and looked inside. Kola was seated on the wooden bed, a letter in his hand.

"'Not a Day without a Scribble'! These letters seem to be an obsession with you," said Simon dryly. He was too deflated for anger.

Kola froze momentarily. Then he flicked off the torch he was using, ducked his head and came out from under the hang of the tent.

Simon stood up again, arms down by his sides, in a defeated pose, as Kola faced him, holding the letter aloft.

"What is this?" asked Kola tensely.

"I have no idea," said Simon wearily. "Isn't it one of your creations?"

"No, it is yours!"

"Oh, I think you're the letter-writer, aren't you?" said Simon. "And stop shouting – I'm too tired."

"I didn't write this one. It was written by Jimoh Igwe, your so-called 'College Son'!"

"My what?" Simon asked blankly.

"You say you don't know Jimoh Igwe?"

"Jimoh Igwe? Yes, I know him – he's a first-year student –"

"So you admit it!" shouted Kola.

"Admit what?"

"Admit you have accepted his offer!"

Simon's deflation was giving way to amazement as Kola began to wave the piece of notepaper in the air. "What offer?" he asked in annoyance. "I don't know what you're talking about!"

"I'm talking about this letter!" shouted Kola.

"I never had a letter from him! And for God's sake, shut the fuck up! We're surrounded by sleeping people here! Look over there! You're waking them up! They've come out to see what's going on!"

"This was in your bag!" hissed Kola.

"*In my bag!* No, it was not! And how dare you –"

"Are you saying I am lying?"

"It *wasn't* in my bag – oh!" Simon's hand went to his mouth as he remembered the exchange with Jan.

"Ah! You remember now! All right. I have listened to you read many letters aloud and laugh your head off at their childish stupidity. Let us see if you will laugh at this one!" Kola flicked on the torch.

"Kola! Listen –"

But, having worked himself into a trembling rage by now, Kola began to read in a violent tone – the effect rather spoiled by the fact he had to whisper and peer awkwardly at the letter in the light of the torch.

"*Dear Teacher,*" he read. "*Top of the day for you over there. Hope there is no trouble. How is your work hope it is go on smoothly if so? Glory be to God.*

*The theme of this letter to you is that I want you to be my College Mother. I will be very grateful if you can consider my letter Ma.*"

Simon listened in growing amazement. Jan had been right. One for the scrapbook indeed. This was a classic. Even in this moment of trauma the thought crossed his mind that something had to be done about the standard of first-year English.

Kola was in full swing. "*Please Ma, do not surprise how I known your address. Then I known your address when as I am one of your student. and have visited you at your house. Then as your performance and the way you behave to me and embrase me made me to know your loving hart and made me writting you as my college Mother.*

*I will be wait for your reply because of my resons you will consider me your college son.*

*I drop my biro here.*
*Yours faithfully*
*Jimoh Igwe."*

Kola paused in his spluttering speech and looked at Simon with withering scorn before adding, "PPS I *apreciate the way you are looking so sexy in your African wrapper."*

He held his pose dramatically, the torch's circle of light still focused on Exhibit A: the letter.

Exhibit A, thought Simon. How did *I* get to be in the dock? And it's not even my letter! A torrent of thoughts and emotions thundered through his head.

Then, as if Kola suddenly felt stupid, he lowered his hand and flicked off the torch.

Anger suddenly ripped through Simon like a bush fire. This bastard was trying to turn the tables on him! Attack being the best part of defence, no doubt! "How fucking dare you?" he hissed in a white fury. "You fucking retard! After what you did to me, you have the nerve to work yourself into a passion about an innocent letter from a kid! You appalling fucking cretin! You're fit for nothing better than your retarded pen-pushing! *Sunshine Boy Advises!* So what's your pen name, may I ask? Arsehole Boy? *Arsehole Boy Lets Off? Arsehole Boy Tosses Off?"*

Kola's expression began to frighten Simon. He knew he was going too far but no force on earth could halt him. "Well," he continued with false briskness, "I had forgotten about that letter – I got it the morning I left Zaria – but, you know, I think I'm going to take Jimoh up on his offer. I mean, since I have a vacancy for a lodger and no doubt he would appreciate a comfortable billet. *Excuse* me!" He pushed his way past Kola and, ducking down, entered the tent.

A moment later a leather drawstring bag came flying like a ball from a cannon, slamming into Kola's groin with a resounding smack.

Simon covertly watched Kola stand for a long time before a dark hand reached down and picked up the bag.

*Don't go*, he thought, *don't go!*

He watched in despair as Kola slowly made his way to the next tent.

## Chapter 14

"'Ere! I must tell you this! I've been *dying* to tell someone!"

Jan was familiar with the little-boy mood but was finding the spectacle of Ned in horizontal position disconcerting. As the sun began to set on another day, he was stretched out, seemingly at ease, ankles crossed, pipe in one hand, weight supported by the other elbow. This pose allowed him to toss his head back when he wanted to chortle – which was often.

Gone were the days (like, yesterday) when he had scorned to sit on a mat. In the space of two days, Ned Bassett had gone native.

She grinned at the notion.

Marie Ogunbesan, still in Tuareg gear, sat on a mat nearby, regarding Ned quizzically.

Marie's arrival at the camp with Anow had earned Jan a scorching lecture from Hetty Coleman. After which the other expats suspected that she had, indeed, smuggled

Marie across the border. Kola, who could have cleared her, had maddeningly and typically kept mischievous silence, thereby confirming every suspicion – and they all had kept discreet silence on the matter, of course, when Marie was around.

"'Ere!" giggled Ned. He hunched his shoulders in little-boy glee at telling his secret. "You know what I found out?"

"About the Tuareg girls?" asked Jan ironically.

"No, no no! Little teases, all of them! Just leading me on! Though I must admit I'm having fun! Ah-hah-hah-hah!"

"So what then?"

"About our friend Cous-Cous."

"Oh! What?" She was immediately fearful of what the answer might be – she didn't need any more ghastly surprises.

"Ah-hah-hah-hah-*hah*! I shouldn't really be saying this in front of ladies – well, you're not a lady, Jan, I know – but Marie is and –"

"Oh, go on, Ned!" said Jan.

"Well . . ." He moved in closer, the better to stage-whisper his news. "He confessed to me –" he hunched his shoulders again and giggled, "that he shags sheep!" Slapping a beefy hand over his mouth to suppress his chuckles.

"Ne-ed!" said Jan, not very amused. "He was joking!"

Marie raised her eyebrows, clearly shocked.

"No, he wasn't!" Ned chortled. "We had several conversations about it – on the road, you know – when we stopped for tea and that. And they were all serious discussions. I questioned him very thoroughly. 'Ere! He explained that it was more often done with goats and camels – or the occasional donkey – as the Tuareg don't actually keep much sheep. Oh, Marie, my dear, I *am* sorry! I'm so used to Jan here and she has no breeding when it comes to sex. I'm sorry if I've spoiled your romantic idea of these Lords of the Desert!"

Marie didn't respond to this and looked a bit frosty. Jan suspected she belonged to that strange group of people she had most trouble understanding: people who *really* would prefer *not* to hear gossip and smut. This was beyond Jan, who thrived on gossip and smut, and would *always* want to know everything about everyone.

"'Ere, Jan! *You* know it's true – you know how earthy they are under all that outward dignity!"

Marie looked enquiringly at Jan, apparently considering her the authority on the matter.

"Well, I have heard of some things . . ." Jan said reluctantly.

"Yes! 'Ere! It's a regular practice! They all do it. Often, he says!"

"But why would he tell *you* such a thing?" asked Marie very astutely. "You are not such good friends, I think,"

"No – but he thinks nothing of it! Nothing! Chatted away about it." He leant forward again, face alight. "Told me how they do it with camels – tricky, that is! In fact, when I was wondering about . . . well," he paused in one of his rare moments of delicacy, "*size* . . . he even offered to show me his – um, equipment. I haven't taken him up on that one! He might take a fancy to use it on me! Ah-hah-hah-hah-hah!" Ned thrashed about in his delight at the notion. "Oh, I'll have to watch out for Roger when we get back to Zaria when Cous-Cous comes visiting! Sounds like he'd 'roger' anything that moves!"

"*Nay-ed! Nay-ed!*"

"Oh, Christ, here they come again!"

It was the same two teases as before, beckoning at Ned to join them.

"Christ! They're wearing me out, you know! And I'm simply wasting my time. Half the time they lead me out into the sand and then disappear! And, crikey, it can be the devil to get back! Yesterday, I was heading off in the direction of Tahoua, it seems – lucky I met with a couple of men from the camp here!"

"*Nay-ed! Nay-ed!*"

"Oh, well!" With a sigh he clambered to his feet. "If I don't turn up by morning, send out the posse – I may be rambling somewhere between this and Algeria. Ah-hah-hah-hah1"

"*Nay-ed! Nay-ed!*"

Hitching up his trousers, he set off once again after the giggling girls.

"Jan?"

Startled, Jan turned back to Marie.

"I'm curious . . . do you think it's possible? From what you know? It is interesting, no? Whether desert people do such things – just like that!" She snapped her fingers.

Oh, the sheep-shagging. Marie had apparently got over her disgust and developed an academic interest in the subject. Jan thought it was interesting too but it wasn't just of academic interest to her. Because she was emotionally involved with the Tuareg she was disturbed and disgusted at the mere notion – even though she was sure it was no more than a notion . . . she thought. An image of the gentle, well-bred Ikus-Ikoos casually rogering a donkey flashed through her brain, followed by an even more unwelcome flash of Anow working on a sheep with gusto . . . she shuddered and, to close the subject, said, "The kids used to tell me that some unhinged men get up to that sort of thing all right . . ." Oh, God: the kids. 'The kids' had included a twelve-year-old Anow . . .

"Well, you know," said Marie, lowering her voice confidentially, "Anow did tell me that too."

Jan gasped. Had she spoken aloud? "Anow?"

"Yes! Please don't repeat this but he told me that when they were kids they used to spy on a certain man . . . I didn't know whether to believe him or not . . ."

Anow had told *her* that? "That must have been a strange conversation . . ." said Jan, as lightly as she could, though her face was flushing, her heart quailing.

Marie shrugged. "Oh, he's so young . . . he is, I think, a bit over-sexed at present."

A cold feeling began to climb up from Jan's gut. It suddenly dawned on her that Marie had no idea about her interest in Anow. She had to force herself to speak. "Oh, I hope he . . . didn't make a nuisance of himself?"

"Well . . ." Marie's mouth twisted wryly. She cast her eyes down and obviously hesitated. Then she looked up, her brow furrowed. "Can I tell you something? I must tell someone! I am feeling so guilty. And you have proved that you can be discreet."

Oh my God, *what*? "OK," said Jan, her head beginning to spin sickeningly.

Marie bit her lip. She leant forward, brown eyes earnest. "No one must know, Jan. *No one.* Do you promise?"

"Yes! I promise!" Tell me quickly! What?

Marie stared at her for a moment more, assessing her

level of seriousness. Then she said, "I allowed Anow to make love to me. Not once but many times! I lost my head after we had crossed the frontier – I can't understand what possessed me! I think I was mad for a little while, the relief was so great! And – and – it sounds stupid now but . . . I was so grateful to him and he was so eager."

She looked intently at Jan, needing a reaction.

A forlorn little "Oh!" was all Jan could come up with.

"I know it was a dreadful thing to do . . . but, Jan, it was so delicious! So young and so vigorous! Look at me! I am blushing!" She covered her face with her slim brown hands with their burnt-orange henna decorations. Then she looked up again, a gleam of mischief sparking in her eyes, a rueful little smile quirking her lips. "But don't you envy me, Jan? Isn't that something any woman would envy?"

Later that evening Tom nervously approached Hetty Coleman as she lounged outside her tent.

"H-h-h-hetty?"

"Yes, Tom?"

He mouthed as he stood there, satchel in his arms.

"Sit!"

He sat.

"H-h-h-hetty . . . I-I-I-I have been thinking . . ."

"Yes, what is it, man? Cough it up!" And she hit him a wallop between his shoulder blades.

It actually helped.

"I-I have something to tell you." He gulped and his Adam's apple did its yo-yo bounce.

"Well, go ahead! We're listening!"

We? Oh, yes, the dog.

"Well . . . if you remember I told you about that friend of mine who used to . . . h-h-howl at the moon?"

"Ah, yes! I certainly do!"

"Well, you see, that was me."

Hetty stared at him. "I suspected that!" she boomed. "Ajax, what did I tell you? I said he was a howler! Excellent!"

Tom was bemused at this response but supposed it must be positive. At least she saw him as an interesting problem. He pressed on. "I-I-I thought you could give me some help in the matter –"

"Help!" Hetty boomed. "Of course I can give you help! You shouldn't have hesitated to ask!"

"Y-y-you w-w-would agree to do a session or two w-w-with me?

"Any time!"

"Thank you." The relief! He continued more bravely, "You see –"

"Do you want to do it now?" There was a wild gleam of enthusiasm in her eyes.

"Well, I hadn't considered doing it *now* but – if you wish . . ."

"Have you seen the moon?" She lifted a sturdy finger aloft.

"Y-y-y-yes! It's making me nervous."

"That's because you are fighting against your urges. Come!"

The command seemed intended for both him and the dog.

Tom rose and followed Ajax in Hetty's wake. This was sudden but why not? Might as well bite the bullet. A psychiatric session in this unusual setting might be painless.

Hetty strode ahead, cotton dress flapping with the vigour of her movement. Tom glanced nervously behind. He didn't really think they should get out of sight of the campfires.

She stopped on a rise. "This should do nicely." She sat down, cross-legged in the sand, and Ajax lined up and sat beside her. It obviously wasn't the dog's first psychiatric session. The huge moon glowered down at them.

"Should I l-l-l-lie down?" asked Tom.

"If you wish – but I find that sitting is more effective."

"Oh, right then." He sat cross-legged facing Hetty, his bag on his lap.

"Turn and face the moon, man."

"Oh, right." He faced the moon, in line with Hetty and the dog.

"Should I begin?" he asked.

She was wearing that wolfish grin again, he was alarmed to note.

"Please do."

He gulped and swallowed, What should he tell her first? About Jan? About Pooh Bear? Should he talk about his fears of becoming a werewolf? Suddenly his Adam's apple felt like a real huge apple-core stuck in his throat. "I'm a bit nervous," he croaked.

"Relax, man! No problem! In that case, let me take the lead."

He nodded gratefully.

Hetty threw back her head.

Tom waited nervously for the first question.

Then Hetty began to howl at the moon, Ajax joining in on cue.

Jan and Kola were interrupted in their labours by the howling of wolves – or dogs – or hyenas? They had carried a mat to the top of a little ridge behind the camp – an excellent vantage point for their purpose.

Earlier that day, Anow had escorted Simon on a camel-ride to visit the local silversmith, intending to spend the night there – which left Jan and Kola free to get up to mischief.

They had planned the meeting earlier that day, before Jan's heart had been put through the wringer by Marie, but now she was glad of something to distract her. She suspected that Kola was in exactly the same state of mind, thankful for a bit of light relief.

They now bent over their labours, helpless with laughter.

"Oh, come on, Sunshine Boy, take this seriously!"

"I wish you would stop calling me that! I have never called myself Sunshine Boy! I *know* Sunshine Boy and he's a retard! Now, I have on occasion called myself 'Art Adidas', 'Stephen Reebok', and 'Johnny Surfer' which are altogether more up-to-date!"

"Kola!"

Kola sobered up and applied himself once more to the task of composing the letter. "OK, OK! How does this sound? *'Dear Ned, My heart beats fast in my bosom at the thought that you may respond positively to this letter . . .'*"

"What's that sodding noise?" Ned went through a virtuoso performance of neck-craning and gaping. "'Ere, do you have wolves out here?"

"No," said Ikus-Ikoos, looking up from his tea-making. "It must be dogs. Unusual."

Ned squatted down uncomfortably, wincing as his thighs took the strain. "'Ere! Cous-Cous! You're looking very pleased with yourself! Have you heard some news about Fatty?"

"Not yet," said Ikus-Ikoos, smiling. "Patience is everything."

"That's fine for you to say! You haven't lost your money! Oh, no! Or your bride-to-be! I'll bet you'll be off for a spot of slap and tickle with a lady-friend later on, by the light of the silvery moon!"

"Umm – maybe so," grinned Ikus-Ikoos.

Ned settled himself on the mat, legs stretched straight out in front of him, taking his weight on a brawny arm. "Christ, those sodding dogs are noisy buggers! Listen to that!"

Ikus-Ikoos had never heard anything like it. Maybe he should go and investigate?

"'Ere! Cous-Cous?"

"Yes?"

"I thought you told me you'd left your inamorata behind in Zaria!"

Ikus-Ikoos's face creased in his lovely smile as he proceeded with his tea-making. In a voice almost gurgling with laughter he said, "Oh, well, courtship is our big business in life here. We don't have TV, you know! Or nightclubs!"

"A girl in every port, wot? Or a camel! Ships of the desert that pass in the night! Ah-hah-hah-hah-hah!"

"Something like that. Will you try some tea?"

"Don't mind if I do."

Ikus-Ikoos began his condensed milk operation.

"So aren't you rushing off to copulate? Ah-hah-hah-hah!"

"Later. It's always better later." Ikus-Ikoos flashed him a smiling glance.

"Keep 'em waiting, eh? That's the policy. Eh? What does *he* want? A suit of clothes for a start! Ah-hah-hah!"

A small naked boy was standing by the mat with a certain formality, for all his nakedness, that suggested business. However, he seemed dumbstruck at the sight of Ned squinting at him at close quarters.

Ikus-Ikoos took his dusty brown hand and drew him close and in doing so discovered that he had a small folded paper in his hand. "A message, it seems!" He gently pulled the little fellow down and cuddled him against his side. He opened the paper and read. "Oh!" He held it out to Ned between two fingers. "It's in English and it's for you!"

Ned goggled at the letter as if it might bite him, then took it.

"I can't read it in this sodding light," he grumbled.

"Here, take this," said Ikus-Ikoos with long-suffering patience. He snapped on a torch and handed it to Ned.

"Ah, that's more like it . . . let's see . . . *Dear Ned*, . . ." He read on.

Then looked up at Ikus-Ikoos. "Well, I'll be buggered! The old fart fancies me!"

"Who?"

"Hetty! Hetty Coleman! She's inviting me for a lovers' tryst in her tent!"

Ikus-Ikoos didn't know what a tryst was any more than he knew what to be buggered meant, but he grasped the idea about Hetty rapidly. He laughed delightedly, hugging the little boy. "It's so appropriate! That is exactly what a Tuareg lady does! Invites a man secretly to her tent!"

"*Listen! My heart beats fast in my bosom in the hope that you may respond positively to this letter. Please come to my tent tonight but not before midnight. Before then do not betray the interest between us . . . Your Hetty!* Ah-hah-hah-hah! My God, she's mad for it! You know, I *thought* so earlier! I noticed her looking at me slyly from under her fringe and hitching up her dress over her bloomers' leg."

"You will go?"

"Why not?" chortled Ned. "Don't mind if I give her an old rummage she won't forget! She's a mad old baggage but quite a handsome woman nevertheless. Gorgeous skin. Fine thighs! Frighteningly strong they look! I hope she's not one of those killer women who like to strangle their victims at the moment of climax! What a way to go! Ah-hah-hah-hah-hah! Oooh, I wouldn't miss it for the world!"

Jan and Kola were playing chess by the light of the moon while they watched from their vantage point and waited for Ned to make his move. Jan had been startled when Kola produced the chess set from the depths of his leather fringed bag – and not a cheapo or nasty little travel-set either. It was made of wood with a fold-over hinged board and fine smooth heavy pieces. The tactile pleasure of handling them, the weight of them in her hand, added hugely to the kick she was getting from the game and the sheer surreal sensation of playing under such circumstances. She knew before they even started that she hadn't a hope in hell of beating him.

"Pawn to Queen's Castle," said Kola half an hour later having already beaten her twice.

"What?"

He indicated with a nod of the head.

Below them, Ned was cautiously crossing the sand to Hetty's tent.

Ned squatted down at the entrance of the tent. A low growl greeted him.

"Hetty? Is that you?" he stage-whispered, creeping inside.

The growl turned to a snarl and Ned remembered the sodding dog.

"*Oh, Christ!*" he yelled.

A deluge of hairy animal descended on him and he found himself pinned flat on his back on the ground, Helpless beneath 80-odd pounds of dog, he braced himself for the ravening fangs to sink into his neck. Instead, as the animal slavered and slathered all over his face, he became aware of a quite familiar rhythm beating itself on his nether regions.

*"Hetty!"* he yelled in horror. *"Your dog is ravishing me!"*

Ajax had already withdrawn, well satisfied, and Ned was lying there practically in tears at the humiliation of being a sex-aid for a German Shepherd, when Hetty's boom sounded from the low wooden bed. "Bassett!"

"Hetty!" he cried peevishly. "Why didn't you help me! I couldn't get up and I was afraid he would bite!"

"No. I don't allow him to bite. Well, come up now, man!"

Ned felt a powerful hand grasp his arm and pull him upwards. He half-rose, then lost his balance and collapsed across Hetty on the bed. But only for a moment, as, with some sophisticated wrestler's move she flipped him over and slammed him on his back on her other side. Eighty pounds of amorous German Shepherd was one thing – but one hundred and fifty pounds of growling Hetty Coleman was something else.

Ned was resigning himself to his fate when he felt a wet tongue licking the palm of his hand and realised that Ajax was coming back for more . . .

Kola carefully packed the chess set into his bag and pulled a handful of roll-your-own cigarettes from one of its pockets. "This is what the doctor ordered," he said. "For both of us."

She opened her mouth to protest that she didn't smoke, then paused and peered. They were joints. She eyed the bag. "Well, aren't you the regular Mary Poppins?" What next? Bronze masks and gold heads? She should have searched the bag properly when she had the chance at the *campement*.

They lay back, stared at the moon and got to work on some serious relaxation.

At length, dazed and drowsy, the edge taken off both pain and pleasure, she turned her head and stared at him. What if? And why not?

Why not take this man on? It would be a far more viable reltionship than any she could have with a Tuareg – bar Ikus-Ikoos maybe.

Why not? Simon why not. Anow why not. Her love of the Tuareg why not.

But especially Simon why not.

She loved that guy.

And there was another 'but' . . .

But . . .

What was the other but?

But, even if she didn't love Anow – and she did love Anow, she knew that now – the trouble was . . .

"Kola?"

"Umm?"

"Do you love Simon?"

"Yes."

That was the other but.

Much later she got the spaced-out notion of spying on Marie and Anow, to see if they were sleeping together. They set out in what she hoped was the right direction, Kola's arm about her, supporting her.

They came upon the little thorn tree so suddenly it seemed to rear up before them and even then Jan didn't see the black-robed figure squatting on the ground, back to them. It rose from the ground and swung around at the same time, facing into the moonlight with a wild cry, a hand to a face that gleamed green around black empty eye-sockets.

Jan's heart nearly stopped and she broke away from Kola and was stumbling across the sand when she heard the urgent and familiar female voice.

*"Jan! Jan! Please come back! Come back!"*

She swung around again and stared.

"Jan! It's only me! Marie!"

It was Marie and there was nothing wrong with her face. As they drew near, she raised a heavy bowl-like object she was holding against her side. "I'm sorry – it was stupid – but I couldn't resist looking at it – I needed the comfort." She gave a little laugh. "And now I will have to explain everything to you."

She shrugged and raised the object again and held it in

front of her face: a mask, bronze and unmistakeably Nigerian.

Hetty was sitting up on her wooden bed, leaning against a tent-pole. Watching her warily, Ned was very fearful that her weight would bring the whole tent down around their ears. Ajax was peacefully asleep next to Hetty on the bed.

Hetty had rummaged Ned, good and proper, rather than the other way round.

"Bassett," she growled eventually. "Thank you for coming. But if you don't mind – I have to ask you to leave now."

"Eh? Oh, that's no bother!" What a relief! "Eh, if I get down on the floor to look for my pipe he's not likely to mount me again, is he?"

"Not at all, man! Can't you see the dog is asleep? Go ahead."

Ned cautiously began to crawl about the ground looking for the pipe, a cautious eye on Ajax.

"Bassett?"

"Eh? Aaahh! Found it!"

"Good. Now leave."

Ned felt honour-bound to protest a little at this abruptness. "Eh, that's not very gracious of you, is it, Hetty? I said I'm leaving!"

Ajax opened an eye and growled.

"Oh, right then! I'm off! Thanks for the – the – encounter." He clambered to his feet and began to feel his pipe over for damage.

"I think you'd better go now," said Hetty.

Christ, the old mare was in some hurry to get shot of

him, now that she'd had her oats. What was her hurry? "You expecting someone else then?" he joked.

"I am not an indiscreet person, Ned," growled Hetty.

"Oh, certainly not! I didn't mean to imply that you were! Well, I'm off now!"

Ten minutes later, Ned, crouched behind a neighbouring tent, was rewarded for his wait by the sight of Tom Purthill, canvas bag under his arm, crawling into Hetty's tent where he was greeted by a chorus of growls and yelps.

Ikus-Ikoos strode across the sand, his heart as high as the moon. He knew there was a silly smile fixed on his face but he didn't care. He had been patient, very patient. But now he would reap his reward. She had kept her word. He ducked his head in embarrassed joy as he thought that he was soon to be, in one blow, a husband and father.

His blood raced. All the tension, all the waiting was worth this moment – all the hours of enduring Ned Bassett's ravings. He had only to stretch out his hand. And stretch it he would. He laughed aloud!

She was so wonderful. He could smell her perfume already – heady, musky, arousing. He imagined what she would say. And do. A shiver of anticipation ran up his spine. Aaah! What she would do!

If there had been any doubt that she truly wanted him, that doubt was fled away. She would walk through fire to be with him!

There!

There she was!

Standing by the palm-tree, her silver jewellery glittering in the powerful moonlight.

There she was – arms outstretched in welcome – just as he had imagined in his dreams.

His pace quickened and his pulse beat hard.

But no – her arms weren't outstretched – he must have imagined that . . .

He was almost upon her. He pulled the folds of his *tagilmoust* further down beneath his chin.

"My Maryam!" he called, his voice thick with desire and emotion.

He strode the last few yards towards her, arms wide.

"Sheep-shaggaire!" shrieked Marie Ogunbesan and, drawing back a well-toned brown leg, kicked him soundly in the balls.

And then added further insult to injury: "*Espèce* de sheep-shaggaire!"

## Chapter 15

The morning after the night before arrived far too early. The Zarians were woken at a ghastly hour, the sky barely streaked with pink, by a combination of goats prancing over their beds, naked kids gathering in throngs to gaze in their half-sleeping faces, old women exhorting them reproachfully to rise as the day was half gone and, in the case of Ned Bassett, by two great globes of flesh prodding him in the face.

He opened his eyes, thinking he was still in Dreamland.

Dreamland or no, it was Fatty! Kneeling on a mat by the wooden bed and reaching up behind his head to get down a charcoal brazier tied to a tent-pole.

He truly didn't believe his eyes. He sat up and put on his glasses. It was her! Sitting there, busying herself making tea.

"Tom! Tom!" he stage-whispered to his bed-partner who was sleeping like a log beside him. "It's her! It's my girl Fatty! Wake up!"

Tom groaned, squeezing his satchel to his chest.

"Fatty!" said Ned.

She smiled. *"Nay-ed! Ina kwana?"* Ned, *how was your sleep?*

It was her! She was now wearing a black veil and had a different hairstyle but he'd know those boobs anywhere. And there was his watch on her wrist besides. He lay back down, though he was dying to relieve himself, and watched her entranced.

They were even bigger than he had remembered in his fantasies. As she went through the motions of making tea they jiggled, they bounced, they swayed, they swung, they got in her way and she pushed them aside, they rested comfortably on her lap when she leaned a little forward. The nipples really were like saucers. Heaven, he thought, I've died and gone to Boob Heaven.

There was a movement at the tent entrance.

"Jan! Jan!" he said delightedly. "Look here! It's Fatty!"

Jan crawled into the tent and stared. "Oh, God," she said.

"What's the matter? I've found her! Or she's found me!"

Jan had her fist to her mouth, her eyes on the woman.

*"Ina kwana, Jan!"* said Fati cheerfully.

"'Ere! How does she know your name?"

*"Lafiya, Jan?"* asked Fati. *Are you well, Jan?*

*"Lafiya kalau,"* Jan answered belatedly, still staring in apparent horror. And then, to Ned, "Are you sure?"

"Am I sure what?"

"That this is Fati?"

"Of course I'm sure, you silly sod! Look! Don't you see? She's wearing my *watch*!"

Jan gaped at the watch, then closed her eyes. Her face had flushed a deep pink-red.

"What's up?" said Ned, squinting. "I *know* they're embarrassingly big. But I thought *you* were used to these naked women."

"No, it's not that . . ." She opened her eyes and shook her head.

"What's the matter with you then? Jealous, are you? Ah-hah-hah-hah!"

"God, Ned . . ."

"What?"

"This is the woman I brought from Zaria . . ."

"*Wot?*" Ned sprang up in shock. "But that's impossible!" he blustered.

"It's not," said Jan in a small voice. "I did."

"But you told me it wasn't her! *You silly sod! How could you not know?*"

"They were calling her Takowilt – I guess it's a nickname. They all have nicknames – like Anow's proper name is Issouf and Ikus-Ikoos's is Ibrahim. I'm sorry – how could I know? And, Ned! She has three children! A small boy and two young girls! You told me she was a virgin!"

Ned was now thrown into a violent state of agitation. His dream-state disrupted, he remembered the true state of affairs – in particular, the loss of his money. *"Three children!"* he ranted. "I knew it! I knew it! I knew she couldn't have sodding great boobs like that without a bunch of suckling infants! I knew I had been cheated! I'm going to get the sly buggers!" He shook his fist and Fati cowered, sheltering behind her veil.

He clambered out of the tent past her and her tea-things, staggering upright outside. "Jan! Jan! Let's find Cous-Cous!

There's the girl, bold as brass, sitting in my tent – wearing my watch – *when they stole my money!* The sodding crooks!"

They found Ikus-Ikoos lying dejectedly on the bed in his tent, *tagilmoust* drawn over his face.

He pulled the veil down an inch and surveyed Jan and Ned with lacklustre eye as they crawled in.

"'Ere! 'Ere, Cous-Cous! They're here! Fatty is in my tent! Did you find them? Contact them? Was it you?" Ned clambered onto the bed and sat, his arse shoving Ikus-Ikoos's legs out of its way.

"No, it wasn't me," said Ikus-Ikoos in a voice that was almost a groan.

"Well, come on then! We must confront them! She's bold as brass in my tent right now!"

Ikus-Ikoos didn't move a muscle.

"*I must get my money!* Come on, you lazy sod! Show a leg!"

For answer, Ikus-Ikoos's eyes flickered.

Christ, thought Jan, what's the matter with him? "Are you ill, Ikus-Ikoos?" she asked, alarmed. "Do you have a fever?"

"No, no," he answered with a groan.

"'Ere, Cous-Cous," said Ned, aggrieved, "you can't let me down now! Fatty could bugger off again! *I must get my money back!*"

Another groan issued from behind Ikus-Ikoos's veil.

They were at a loss.

"Cous-Cous!" wailed Ned.

With a sigh Ikus-Ikoos pushed himself upright, pulled his legs sluggishly around Ned's backside and swung them to the ground – wincing as he did so – and adjusted his veil.

He clasped his hands and began to fidget with his silver rings.

"Ned," he said ominously.

They waited.

He reached inside the huge pocket in the front lining of his cotton gown and withdrew a thick bundle of naira notes, tied with an elastic band. He handed this to Ned.

"You already got it!" cried Ned in delight. "You got my money!" He pressed the bundle to his lips. "Ummm-mah!"

There was a silence from Ikus-Ikoos. Then another deep sigh. "No," he said wearily.

"No, what?" asked Ned.

"No, I didn't get it . . . I had it all the time."

"Eh?"

"I never gave the bride-price to Fati's family. Her mother absolutely refused to allow her to marry you."

"What? What? What?" spluttered Ned. He was flummoxed. Even his paranoia couldn't square Ikus-Ikoos with the idea of daylight robbery. "But – but why did you keep it? W-w-were you trying to cheat me?"

"No. I always intended to give it back. But I had my reasons for wanting to cross the border in your company."

"Wanting to cross the border! What do you mean? I had to *beg* you to come with me!"

Ikus-Ikoos sighed again. "No, no. I was leaving for Niger that morning in any case."

"But . . ." Ned gaped.

"In fact, I . . . well, it was I who manipulated you into going . . ."

"*What?*"

The real question is 'Why?', thought Jan. But she knew the answer – and many other answers – after hearing Marie Ogunbesan's confessions.

"Well . . . you saw how aggressive the custom officers are. I thought it would be safer for me to cross in the company of a European, a Senior Lecturer," said Ikus-Ikoos.

And that was only half the story, thought Jan.

"Oh, I see," said Ned, flattered. "I suppose that makes sense. They were very aggressive, it's true." He stared at his pile of money. Then back at Ikus-Ikoos in wonder. "So all that to-ing and fro-ing between you and Fati's people was fake?"

"Oh, I was negotiating marriage for you all right! But they never agreed."

"So you told me they had scarpered with my money!" The enormity of the fraud perpetrated on him was keeping him on the calmer side of aghast.

"But how did you know Ned would follow them to Niger?" asked Jan.

"I didn't. It was just a gamble – that paid off." And he stretched himself out again on the bed in a gingerly fashion and covered his face with his *tagilmoust*.

Ned was in a state of shock.

"Come on, Ned," said Jan. "Let's go count your money – make sure it's all there, you know." She tugged him by the shirtsleeve and began to crawl out of the tent. She wanted to get him away before his bemusement turned to rage.

"Eh? Yes, yes."

To her relief he followed her like a lamb.

"Well, I'll be buggered!" he gasped as he exited.

"Oh, by the way, Ned!" Ikus-Ikoos called hollowly after

them. "That reminds me – last night I discovered in the most painful way what 'sheep-shagging' means."

Jan had never seen such a sorry bunch of travellers as assembled to leave for Nigeria two days later.

Hetty wasn't ready to go yet so there were just the two cars: the Land-Cruiser and the VW beetle. Without Fati-Takowilt and family, there was plenty of room but the seating arrangements were made complicated by rampant emotions.

Ned (by now in a thorough rage) wouldn't travel with Ikus-Ikoos, Simon wouldn't travel with Kola. But Jan didn't want Anow to see her head off with Kola nor did Kola want Simon to see him head off with Jan.

Ned climbed into the Land-Cruiser; Ikus-Ikoos got into the VW.

That left Kola in a quandary, like piggy-in-the-middle.

He stood between the two cars at a loss.

Around the cars stood those who were staying behind, each separate from the other, like mourners around a grave-site: Marie, Anow, Hetty, Ajax, Fati. Behind those again assorted nomads, goats, dogs and children.

At length Kola shrugged his shoulders and strode over to stand beside Hetty, dumping his bag on the sand at his feet.

Jan took it that he was staying.

She glanced over at the VW and saw Simon turn a ghastly white. Suddenly her eyes blurred and she slammed on her dark glasses as tears began to slide down her cheeks. She glared out the driver's window, away from Anow.

"Just a tick, Jan," said Ned thickly. He slid from the passenger seat and beckoned to Anow. Embarrassment evident in his every move, he then made his way to where

Fati-Takowilt stood, making a wide and wary circuit around Ajax who sat there at dignified attention, sporting a brand-new Tuareg red-and-green leather charm around his neck. Ned earnestly began to address Fati through Anow's translation.

Damn! thought Jan, fuming at this hijacking of Anow. She had been hoping against hope that he would abjectly approach her, begging to be taken back to Zaria. She would have refused, of course. Probably.

Tom, next to her in the Land-Cruiser with his satchel on his knees, was smiling coyly out at Hetty.

Hetty raised a hand. "See you in Zaria!" she boomed. "Full moon, remember!" Ajax barked – once, twice, like a salute.

Of all of them, Jan thought, the dog was making the most dignified farewell. And even as she thought this Marie came darting forward and laid a shaking hand on Ikus-Ikoos's elbow where it rested on the window of the VW. She seemed to be pleading. He didn't even turn his head to acknowledge her. After a few moments she let her hand drop and walked away, face twisting in tears.

Jan was able to interpret that. The dispute between the lovers was no longer about sheep-shagging. Anow had put his foot in it. Unwittingly, he had approached Ikus-Ikoos and begged him to plead with Jan on his behalf – beg her forgiveness for the fact he had been screwing Marie on the road to Tahoua. Ikus-Ikoos had on the instant abandoned his attempts to convince Marie that he had never shagged a sheep and, broken-hearted, decided to return to Zaria.

What a fucking disaster the whole expedition was, thought Jan.

Well, not altogether . . . Marie Ogunbesan had done well; she had escaped her violent husband with her children and her million-dollar mask – or at least her share in the proceeds if she could get it as far as a certain airstrip outside Agadez. Plus, of course, her percentage of the proceeds from the two gold heads smuggled out by her accomplices . . .

But she'd lost Ikus-Ikoos.

Ned had got his money back but had lost Fati – or had he? Yes, he had given up on his pleadings or offers and was trudging back to the car.

Tom had also done well. He seemed to have gained a dominatrix, an amorous German Shepherd, a future and possibly his sanity. Oh, and Pooh Bear was safe.

Simon had lost on every count.

So had she. Well, Anow was safe, at least. And there were the memories of Kola . . .

Kola?

What Kola had lost or gained was typically obscure. Still a conundrum.

Jan turned on the ignition and drove out of the camp, pursued by yelping dogs and children. She saw Ajax, off to the left, keeping pace with the Land-Cruiser for quite some time as it swayed through the sand. Then he halted and she felt utterly bereft as he put his tail between his legs and loped away.

Ahead lay Zaria, a gruesome last term and an unavoidable encounter with a certain gentleman not worthy of the name.

## Chapter 16

Jan knocked on Langley Forrest's door.

"Enter!"

Yes! At last, a whole week since her return to Zaria, she had caught him in his office.

"Ah! Jan!" He looked exactly as he had on her last visit – no – then the embroidery on his black shirt was silver. This time it was gold. Well, that was appropriate – he was coming up in the world after all.

She sat and studied him. He was apparently stone-cold sober for once in his life.

He smoked and surveyed her ironically through slitted grey eyes that glinted like mercury. So he knew she knew.

"I thought you would have retired on the proceeds by now," she said at last.

His eyes opened wide and his chin dipped, giving her the benefit of his best combination of little-boy charm and avuncular reproach. "I'm in no hurry, my dear. Contrary to popular opinion, I like it here."

"Well, it's a safe place to bide one's time, I suppose, and look forward to a pleasant and well-moneyed old age." *If he should live that long.*

"Oh, Jan, Jan, Jan! On your moral high-horse again? You're *still* so wet behind the ears. It's such a pity! I *do* like you! But what's to be done about your essential innocence? You wear it like an albatross around your neck." He sucked at his cigarette and stubbed it out.

"I wish *you* were wearing something around your neck! Like a noose, for instance!"

"I'll take that as a joke. Though I could be hurt by it."

"Hurt? *Hurt?* After what you did?"

He cocked an eyebrow and lit another cigarette. "Aah . . . so, Jan . . . you stumbled upon the truth –"

"Yes, in the guise of Marie Ogunbesan peering through a bronze mask."

He smiled and shook his head. "So stern, Jan, so intransigent! Ah, well, there will be time to mellow later. Leave wisdom to the aged – like me."

Wisdom, he called it. She was wasting her time. "Has Marie been in touch with you?"

"Not directly. Too risky. But I do know Marie delivered the mask and the other artefacts safely to the buyer from Saudi in Agadez – and collected her percentage – which was sizeable. I had decided to be generous with Marie – I am very fond of her. And after all, I do it for fun, you know – the money is secondary. Such a giggle and usually as easy as falling off a log – but never so laughably easy as this time! I had never actually been the curator of the objects of desire before!" He stubbed out his cigarette, smiling beatifically. "Do you know, the artefacts weren't even *in* the exhibition storeroom the night of the 'robbery'! Doesn't that take the proverbial biscuit?"

It did, really. But she refused to applaud. "Yes, I know. You'd taken them home."

"It only worked, of course, because it never dawned on the Nigerians that there should be a guard *inside* the building. To them, the proper place for a nightwatchman was outside. The guards, by the way, had wisely fled by the time the 'break-in' was officially discovered next morning – the faulty catch on a window and disruption in the storeroom. Oh, child's play! Such fun!"

"Fun! Yes, for you – sitting here in Zaria in comfort!"

He was looking at her benevolently as he lit up once more.

"But answer me! How could you put people – friends – at risk like that? Using us all as pawns in some game of chess!"

"Friends? Well, yes, of course – that was the point. Who else could I have trusted but friends?"

"So why not simply send your 'friends' to Kano with the stuff and get the Saudi buyer to come there?"

"Oh, no, no! He has a well-tried and tested system battened down in Agadez – he refused to pick up the stuff anywhere else. Besides, where would be the fun in just sending people up the road to Kano!"

"Oh, God!" Jan was speechless.

"Oh, come now, Jan! There was very little risk!" He smiled, leant on an elbow and shakily wagged a finger at her. "Now be a good girl and listen. My game of chess, as you call it, has freed Marie from a miserable marriage and ensured that she and her children are well provided for until she finds her feet. By now she must be safely in Algeria with her Tuareg paramour. You and your little boy are happy, I presume. Tom Purthill can afford a nice psychiatrist when he returns to England and your loopy faggot friend should now have a hold on that Yoruba which will never let go. And Ned – well," inspiration failed him, "Ned, I suppose, will always be Ned."

Jan frowned, perplexed by much of that – but said nothing, not wanting to give him the satisfaction of knowing she was in the dark. "But the *risk*!"

He dragged at his cigarette and smiled broadly. "I'm a *gambler*, Jan. A *gifted* gambler. And I don't lose when I feel inspired." He stared at her encouragingly through a drift of smoke, as if waiting for a light bulb to click on over her head or a speech-bubble to appear declaiming '*Now* I understand!'

When neither happened he looked pained. "Don't you see? *Everything* we do is risk. If we drive a car, fly, give birth, inoculate our children. We are *born* to take risks. What we must learn is how best to calculate them." He stubbed and sighed. "But such fun, Jan! I do wish I had been there! Such ingenuity! They all richly deserved their pay-offs! Who would have thought Tom Purthill would have the nerve? The gold head inside his teddy bear! Oh, that's rich!"

Jan smiled faintly. It was, in fact. And only one in his demented state would have risked simply popping it into the nearest loo or up a tree to get it past the police.

"And Ikus-Ikoos!" Langley rhapsodised, his grin wicked and glistening. "That was so clever! A sugar-cone with a cavity inside! Tom told me the Tuareg silversmith had done a beautiful job on it!" He stubbed and lit up. "And, best of all, my amateurs managed to fool the intelligence agent. That amazes me, I must confess."

Now Jan couldn't help but gape. "Agent? What agent?"

"Oh, don't you know?"

"No," said Jan hesitantly, still hating to concede an iota.

A wonderful smile transformed Langley's face – like one who hears the choirs of angels as he approaches the Throne of God. "You really don't know?"

"No, I don't," Jan said faintly. "Oh, my God! Hetty!"

"No, not Hetty!" said Langley. "Don't be silly!" He lit up another cigarette and inhaled deeply, eyes closed, face alight with the bliss of one-upmanship. Then he opened his eyes, stubbed out the cigarette and made a grab for the thermos flask by his elbow, knocked it over, righted it, unscrewed the cup and the cap –

Oh, n-o-o-o-o! thought Jan. Not the coffee routine!

Helpless, she watched as Langley went through the process of pouring, raising the plastic cup in a shaking hand, slopping it, sipping it, smacking the lips, taking a deep draught, smacking the lips again, closing the eyes, sighing blissfully, taking a drag from his cigarette, exhaling, sighing even more blissfully –

"I really must apologise to you, Jan," he said, eyes springing open. "I have no other cup here to offer you coffee –"

"Oh, bugger the coffee!"

His open-eyed mock-startled gaze was pure innocence. "Oh, don't be annoyed! I really *am* sorry – I *must* get Prissie to bring in some extra cups for the office."

She didn't trust herself to speak.

"Yes," he said at last. "Simon's paramour."

She waited. He didn't continue. "What about Simon's paramour?"

"He works for central intelligence, you know."

She couldn't believe her ears. "Who?"

"Who? Simon's live-in lover. Aboyade."

She stared. "You're telling me Kolawole Aboyade is a-a-a kind of detective?"

"Oh, yes." He beamed at her. "And a very good one, capable of the inspired hunch. He was on the trail right from the start."

Jan gaped. "On the trail! But I picked him up hanging around the market in Funtua!"

"*He* picked *you* up, my dear!"

"You mean he'd been *following* me! He suspected *me?*"

"Well, you see, he's crossed swords with me before – and I suspect that Simon Cullen told him about our interview regarding Tom Purthill and Immigration – sorry about that, by the way – I did have to exaggerate the situation rather. So, he did a clever bit of deduction and came very close to the right conclusion – in fact, if you had agreed to take Marie as I had planned, he would have been precisely right. But clever as he is, he wasn't quite clever enough to catch any of my people."

But he had caught them. And Marie had made a full confession that night in his hearing.

But he had done nothing about it.

"How do you know about any of that?" she asked. "About him?"

Langley smiled like an angel. "Well, of course, the police have been keeping me up to date on all their progress – and, wanting to impress me with all that was being done, were a little indiscreet."

"So that was the real reason Kola was on the road to Niger . . ." The implications of this sank in. "Oh, God, it had nothing to do with his feelings for Simon at all . . . or the Agony Aunt letters or anything . . ." Or me, she thought. "The pregnant Hausa girl was just a coincidence he used to cover his tracks. Oh, God . . . where does that leave Simon?"

"In a very strong position I would imagine, if you let him in on the secret – why, he'd have him over a barrel which is, I presume, *exactly* where he wants him! But, tell me, Jan, where do pregnant Hausa girls and Agony Aunts come into it?"

"Oh, there are some things you don't know, Langley."

Figuring that was as strong a parting-shot as was likely to come her way, Jan got up and made for the door.

"Jan! Wait, Jan! Tell me one thing – why did Hetty Coleman back down?"

Oh, wonderful! Langley begging her for information! She looked back and grinned spitefully at him as he sat, elbow on desk, stubbed-out cigarette poised, quizzical expression in place. "Oh, it must have been something to do with the phase of the moon, Langley."

To her delight, his expression of bafflement deepened.

She closed the door on the sight of him attempting to take a nonchalant drag from the stubbed-out cigarette.

Yes! thought Jan. Thank God for petty victories.

She took her courage in her hands and went to see Simon. She hoped he might be comforted by the fact that Kolawole had been stuck between quite a different rock and hard place than he'd imagined.

She wasn't prepared to find him entranced by the whole business.

"Oh, it's so romantic!" he breathed in girlish mode. "A Secret Service agent! James Bond, no less!"

"James Bond? Oh, come off it, Simon, he's just an undercover policeman! A cop with a skeleton in the closet, what's more, or in Box No 007. And I don't mean you – I mean Sunshine Boy or Sony Adidas or whatever he calls himself."

"Oh, that's probably just a cover!"

And *you're* probably just a cover, she thought. But she said, "How can it be a cover when no one knows about it, idiot?"

But Simon wasn't listening. "Oh, if only I had known!" he sighed.

"What? What if you had known?"

"Oh, I created all kinds of difficulties for him! And he was so patient!"

"Simon –"

"And he let us get away with the crime! To the detriment of his career! He could be a high-ranking officer down in Ibadan or Lagos now! Instead he chose to sacrifice himself, everything, to stay here with me! And I rejected him!"

Jan stared at him in exasperation. But what would be the use of a reality check? It wasn't as if she could make any more sense out of Kola's motives than Simon's romancing just had.

"Oh, I never dreamed I would be loved with such unselfish heroism!" Simon hugged himself in glee, starry-eyed.

"Oh, for God's sake . . ."
"Iced coffee?"
"Er, yes – that would be lovely."

Hetty Coleman had certainly been on the ball, mused Jan as she drove home. Not such an insane old bag after all. Had she guessed about Langley? Had he, in his megalomania, let something slip? All the more reason why Hetty should have moved in for the kill. A pleasant image of Ajax tossing Langley about like a rag-doll entertained Jan for a while.

Instead the bellicose Hetty had called the hounds off. God, she had taken a serious fancy to Tom Purthill. Extraordinary. They hadn't a thing in common.

But, for him, she'd laid aside her moral qualms.

Well . . . Jan herself had paid precious little attention to the moral issue of the fate of the artefacts. Marie's and Tom's needs had been too desperate, her own too all-engulfing.

Hetty should be back soon – with Kola presumably. Into her head flashed another image: Anow in Hetty's passenger seat, eagerly scanning the campus . . .

She shooed the treacherous image away. Anow would have escorted Marie to Agadez and was no doubt now fucking her on a flying carpet somewhere between Agadez and Algiers . . .

And good riddance?

It was at this point, as she passed Samaru market, that she spotted a familiar Tuareg figure striding along the roadside carrying a suitcase. And a goatskin bag.

Alarmed, she pulled up alongside him.

"Jan!" said Ikus-Ikoos.

She leant out of the window. "Ikus-Ikoos! What's up?"

His smile set his face alight. "I'm going back."

"To Marie?" she asked eagerly.

"Yes."

"So you forgive her?"

"Do you?" he countered swiftly, looking at her knowingly.

"Yes," she said, flushing.

But what if Anow was with Marie? Had Ikus-Ikoos considered that?

"But . . ." She groped for the right words. "Where is she? She went to Agadez after we left – how do you know she hasn't left Niger already?"

"I don't. But I feel in my blood that she will not leave without me." He seemed to hesitate and then he said, "I had a dream last night. I dreamt she is waiting in Agadez, hoping I will come."

Jan stared at him, his faith flooding into her, bringing her hope like water to parched earth. Tears sprang to her eyes. He was right. Marie would wait. And Anow . . . what would Anow do?

"In any case, I will find her wherever she has gone," said Ikus-Ikoos. "Even France."

"So you won't be back? I won't see you again?" she asked then, a lump in her throat.

"Oh, I will write from Algiers – or France – or wherever! You can visit us!"

"Well . . ." she swallowed her tears, "I wish you luck!" She did, with all her heart. Fuck the artefacts. They'd probably be sold back to Boston museum again through the black market in any case. "Goodbye, my friend!" And shook his hand in proper lingering Tuareg style.

"For a while," he answered in Tamajegh and tears glimmered in his eyes.

She watched him walk on and turn into the roadside taxi station.

Two evenings later, as she sat on her little patio, pretending to herself that she was watching the sun set, she saw Hetty's Land-Rover tearing down the Sokoto road. It took the turn-off across the green that would lead it to her bungalow and was practically upon her before she was sure she wasn't hallucinating.

She stood up, breaking out in a sweat, clasping the wooden rail of the verandah to steady herself.

There were Tuaregs on board, definitely – she could see the turbans. Who? *Who?*

There was Ajax in the middle, hale and hearty. And Kola – it had to be Kola – in his straw hat next to him.

Kola! Kola being dropped off! Oh, no! The Land-Rover drew to a halt as thoughts skittered through her head. She couldn't let him stay! Simon would gut her!

But it was Anow who got out to stand uncertainly, looking towards her with his bag at his feet.

As she moved forwards, shaky with joy, the passenger-door flew open and seconds later she found herself engulfed in a combined embrace from Kola and Ajax – the dog unfortunately embracing her from behind.

"Hetty! Hetty! Christ! Call off your dog!"

"Ajax! Inside!"

Ajax backed off and a laughing Kola released her.

"*Madame* Jan! *Madame* Jan!" A hefty indigoed arm was raised in salute in the back of the Land-Rover and out clambered Fati-Takowilt, her three kids, Aberfekil, Daud and Fati's mother and father.

What the fuck?

"Takowilt!" said Jan faintly. "Eh – you all came back?"

"Yes, *Madame*, we came back!" cried Fati, throwing her arms about her, engulfing her in breasts. "We missed you!"

Kola was grinning fit to bust. "I think they're intending to have another go in the marriage stakes. But far away from Ned Bassett, I imagine."

"Well," boomed Hetty from the driver's seat, "I'll be off! Ajax needs to be fed!"

*What!* "Hetty!" shrilled Jan. "Wait!" She ran around to the driver's side. "Hetty! You can't be leaving them all here surely?"

"Must do," said Hetty. "Must feed Ajax and go see Tom Purthill without delay. Want to offer him a job. Back in England."

"Oh, great but –"

"Brilliant man. That marvellous, original idea of his! A combined dog and human clinic: *Dogs 'R' Us*. Well, I thought of the name after he left. I intend to employ him as my 'ideas man'. Must go seal the deal. Goodbye now."

'Ideas man'! *Dogs 'R' Us!* Jan stared, gobsmacked, as the Land-Cruiser bounced enthusiastically away.

She turned to survey the motley bunch of people settling themselves down on her verandah. Only Anow was still standing in the garden, bag in hand now, leaning on the rail. She could see his dark eyes glinting through the narrow slit of his *tagilmoust*.

She walked past him, without acknowledging his presence, climbing the two steps to the verandah, and went to where Kolawole had sprawled out on a wooden garden chair. She stood over him, hands on hips.

He grinned his lovely white-toothed wide grin up at her.

"You!" she said. "On your feet! You're going home! Come on."

She marched back down the steps and out onto the green. Then she turned and waited for him to catch up with her. "You can catch a taxi on the road," she said when he drew level.

He was smiling – cool as a cucumber. "Home? Do I have a home here? Tell me, what kind of a reception am I likely to receive from Simon? Has he calmed down?"

"Oh, I think you should have no problem," she said. "Just play it cool. You're good at that." She grinned. "Think panache. Nonchalance. Humour. And you'll be fine."

He smiled, lifted her chin with a long dark finger and kissed her sweetly with his gorgeous cushiony lips. "Thanks," he said. "It was fun."

As he strode off she had a thought. She called after him. "Hey, Kola! Bet you ten naira he asks you if you want it shaken or stirred!"

He turned, frowning, perplexed, but she was on her way back to the house. "I don't know what you mean! But you're on!" he called into the gathering darkness.

Kola was prepared for anything as he approached the house with the adrenalin rushing through his veins screaming fight or flight. He was prepared for tears, ice, ridicule, an African artefact to the skull or Jimoh Igwe in residence.

But he wasn't prepared for a radiant Simon sporting a flirtatious under-the-lashes smile.

"Welcome home!" Simon cried joyously, scattering a bundle of essays he had been correcting every which way as he sprang up to greet him. He sidled towards him, a red biro stuck behind his right ear and a blue behind his left. "Oh, is that a gun I see in your crotch or are you just glad to see me?"

Kola was wary. Had Simon been drinking? Simon was often frivolous but never silly. And that was a silly greeeting.

Cautiously, he put his bag and hat down. He looked about for telltale signs of a male presence.

"Looking for clues?" said Simon archly.

"Yes. But I don't see any." Cool as a cucumber, Jan had advised. Nonchalance. Humour. He tried a lazy grin. "I take it your College Son isn't in residence?"

"Jimoh?" laughed Simon. "Oh, darling, never fear! He doesn't have an ounce of your panache!"

Panache? That was the word Jan had used. They must have been gossiping about him again.

He stared at Simon who was posturing in front of him and shook his head slowly in perplexity. "I will never understand you. You're more impossible than any woman."

"Oh, darling!" said Simon. "That's the nicest thing you've ever said to me!" And stepping forward confidently, grinning, laid his two outstretched arms on Kola's shoulders. "Well, come on then!' he said huskily. "Let's get down to debriefing!"

That, at least, Kola understood. He put his arms around him, embracing the strange angular height of him.

"So how do you want it?" breathed Simon against his ear. "Shaken or stirred?"

Good God! How had Jan known he'd say that? Now he owed her ten naira. Shaken or strirred? It did sound familiar . . . oh, yes, cocktails, wasn't it? "Eh – on the rocks."

For some reason, this sent Simon into gales of laughter.

Oh, well, thought Kola, this is crazy but a damn sight better than a kick in the balls. At any rate, it looks like I'm home.

Jan and Anow sat cross-legged, facing each other on a mat out in the garden, nose to nose, holding hands – the house at long last quiet and sleeping behind them. His hands were strange, she dreamily thought, more fine and light and gentle than she had remembered. Almost too gentle – as if he were handling a newborn kid – or a precious object. Or was simply being very tentative. They pressed noses together and breathed in each other's breath until she was dizzy with it. Then she kissed his nose and his cheek and his lips and he kissed her lips and her cheek and her nose and her eyes and her chin.

They had agreed to discuss their differences. She supposed they were doing that.

She was so bloody glad to see him.

She wrapped her arms around his slim young shoulders and he locked his hands behind her back.

She laid her head in the curve of his neck and inhaled some more. And he lowered his head to her shoulder and breathed against her.

It was perfection. They sat like a little sculpture smoothed into a ball by sand, round as the still perfect moon above them.

But nothing ever stays still, not even the moon, and they could not remain there like a little sand sculpture. They were alive and that meant that their hands could not stay still – that his must grasp her breasts and that hers must reach around behind to grasp his buttocks.

"I want you," he said, which is what you said in his language and was very accurate and practical.

"I love you," she said in English, which was something else altogether and was vague and metaphysical.

But hopefully they meant the same thing.

The good thing about his statement was that they could meet its demands on the spot.

She opened the knot in the drawstring of his trousers and opened the trousers up like a black flower unfolding. And there was this miraculous stamen protruding from the centre of the black petals.

It was the sexiest thing imaginable and her eyes ate it up.

She might have to review her findings on the subject of underwear.

She stirred and felt her body sway on a warm sea of contentment.

She almost could hear the resounding ebb of last night's pleasure.

Turning her head, she gazed at Anow. The poignancy of the youthful line of his shoulder and waist and hip made her pleasure at once keener and less pure. Christ, if she were a sculptor – to catch the beauty of that line. She sat up gently and leant forward to kiss that hip.

He had got thin. She must feed him up.

Milk – the Tuareg's beloved staple. They must get into the habit again of driving to the university farm in the early morning and buying fresh milk.

She kissed the cloud of blue-black hair and her happiness wept at the thought of ever losing him.

He stirred and turned half on his back. "*Matare, tantout?*" he murmured sleepily without opening his eyes. *What is it – what do you want, woman?*

"I – want – you," she answered, leaning over him.

He was still half-asleep but he smiled as he settled onto his back and pulled her up to sit astride his early-morning glory.

All too soon she had to tear herself away. There were essays she had to drop off at the office and, though it was too soon, every day she checked for a letter from Ikus-Ikoos or Marie. Anow had no news of them – he had not accompanied Marie to Agadez after all.

But Jan's mail, when she reached the department, was a solitary sea-swept postcard from home.

She went back to the carpark and had reached her car when she heard the shout.

"*Jan! Jan!*"

In her side-mirror she saw the figure of Ned Bassett bearing down on her. He was wearing his familiar pink shirt and brown trousers today and was waving a sheaf of papers aloft.

"*Jan! Jan! About these sodding essays!*"

She flung herself into the driving-seat and started up. She could just make it. Fixing a bland smile on her face, she concentrated on the thought of Anow's warm body still deeply sleeping in her bed. She bent the smile on Ned and waved airily as she swung past him out of the parking area.

"'*Ere! Jan! Wait! You'll never believe this! I am a daft bugger! Ah-hah-hah-hah-hah!*"

There he was in her side-mirror, bent double in glee.

Oh, sod it, she sighed to herself in Ned-speak, and stopped the car.

He strode briskly after her.

## THE END